Acclaim for Walter Mosley's

FORTUNATE SON

"Walter Mosley may be considered one of the greatest prose writers of all time. . . . In *Fortunate Son* readers will get a taste of the powerful, insanely rhythmic voice that made him a literary rock star." — *Black Issues Book Review*

"Masterful. . . . *Fortunate Son* wrestles with a variety of issues, including the corruption and incompetence endemic in the U.S. justice system, the role of fate, and the ability of the human spirit to overcome. Importantly, the novel demonstrates how easy it is to end up on the wrong side of the tracks without fully grasping what is happening before it's too late." — Russell Myrie, *Independent* (London)

"From the moment Thomas Beerman and Eric Nolan appear, Walter Mosley has the reader in his hands. . . . In the quieter moments of the boys' lives, Mosley's writing shines." — Angela Townsend, *Cleveland Plain Dealer*

"A fierce little fable of loyalty and redemption. . . . The entertainment and pathos are held perfectly in balance with the polemics. . . . By the final pages you'll still be on the edge of your seat." — Elaine Richardson, *O Magazine*

"The gripping descent into loss and acceptance plays out brilliantly in *Fortunate Son*." — S. A. Fuller, *Upscale Magazine*

"Mosley is a master storyteller. . . . *Fortunate Son* is one of his best." — Paul Roberton, *Regina Leader Post*

"A work of magical naturalism. . . . We can see the lingering influence of Zola in the social typicality of the central characters and in the peripheral characters who spring to life in this and other Mosley fictions."
— Michael Helfand, *Pittsburgh Post-Gazette*

"The writing is crisp and the plotting impeccable. *Fortunate Son* deserves to be on the shelves of every library."
— *Library Journal*

"Mosley writes in spare, evenly cadenced prose reminiscent of Richard Wright or Raymond Chandler."
— Mary Fitzgerald, *New Statesman*

"Mosley's somewhat Dickensian novel is remarkably rich in its detail. A vibrant and earthy story about human relationships and the human condition, it is dense with incident, violence, and sex, and with examples of ugliness, beauty, sadness, hope, and love. . . . This is the always good Walter Mosley at his best."
— Tom Bonzca-Tomaszewski, *Independent on Sunday*

"Mosley weaves the themes of race, destiny, and redemption into an astonishing tale of unlikely siblings and unconditional love."   — Allison Block, *Booklist* (starred review)

"An immensely readable urban fable. . . . It's a great credit to Mosley, an articulate storyteller and profound social critic, that *Fortunate Son* feels organic. . . . His spare, dark prose gives bottomless soul to his characters, who seem to live and breathe. This is a fiercely perceptive observation of modern-day America and its black and white world. . . . Mosley reveals the world in its most desperate shades of gray."
— Clayton Moore, *Rocky Mountain News*

"Walter Mosley is so brilliant a writer that he can bring cardboard to life. He can outline a character on the thinnest of materials, color it, run his scissors around the edges, and bid his creation rise and move through the pages of a novel."
— Michael D. Schaffer, *Philadelphia Inquirer*

"Suspenseful . . . entertaining all the way."
— Jack McCray, *Charleston Post and Courier*

"Everything is possible in Walter Mosley's *Fortunate Son,* where love transcends all boundaries."
— Diane Sharper, *Wilmington News Journal*

"Engrossing. . . . A modern twist on *The Prince and Pauper.* . . . Only Mosley can make us feel outrage and joy on a single page."
— Nazenet Habtezghi, *Essence*

"With the lightest, slyest of touches, Mosley shows how a certain kind of inarticulate, carnal, involuntary affection transcends just about anything. It's not love, it's fate, and it's breathtaking."
— *Publishers Weekly* (starred review)

"More than any other contemporary novelist's, Walter Mosley's work affects the reader on an immediate, visceral level. His anger is as infectious as his humanity. . . . His lucid style resists sentimentality while constantly offering fresh insights into the mind-set of complex characters, drawn from a wide spectrum of American race and class. . . . Both furious and forgiving, he assumes our common awareness of social injustice and concentrates instead on what we might have missed. And on the strength of this remarkable book alone, his best to date, Mosley must be considered one of our great novelists."
— Michael Moorcock, *Guardian* (London)

FORTUNATE SON

Walter Mosley

BACK BAY BOOKS

Little, Brown and Company

New York • Boston • London

Back Bay Books / Little, Brown and Company
Hachette Book Group USA
237 Park Avenue, New York, NY 10017
Visit our Web site at www.HachetteBookGroupUSA.com

Originally published in hardcover by
Little, Brown and Company, April 2006
First Back Bay paperback edition, August 2007

The characters and events in this book are fictitious. Any similarity to real
persons, living or dead, is coincidental and not intended by the author.

The interview with Walter Mosley that appears in the reading
group guide at the back of this book was originally published in
the *San Jose Mercury News* on May 14, 2006. Copyright © 2006
San Jose Mercury News. Reprinted with permission.

Library of Congress Cataloging-in-Publication Data
Mosley, Walter.
Fortunate son / Walter Mosley. — 1st ed.
p. cm.
ISBN 978-0-316-11471-4 (hc) / 978-0-316-06628-0 (pb)
1. Conduct of life — Fiction. 2. Male friendship — Fiction.
3. Social classes — Fiction. 4. Race relations — Fiction. I. Title.
PS3563.O88456F67 2006
813'.54 — dc22   2005024477

10 9 8 7 6 5 4 3 2

Q–MART

Book design by Jo Anne Metsch

Printed in the United States of America

FOR
Mark Douglas Neiman

FORTUNATE SON

1

Thomas Beerman was born with a hole in his lung. Because of this birth defect, he spent the first six months of his life in the intensive care unit at Helmutt-Briggs, a hospital in West Los Angeles. The doctors told his mother, Branwyn, that most likely he would not survive.

"Newborns with this kind of disorder, removed from the physical love of their mothers, often wither," kind-eyed Dr. Mason Settler told her.

So she came to the hospital every day after work and watched over her son from six to eleven. She couldn't touch him because he was kept in a glass-enclosed, germ-free environment. But they stared into each other's eyes for hours every day.

Branwyn would read to the little boy and talk to him through the night after her shift at Ethel's Florist Shop.

"I know you must wonder why it's always me here and never your father," Branwyn said to her son one Thursday evening. "Elton has a lot of good qualities, but bein' a father is not one of them. He left me for one of my girlfriends less than a month after we found out I was having you. He told me that he'd stay if I decided not to have the baby. But Elton had the choice to be with me or not and you didn't. I couldn't ask you if you minded if I didn't have you and if you didn't have a life to live. No sunshine or sandy beaches. You don't even know what a sandy beach is. So I told Elton he could leave if he wanted to but I was havin' my baby.

"May Fine said that she'd be happy to be childless with a man like Elton. You know, your father is a good-looking man. He's got big muscles and a nice smile."

Branwyn smiled at Baby Thomas, who was then four months old. He grinned within his bubble and reached out, touching his mother's image in the glass.

"But you know," Branwyn continued, "May is gonna want a baby one day, and when she does, Elton and his good looks will be gone. And then she'll be worse off than me. It's like my mother said, 'That Elton's a heartbreak waitin' to happen.'

"So he's not here, and he probably won't be comin' around either. But that doesn't matter, Tommy, because I will be with you through thick and thin, rain and shine."

Branwyn brought children's books and read and sang to Thomas even when he was asleep and didn't seem to know she was there.

DR. MINAS NOLAN was a heart surgeon who had temporary offices across the hall from the intensive care unit where Thomas and his mother spent that half year. Nolan was a widower, young and hale. A week after Thomas was delivered, Dr. Nolan's wife, Joanne, had borne them a son. She died of complications thirty-six hours later. His son, Eric, came out weighing twelve pounds and twelve ounces, with a thick mane of blond hair, and arms and legs flailing. One of the nurses had commented that it was as if Eric had drained all of the life out of his mother from the inside, and by the time he was born, she was all used up.

Dr. Nolan often worked until eleven at night, when the ICU nurse on duty was forced by hospital regulations to ask Miss Beerman to leave. Branwyn always hesitated. She would have happily spent the whole night sleeping in a chair next to her baby. Then in the morning she could be the first thing he saw.

One evening, noticing the new mother linger at the unit door, Minas offered to walk Branwyn to her car.

"Oh, I don't have a car, Doctor," she said. "I get the bus down on Olympic." The dark-skinned Negro woman had a beautiful smile and nearly transparent gray eyes.

"Well, then let me drive you," the doctor offered.

"Oh, you don't have to do that. I live very far away."

"That doesn't matter," the doctor said. "I don't have much to go home for. You see, my wife died in childbirth recently —"

"You poor thing," Branwyn said, placing a hand on his forearm.

"Anyway, Eric, that's our boy, is usually asleep when I get home, and there's a nanny there . . . and I'm not very tired."

Branwyn was taken by the doctor's handsome Nordic features. He was blond and blue-eyed, and his smile was kind.

They drove down to Branwyn's neighborhood near Crenshaw. He parked his silver Mercedes in front of her apartment building, and she said, "Thank you so much, Doctor. You know, it's a long trip on that bus at night."

There was a moment when neither of them talked or moved.

"Are you hungry, Miss Beerman?"

"Why . . . yes I am, Dr. Nolan."

She wasn't really, but the way the doctor asked the question, she knew that he needed company. A man losing a wife like that would be lost in the world, she knew.

There was an all-night place called the Rib Joint on La Brea, run by a wild character named Fontanot. He was a six-foot-seven Texan who smoked his ribs in the backyard of the restaurant and whose great big laugh could be heard from a block away.

Fontanot had a long face and sad eyes. He was very dark-skinned and powerful, in both his limbs and his will. At that time, the Rib Joint was very popular with the Hollywood set. Movie stars, directors, and big-time producers came there every night. They ordered Fontanot's ribs for their private functions and often invited him to come along.

"I ain't got time for no parties," he'd say, shunning their invitations. "Make hay while the sun shines, that's what my mama always told me to do."

Fontanot did not fraternize much with the muckety-mucks from Hollywood. He laughed if they told a good joke, and he put ribs along with his homemade sauce on their tables.

When Minas and Branwyn came into the restaurant, sometime just before midnight, there was a line of at least a dozen parties waiting to be seated. Men and women were laughing and drinking and trying to get their names put ahead on the list. Minas hunted up a stool and put it against the jukebox so that Branwyn could get off her feet.

When Fontanot saw this simple gesture from the tiny window that looked out from his kitchen, he came out and shook hands with the doctor.

"Ira Fontanot," the restaurateur said.

"My name's Minas. Minas Nolan. And this is Miss Beerman."

"You two are in love," the sad-eyed giant informed them.

"Oh, no," they both said at the same time.

"You might not know it yet," Fontanot announced, "but

you are in love. There's no helpin' that. All I need to know is if you're hungry or not."

"Starving," Minas Nolan said with a deep feeling in his tone that struck Branwyn.

"Then come on back to my special table and I will serve you some barbecue."

To be seated at the special table was the desire of every powerful customer at the Rib Joint. That table was there for Ira's mother and for his new girlfriend.

Minda, Ira's sainted mom, said that her son's girlfriends were always new.

"The lady he's seein' might be with him for one birthday, but she'll never see two," Minda would say through her coarse smoker's rasp.

Other than that, the special table, set in the corner of Ira's kitchen, usually went empty. When a famous director like Heurick Roberts would ask Ivy, the hostess, to give him that table, she'd grin, showing her gold tooth, and say, "If I was to sit you in there with Fontanot he'd skin ya and clean ya and slather yo' ribs wit' sauce."

But Minas and Branwyn didn't know anything about the kitchen table and its special status. As a matter of fact, Branwyn thought that it was probably the worst seat in the house, being in the noisy kitchen and all, but she was willing to sit there because of that note of deep need in Minas's voice when he declared his hunger.

Minas asked for ribs, but Fontanot told him that if he was hungry he wanted the restaurant's special smoked sausages.

"Sausages stick to your ribs, boy," the big chef declared. "An' what will you have, Miss Beerman?"

"I don't eat much meat," she admitted with a slight bow of her head.

Minas thought that she was such a kind woman that she was afraid that her appetite would somehow bruise Fontanot's feelings.

"I got catfish come up ev'ry day from Lake Charles, Louisiana," Fontanot said. "They's a farm down there where they introduce wild fish every six weeks. You know, the big catfish farms got they fish so inbred that you might as well call 'em sole."

This made Branwyn laugh.

Minas looked at the young, beautiful woman and wondered where she could have possibly come from. He was about to ask her, when Fontanot put a big oval plate of steaming sausages in front of him. One bite and Minas couldn't stop eating. The sauce was extremely spicy-hot, and so the doctor ate plenty of bread and downed glass after glass of ice water through the meal. But he didn't turn away the second plate when Fontanot placed it in front of him. Something about Branwyn's company and the kitchen and loud, loud Ira Fontanot made the doctor ravenous.

Branwyn picked at her catfish, which was very good, and watched the heart surgeon eat. She imagined that he probably hadn't had a good meal since the day his wife died.

Rich white doctor or no, she thought, *it's an unlucky star that shone down on this man's backyard.*

"I'm not usually such a pig, Miss Beerman," Minas said when he noticed her smiling at him.

"Appetite ain't nuthin' to be shamed of, Doctor," she said. "I wish that I could see my son eat like you."

"You should see my boy, Miss Beerman," Minas replied. "He sucks down formula by the quart. When he cries it's almost as loud as Mr. Fontanot here."

"Maybe he'll be a singer," Ira Fontanot said. "That's what I always wanted to be. But my voice was too strong, and they made me lip-synch in the church choir."

"That's awful," Branwyn said. "A boy or a girl should always be let to sing. When you gonna sing but when you're a child?"

"And who has more reason?" Minas added.

The three were silent a moment, appreciating how much in line their thinking was.

"More sausages, Minas?" Fontanot asked.

"I wouldn't be able to get in behind the wheel if I had them, Ira."

"How's your fish?" the big cook asked Branwyn.

"The best I've ever eaten," she said. "But don't tell my mama I said that."

BACK IN THE CAR, Minas related a long and convoluted joke about a poor woman who fooled a banker into being the shill for a hoax she was pulling on a fancy-pants lawyer.

The story took so long to tell that he had driven to her apartment building and parked in front of the door again before it was through.

Branwyn liked a good story, and she was happy at the end when the trick made her laugh and laugh.

"That's really beautiful," Minas Nolan said.

"What?"

"Your laugh."

This caught the young mother up short. She had never in her wildest dreams imagined that she would be sitting in a car in the middle of the night with a rich white doctor calling her beautiful. White people were fine by her, but she never responded to any flirtation that she got from white men. She wasn't interested in them. She liked men like Elton, with his jet-black skin and deep laugh.

But Minas Nolan wasn't flirting. He really thought that she was beautiful, and he was honestly happy to be sitting there next to her.

"I should be going," she said. "It's very late."

"Thank you for keeping me company, Miss Beerman," Minas said.

They shook hands. Branwyn thought that she had had kisses less passionate than the way that surgeon held her fingers.

THE NEXT EVENING, Minas was waiting outside the ICU at eleven.

"I don't expect you to have dinner with me or to do anything except to accept a ride home, Miss Beerman," he said quickly, as if to keep her from protesting.

"You don't have to do that, Doctor," she said.

She had been thinking about Minas throughout the day — whenever she wasn't thinking about her son. Before their night at the Rib Joint, Branwyn would spend her days thinking about what it would be like if Elton came back and Tommy got better and they all moved to a house out toward the desert where they could have a backyard with a garden and a swing.

But that day, she hadn't thought of Elton at all — not once. This wasn't a pleasant realization. If just one impossible night with a man who couldn't ever really be a friend made her forget the father of her child, then what would two nights bring? She might forget about Tommy next.

Dr. Nolan could see the rejection building in Branwyn's face, and before it could come out, he said, "Last night was the first time I got to sleep before sunrise. I had a good time just driving you home. It was something I could do. You know what I mean?"

She did know. It was just as if he knew how she understood things. His few words spoke a whole volume to her understanding of the world and loneliness. She couldn't refuse him the release of that drive. If she went home on the bus now, she would never get to sleep because she'd be up thinking of that poor man lying awake, thinking about his dead wife.

"I can't go to dinner though," she said as if in the middle of a much larger conversation.

Dr. Nolan drove Branwyn straight home. They talked about flowers that night. She explained to him how she thought about arranging different kinds of blossoms and leaves. He listened very closely and asked astute questions.

The next night he told her about the first time he cut into a living human body.

"I was so scared that I threw up afterward," he admitted. "I decided that I wasn't meant to be a surgeon."

Branwyn grinned at that.

"What are you laughing about?" the doctor asked.

"You."

"Because I was afraid?"

"Because you seem like you're not afraid of anything," she said.

"I'm scared plenty."

"Maybe you think so," Branwyn replied. "But people really afraid hardly ever know it."

"What does that mean?"

"Well . . . the way I see it, a man who's afraid stays away from the things he fears. A man afraid of cutting into another to save his life would never put himself in the position to do that. He'd become an artist or anything else and then talk about surgery like he was some kinda expert. Fear makes men bluster. They do that so you can't tell how they feel, and after a while, neither can they."

The next night they were both quiet on the drive. The only words the doctor spoke were "thank you" when Branwyn got out to go to her door.

She liked it that Minas stayed in front of her apartment until she was well into the building.

MINAS NOLAN WORKED nearly every day after his wife died. And almost every night he stayed late and drove Branwyn Beerman to her door. After many days had passed, he made an appointment to talk to Dr. Mason Settler about Thomas Beerman's condition.

"There's nothing more I can do, Minas," Dr. Settler, head of the pediatric section of the ICU, said. "I'm surprised that the boy has lived so long. You know, his immune system is off, and I don't like the way he's breathing."

"You can't just let him die without trying something, Doctor," Minas said.

"What?" the elder Dr. Settler asked.

"Something."

TWO WEEKS LATER, when Minas and Branwyn pulled up in front of her building, she hesitated before opening the car door.

"Dr. Nolan."

"Yes, Miss Beerman?"

She took a deep breath and then said, "I have something I want to ask you."

"What's that?" he said in a whisper.

12

"Do you ever plan to kiss me?"

Dr. Minas Nolan had never in his life been without words. And even then he thought he had an answer to Branwyn's question. But when he opened his mouth to speak, nothing came out.

"Never mind," Branwyn said, and she pulled the handle on the door.

Minas reached out for her arm.

"No," he said.

"No what?"

"I . . ."

"What?"

"I never, I never thought that you wanted me to . . . and I was afraid that you'd stop coming with me if I . . ."

Branwyn turned toward the doctor and held out her arms. He rushed into the embrace, and they both sighed. They hugged without kissing for the longest time. It seemed that with each movement of their shoulders they got closer and closer, until one of them would groan in satisfaction and chills would jump off their skin.

"Let's go back to your place," Branwyn said finally.

That's when he first kissed her.

He turned the ignition and slipped the car into gear.

She touched the side of his neck with two fingers and said, "You drive me crazy."

THEY NEVER WENT to sleep that night. The first rays of the sun found them nestled together, thinking very close to the same thoughts.

"I'm worried about Thomas," Minas said after a very long, satisfying silence.

"What do you mean?" Branwyn asked, rousing from her lassitude. She had just been thinking that she had enough time to go see Thomas before she had to be at work.

"Dr. Settler doesn't know what he's doing for the boy. He just keeps him in that bubble, waiting for him to die."

"No."

"Yes. He has no positive prognosis. I think you need to try something else."

"Like what?"

"You need to take him out of that place and hold him and love him. Maybe he'll live."

"Maybe?" Branwyn asked, knowing that this man cared more for her than the whole of Helmutt-Briggs Hospital and every other doctor she had ever known.

She was thinking over what he had said when loud crying erupted from somewhere outside the master bedroom. Minas jumped up, and Branwyn followed him into the room across the hall. There, in a large crib, sat a giant baby with golden hair and eyes the color of the Atlantic Ocean. He was hollering, but there was no pain or sorrow in his face, just mild anger that he'd become hungry a moment before the nanny brought his food.

The nanny was a small Asian woman (later, Branwyn would find out that Ahn was from Vietnam) who seemed too small even to lift the child tyrant — Eric. But she hefted the thirty-five-pound infant from his crib and stuffed the rubber nipple of the plastic bottle into his mouth.

"He's so big," Branwyn marveled. "Twice the size of Thomas. And his eyes so blue. I never seen anything like it."

Eric, nestled in the tiny nanny's arms, suckled the bottle noisily while staring with wonder into Branwyn's eyes.

"He like you," Ahn said with a nod and a smile.

Branwyn tried to figure out how old the woman was. She couldn't tell by the weathered face or the tiny features. She smiled at the woman and held out her arms, taking the behemoth baby to her breast.

Eric dropped his bottle and stared open-mouthed at the woman holding him. He made a soft one-syllable sound and put his hands on her face.

"Ga," he said.

"Ga," Branwyn replied with a smile.

Suddenly Eric started crying, hollering.

"You stop that crying right now, Eric Nolan," Branwyn said in a stern but loving voice.

Abruptly baby Eric stopped, surprise infusing his beautiful, brutal face.

Ahn smiled and hummed.

"That's the first time he's ever obeyed anybody," Minas said softly so as not to break the spell. "Usually when he cries, there's no stopping him."

"That's because Eric and I understand each other. Don't we, boy?"

Eric laughed and reached out for Branwyn's face like a man come in from the cold, holding his hands up to a fire.

Ahn made breakfast while Branwyn, Eric, and Minas went to the drawing room on the first floor. There they sat on the divan that faced a picture window looking out on the Nolans' exquisite flower garden.

"It's so beautiful, Doctor," Branwyn said while bouncing the baby on her lap. "You have more flowers than the florist I work for."

"My wife loved flowers."

"So do I."

Minas was looking at his son's white body beaming against Branwyn's dark-blue dress and darker-still skin.

"Don't you think that you should call me Minas or honey or something like that?"

Branwyn laughed and so did Eric.

Then a deep sadness invaded the woman's face.

"Did I say something wrong?" Minas asked her.

"I shouldn't be happy like this when my baby can't even be comforted by my arms."

Minas opened his mouth to say something, but again he could not find the words.

Eric opened his mouth too, and Ahn — who had just entered the room carrying a platter of sliced fruit, cheese, and bread — had the distinct feeling that the baby could have spoken if he wanted to. But Eric just stared at the black woman with the intensity of a much older child.

"I have to go to the hospital . . . , Minas."

"I'll drive you," the handsome doctor said.

ON THE RIDE, the doctor said again that Thomas would never get better as long as he was in that bubble.

"He needs his mother's arms and the sun," Minas told her.

"That's what I told Dr. Settler, but he said that with Tommy's lung like it is he's liable to get an infection and die if they let him out."

"He won't grow in there," Minas said, "and he won't get better."

"But what will happen if I take him out?"

"He'll be your baby in your arms."

"But will he die?"

"I don't know. He might. But one thing's for sure . . . he'll never grow to be a man in the ICU."

THE DOCTOR DROPPED Branwyn off at Helmutt-Briggs and then drove back to his home in Beverly Hills. Before he was in the front door, he could hear Eric's howls. Minas found the boy and Ahn in the nursery. She was holding him, and he was battering her face with pudgy fists. The boy had been screaming at the top of his lungs until his milky skin turned red.

"He won't stop," Ahn told the doctor.

Minas took the boy in his arms. Eric fought and struggled and screamed and shouted and hollered. Hot tears flooded out of his eyes. Every now and then he'd stop long enough to be fed, but as soon as the bottle was empty, he started in crying again.

It was like that all day. Dr. Nolan examined the boy for gas and then infection, but he couldn't find anything and the baby couldn't talk. All he could do was yell and cry.

At four thirty in the afternoon, after what seemed like three years of tears to the doctor and Ahn, the telephone rang. Minas rushed to it, hoping for some heart attack or stroke that would take him to the peaceful operating room.

"Dr. Nolan?" a woman asked.

"Yes."

"I'm calling from the ICU at Helmutt-Briggs. We were told that you're familiar with a woman named Branwyn Beerman."

"Yes."

"Well, Doctor," the woman said, "we think that she removed her son from the isolation unit he occupied. He's gone from the hospital, and the number we have for her on file has been disconnected."

"What do you want from me?"

"Do you know how we can get in touch with her?"

Eric was screaming two rooms away.

"Don't you have an address for her on file?" Minas asked.

"We don't have the staff to send, Doctor, and the head of the unit has ruled out calling the police."

"So, again, what do you want from me?" Nolan asked.

"We thought that maybe you knew how to reach her. Her baby might die outside of the isolation unit."

"No."

"No what?"

"No, I don't know how to reach her."

MINAS NOLAN, THE Vietnamese nanny, Ahn, and Eric all piled into the silver Mercedes and drove down to a street off Crenshaw. There were no buzzers at the front door, and the mailboxes had numbers but no names.

On the first floor of the dilapidated, modern building, only one apartment door in the long corridor of doors was open; just inside sat an extraordinarily thin black man wearing only a pair of black cotton pants.

"Evenin'," the man said to Minas as he hurried by with his son and the nanny looking for some sign of Branwyn.

"Hello," Minas replied. "Excuse me, sir."

"You lost?" the old man asked. "You look lost."

"I'm looking for Branwyn Beerman."

"You from that hospital?" the man asked suspiciously.

"I'm a friend of hers."

"Then why don't you know where she live at?"

"I've never been up to her apartment. I've only ever dropped her off at the door."

"Oh," the man said, smiling now. "You're that doctor always takes her home after she visits with her poor baby."

"Yes. That's me."

"You not comin' to take her baby away now are ya?"

"No, sir. I'm the one who suggested that she take Tommy out of there."

The whole time in the car and while they stood in the hall talking to the old man (whose name was Terry Barker), Eric screamed deafeningly. Nothing that Ahn or Minas did or said could stop him.

Terry told them that Branwyn lived on the fifth floor, but the elevator didn't work.

They scaled the stairs and made it to 5G. The door came open before they knocked. Branwyn was standing there, beautiful with babe in arms.

"I heard Eric from out on the street," she said. "I would have come down to meet you, but I didn't want to jostle little Tommy."

Thomas Beerman was small and still in his mother's arms. He moved his head only to keep an eye on her face. His hands were holding tight to her thumb and forefinger.

Eric stopped crying when Branwyn appeared.

"Can we come in?" Minas asked, relieved at the silence Branwyn brought into his life.

MINAS NOLAN CHECKED baby Thomas for signs of disease or decay.

"His breath is a little labored," Minas announced. "It would probably be best to put him in an oxygen tent for part of each day."

"I don't have no oxygen tent," Branwyn said.

She was sitting on the bed with both boys. Thomas was in her lap, while Eric nestled up against her thigh. At one point Eric raised his head and looked at Tommy. He brought his hand down with some force against the recently liberated baby's head. Thomas didn't cry but merely frowned at the pain.

Branwyn grabbed the offending forearm and said, "Eric Nolan, you are welcome in my house but only if you are kind to my son, Tommy. Do you understand me?"

Eric's face twisted into agony. He was about to let out a scream.

"I don't want any'a that yellin' in my house," Branwyn said, and Eric's expression changed into wonder.

"I had an oxygen tent brought over to my place for Joanne when she had pneumonia last year," Minas said. "Why don't you come and stay with us until young Thomas here has built up his strength?"

Branwyn thought about saying no, but Tommy needed a doctor and it was plain to see that Eric needed a mom.

2

MOTHER AND child moved into Minas Nolan's home the next morning. Branwyn expected to stay there only until Tommy could live without an oxygen tent. Minas gave her her own room and told her that he'd like to take her out for dinner the first night she was there.

Tommy and Eric were sleeping peacefully and Ahn had Dr. Nolan's beeper number. Branwyn hadn't eaten in the last twenty-four hours and so she said, "Okay."

Over sausages and catfish served at the table at Fontanot's kitchen, Minas said, "I am very attracted to you, Branwyn Beerman, but I don't want you to feel any pressure. I have you in my house so that Thomas can heal. And it doesn't hurt that you're the only person who can make Eric stop his crying."

"So you don't mind if I sleep in my own bed?" Branwyn asked.

"No, ma'am."

She smiled, and Fontanot delivered a plateful of home-made corn bread.

That night they went to Minas's room. From that day on Branwyn dressed and kept her clothes in her own bedroom, but she always slept with the doctor — though three or four nights a week she sat up with her son. Thomas was very sick for the next eighteen months. He came down with pneumonia and a dozen other minor and major infections. He suffered from high fevers every other week, but between the ministrations of Minas and Ahn and Branwyn he survived. By Thomas's second birthday, Minas declared that the former bubble boy should be able to live a normal life.

Branwyn offered to move out a week later.

"If you want me to bawl like Eric I guess you can," Minas said.

And so Branwyn stayed on. She kept her job at Ethel's Florist Shop. Minas taught her how to drive and bought her a blue Volvo.

Eric was jubilant. He broke glasses and windows, the dog's leg, and three bed frames just being a "force of nature," as Branwyn said. Meanwhile, Thomas made his way quietly through the large house, watching his foster brother and other wild things, like insects and birds and trees.

Thomas didn't cry much, and he always stood aside when Eric came hollering for Branwyn. He got colds very often, and even the least exertion made him tired. Eric pushed him sometimes but that was unusual. As a rule the big son of Minas Nolan showed kindness to only Branwyn and Tommy. It wasn't that he was mean to his father or others but merely that he took them for granted. People were always bringing him gifts and complimenting his size and handsome features. He learned things easily and dominated other children on the playground and later at school.

Thomas loved his brother and mother. He was also very fond of Ahn, who often sat with him when he was sick, and Minas Nolan, who liked to read to him from the red books on the top shelf in the third-floor library.

Eric had scores of cousins, four grandparents, and more uncles and aunts than either he or Thomas could count. At least one of these relations brought Eric presents every week. They never gave Thomas anything, nor did they pay much notice to the little black boy.

He didn't seem to care though. He'd spend hours wandering through the flower garden finding rocks and sticks that he'd bring to his mother. There in her room, they would make up stories about what kind of treasure he'd found. Afterward, when Eric's family had gone, the robust blond child would ask Thomas about what he and Branwyn had done. He'd sit on his tanned haunches listening to the soft words that Tommy used to tell about his adventures with pebbles and twigs.

Every now and then Branwyn's mother, Madeline, would come over for lunch, usually when the doctor was away.

"Does that man ever intend to make a honest woman outta you?" Madeline would say to her daughter, and before Branwyn could answer, "Not that I think you *should* marry a man like that. A man that takes a woman to his bed not even six months after his wife has died an' gone to heaven. But here you are so far away from family an' friends, an' they treatin' your son like he was a servant's child. And you do so much for him, and then he makes you work at that flower shop. That's not right, Branwyn. You shouldn't put up with it. Either he should marry you or at least put something away for your future an' your boy's future. Here he have you all to himself so that you can't meet no eligible man, an' he ain't doin' nuthin' for you either."

The first few times her mother said these things, and more, Branwyn tried to argue. She didn't want to marry Minas. They had different lives, and there was no need. He was a kind man, and no matter what his family felt, she and Tommy were always at the table for dinner and he never went anywhere without asking her and her son to come along.

"I want to work and to make my own money," Branwyn said. "And Tommy's special. He needs a lot of attention. His growth was so slow after that long time in the hospital. I can't ask Minas to be responsible for another man's child."

But Madeline never seemed to care. In her eyes the doctor was taking advantage of her through her daughter.

"White people like that," Madeline would say, "just like that arrogant boy that's got Tommy runnin' after him like some kinda slave."

"The boys love each other, Mama," Branwyn would argue.

"That white boy just run roughshod over Tommy, an' you cain't even see it," her mother retorted. "He treatin' Tommy like his property, his slave."

This last word was Madeline's worst curse. She would take Thomas in her lap and call him "poor baby" and tell him that he could come live with her whenever he wanted.

Thomas would look up at his grandmother and smell her sweet rose scent. He loved her, but he didn't want to leave his mother. And he didn't understand why she was always so angry. He would bring her green pebbles and seed-heavy branches that he sculpted to look like snakes. But this just seemed to upset Madeline more.

"Here he livin' in Beverly Hills an' all he got is sticks for toys," the Mississippi-born Madeline would cry.

And what could Branwyn say? Any toys that she or Minas bought for Tommy wound up in Eric's room. Whenever the blond Adonis would want to play with Tommy's trucks or handheld electronic games, Tommy always handed them over, and after a while both he and Eric forgot who the original owner was.

One day Minas went into Eric's room and gathered up all of Tommy's toys and put them into a box. Eric bellowed and cried. He fell to the floor and pounded it with his fists and feet. Even Branwyn couldn't console him. Minas brought the cardboard box to Tommy's room on the third floor while Eric bawled and yelled on the second.

Sometime during the night, Tommy dragged the big box of toys to Eric's room and left it outside the door.

"Why you do that, baby?" Branwyn asked her son the next morning. "Those toys belong to you."

"It's okay, Mama," the tiny four-year-old replied. "Eric always wants to play with me and I don't care. I don't like those toys too much. They're too bright anyway."

How could Branwyn tell her mother that?

A year earlier Minas Nolan came home with a two-carat yellow diamond pin for her hat. He gave it to her at the dinner table so that the boys and Ahn could share in their happiness. But Branwyn put the pin away and did not wear it. Then Tommy remembered the jewel and asked his mother why she never put it on.

"It's too bright, honey," she'd said. "Like a big headlight on your head."

And so he collected dead insects and pitted stones that had faces in them.

Branwyn sometimes worried that Eric took advantage of his smaller brother, but when she saw them together the fears dissipated. Eric and Tommy would go into the backyard every day after kindergarten and talk. Actually, Eric did most of the talking. Tommy was the listener, but Branwyn could see how much they loved each other.

One Saturday, just after they both had turned six, Eric had finally persuaded Tommy to play catch with their new baseball and gloves in the garden next to the glass-walled greenhouse. Branwyn was in her fourth-floor bedroom looking down on the boys. Tommy didn't usually play catch with his brother because Eric was almost twice his size and threw too hard. But that day at breakfast, Eric promised to be careful. He was throwing underhand balls, and Tommy was smiling. But then Eric seemed to be urging the smaller boy to do something else. He kept saying, "Come on, Tommy, try it." Finally Tommy threw the baseball overhand. It flew high and shattered one of the panes in the greenhouse wall.

The boys ran into the house.

A big yellow cat came out when they were gone. That was Golden, Ahn's pet. She always followed the boys but never came out around them. Branwyn watched the cat stretch out on the spot where Eric had been standing. She wondered what the animal was getting from that piece of ground. It was as if the creature knew somehow that the places where the doctor's son passed were blessed.

She sat there for much longer than she'd intended, just thinking about blessings and the yellow cat Golden. She thought about Eric, who took everything, and Tommy, who kept nothing. Eric the pirate. Eric the cowboy. Eric the spaceman. He could already read books on a third-grade level, but he was stubborn and never agreed to perform for his father's friends.

Tommy rarely pretended to be anything. He got sick all the time and had not even met his own father.

Branwyn wondered how two such different human beings could even exist in the same world. Then she went down to see what they had to say about the baseball and Minas's beloved greenhouse.

The boys were standing side by side next to the dishwasher in the kitchen when Branwyn entered the room. Minas, wearing his golf clothes, stood frowning over them. When she walked in, he smiled for her. This was probably why she found it so hard to leave: the happiness that she felt in everyone's eyes whenever she entered a room.

"Eric threw a ball and broke a pane in the greenhouse wall," Minas said.

"What?" Branwyn asked.

"Eric wasn't careful, and he broke a window."

"Is that true, Tommy?" Branwyn asked her son.

"Yes," Eric said.

"No," Tommy added. "I did it. I threw overhand and broke the window."

"But I made him do it," Eric said. "I kept tellin' him to throw overhand. He didn't wanna, an' so it was my fault."

Minas looked at Branwyn, bewildered at the turn of events. He often felt like this around her. He was so straightforward and certain, taking up facts like Tommy collected stones. But he never looked closely enough at what he saw. Without Branwyn, he often thought, he wouldn't have understood the children at all.

After the boys had been chastised, they went out to play catch again. Branwyn and Minas sat at the butcher-block kitchen table.

"Will you marry me, Branwyn Beerman?" Dr. Minas Nolan asked for what seemed to him like the hundredth time.

Branwyn sighed and took his hand. She shook her head gently.

"Why not? Don't you love me? Don't you think I love you?"

She didn't answer him. Her life for the five and a half years before had been like a dream. A rich and handsome doctor, a brother for her son, her son's survival, and the flower garden. All of these things made Branwyn so happy that sometimes, when she was all alone, she cried.

At first she refused the doctor's proposals because she felt that he needed her for Eric and not himself. His headstrong son would only heed her for the first few years. She thought that maybe Dr. Nolan looked on her the way he saw Ahn, a domestic with a few other qualities. But as time passed, she came to believe that he loved her as a woman. They went everywhere together. When they stayed in hotels, she was automatically registered as Mrs. Nolan. After a time marriage seemed like the right thing.

But then Elton came into Ethel's Florist Shop not long after Tommy's sixth birthday.

She hadn't seen the tall, fine-looking Elton in Tommy's whole lifetime, but he still made her heart skip and her breath come fast.

"Hey, sugah," Elton said as if he'd only been away for the weekend.

"Don't sugah me, Elton Trueblood. That's the last thing in the world I am to you."

Elton smiled, and Branwyn kept herself from bringing her hand up to still her breast.

"Don't be like that, baby," he said. "You know I just wanted to come an' see how you doin' an' what's goin' on."

"Your son is six years old an' he hasn't even met you," Branwyn stated.

"That's why I'm here," Elton said. "I want to know about my boy."

"Why?"

"Does a father need a reason?"

"The way I see it, you're less a father and more like a sperm donor." Branwyn had been waiting for years to hurl that insult. But the minute she did, she realized that all it proved was how strong she still felt about the man.

"Baby," he said. "Tommy is my son."

"How you know his name?"

"Your mother told me," Elton said with a sly smile. "I know all about you, sugah. Your doctor boyfriend who won't marry you —"

"At least he don't mind a woman with a child. At least he don't mind if that child sit on his lap and ask what the stars is made'a."

But Elton would not be hurt.

"Come on and have lunch with me, girl," he said. "Tell me about my boy."

She said no and told him that she had to get back to work. When he left, she breathed a deep sigh but still didn't feel that she had gotten enough air.

The next day Elton came back. The first time he appeared he wore sports clothes — a black dress shirt under a lime-green jacket. But today he appeared with gray-and-black-striped overalls.

"I got a job as a mechanic trainee at Brake-Co," he told her. "In eighteen months I'll be a licensed mechanic. I could even fix that Volvo you drivin'."

"That's very good for you, Elton," Branwyn had said. "I'm sure that May must be very happy that you're thinking about your future."

"May? Shoot. I moved that heifer out. You know, she quit her job, got big as a house, and had the nerve to tell me that I was supposed to provide for her. Shoot. I provided a open door for her to go through and bus fare to take her home to her mama."

"You just kicked her out? An' she ain't got no job?" Branwyn asked. "How's she gonna live?"

"She moved out my house and three doors down to August Murphy's apartment. Never even got on a bus. Just walked down the street, knocked on his door, an' went in. Now you know she had to know the brother pretty damn well to move in with only five minutes' notice."

"What did you do about that?"

"Nuthin'. I was glad she was gone. All she evah did was lie around the house and talk about how this girl had bad extensions and that one was a cow."

Branwyn remembered how May, when she was in a bad mood, had a sour nature. She would bad-mouth everybody except the person she was talking to at the moment.

"So you got tired of all that mess she talked, huh?" Branwyn asked, forgetting for a moment that he'd walked out on her when she was pregnant with his child.

"Even before we started fightin' I was thinkin' about you, Brawn," Elton said. "'Bout how you always had a good word to say 'bout ev'rythang. An' I was thinkin' 'bout my son. You know, as soon as I found out that he was home I come ovah . . . but you'as already gone."

Branwyn loved Elton's simple language and his artfully told lies.

"Why didn't you come after you found out where I was?" she asked, swinging her words like an ax.

"I didn't know, Brawn," he said, his voice rising into a higher register. "I swear. I went to your mama, but she was mad at me for bein' a fool. It was only when she seen I was serious about a job and I left May, then she told me about where you was."

"What do you want with me, Elton?"

"I just wanna see my son, baby."

"Now how am I supposed to believe that? You left me three weeks after the doctor told me I was expecting. You never came to the hospital once to see your son."

"I was scared, honey," Elton said in a forced whisper. "I didn't wanna see my boy with a hole in his chest, in a glass cage."

The bell over the door rang, and a small white woman, who had a tiny hairless dog on a leash, came in.

"Hello, Mrs. Freemont," Branwyn said. "I'll be right with you," and then to Elton, "You got to go."

"What about Thomas?"

"Leave now, Elton. I don't wanna lose this job over you."

Elton gave Branwyn a hard look that she withstood with stony silence. Finally he turned away and walked out.

ELTON CAME BACK four more times before Branwyn agreed to have lunch with him. The florist was on Pico, near Doheny. There was a hotel a few blocks away that had a restaurant Branwyn liked. They prepared a delicious tuna salad that she made sure to have twice a week.

Elton was wearing a T-shirt with a three-button collar and tan pants that hugged his butt. Branwyn had been dreaming about his lips and those hips for the two weeks since he'd first appeared at Ethel's.

Why does he come by so often? she wondered each night. On one of those nights, the doctor had made love to her. And while he did, she closed her eyes and remembered the fever that took her over when Elton was in her bed. And when she remembered Elton and the things he did to her, she got so excited that she had one of those soul-shaking orgasms that left her shivering like a leaf — and crying too.

Afterward she couldn't even talk to Minas. He lay back with his hands behind his head, proud of the way he'd made her holler and cry. He didn't know, she thought, that she was cheating on him even while they were making love.

That was why she refused the doctor's proposal of marriage that day after Eric took the blame for her son's misdemeanor. If he knew the passion in her heart, he'd never give her a ring.

It wasn't that she wanted to marry Elton. She didn't dream about a house with him and Thomas anymore. She knew that as time went by, he'd come home later and later each night until finally he'd start skipping nights and then weeks and then he'd be gone. Her mother was right the first time when she compared him to heartbreak. But none of that changed how much she wanted him to kiss her and lay the flats of his hands on her sides.

How could she say yes to Minas Nolan when she was wanton in her heart? And why wasn't Elton the kind of man that she could run to and live with until she was old and half-blind?

ON THE DAY she was to meet Elton for lunch, Branwyn brought Thomas to work with her. She made him wear his nice gray cotton pants and the maroon sweater that Eric, with the help of Ahn, had given him for his birthday.

Ethel Gorseman loved little Thomas because he never got into trouble when he was alone. If Eric came into the shop for any reason, the florist kept her eye on him every second. She liked Eric too, but he was a "walking disaster" in her opinion. If Eric ever came in alone with Branwyn, Ethel would hire Jessop, who owned the small arcade across the street, to look after him. She'd give Eric five dollars so that he could eat hot dogs and play video games instead of breaking her vases and tipping over her shelves.

Tommy wished that she would give him five dollars and

send him over to visit Jessop when he was there, but she never did. Instead she would tell him about how florists keep flowers alive and why it was such a good job.

That day Branwyn had kept Tommy out of school. The excuse she gave Minas was that he had a cold, but that wasn't so remarkable. Thomas was used to runny noses and coughing. Most of his life he'd been sick with something.

When Elton came in at noon, wearing his mechanic's overalls, Branwyn pushed Thomas forward and said, "Elton Trueblood, this is your son, Thomas."

She said these words almost as a challenge. But when she saw the love and joy in Elton's eyes, she bit her lower lip and tasted salty tears coming down into her mouth.

Looking at them together, anyone would have known them for father and son. Elton reached out his hand, and Thomas shook it like he had been taught to by Minas.

"I'm your father," Elton said.

"Pleased to meet you, Daddy," Thomas said.

For a long time he had been wanting to call someone daddy. Eric said that to Minas, but Branwyn had always told Thomas that Dr. Nolan wasn't his father. Minas would say that he wished that Thomas was his son too, but that only meant that he wasn't.

Eric called Branwyn "Mama Branwyn." But Thomas knew that that was okay because Eric's mother had died.

Looking up into Elton's hard, dark face, Thomas was a little scared, but he knew that he had to be nice to Elton because his mother had made him wear nice clothes. And so he let the big man hold his hand as they walked down Pico to the hotel where his mother liked to eat.

Elton kept asking the boy questions. *What's your favorite color? Do you have a girlfriend at that white school?*

While they were sitting in the restaurant, Elton gave little Thomas a problem to solve.

"There's a man," he said, "with a fox, a big rooster, and a sack'a corn. He comes to a river where there's a tiny li'l boat. The boat is so small that the man can only carry one with him across the river at a time. But if he takes the corn, the fox will eat the rooster, and if he takes the fox, the rooster will eat the corn."

"Then he should take the rooster 'cause the fox won't eat corn," Thomas said with a smile.

"Then what?" Elton asked.

"Then he could come back for the . . . the fox."

"But if he leaves the fox on the other side when he goes back to get the corn, the fox will eat the rooster," Elton said with a sly smile.

Watching his father's smile, Thomas forgot the riddle. This was his father he was looking at. His father like Dr. Nolan was Eric's father. He had the same black skin that Thomas had and the same kinky hair.

"Stop bothering him, Elton," Branwyn said, feeling that Thomas was confused by being cross-examined like some criminal.

"I'm just doin' what a father's s'posed t'be doin', Brawn," Elton said. "Helpin' him to understand how hard the world is to see sometimes. Is he a li'l slow in school?"

"No."

"I mean, it's just a child's riddle really," Elton continued. "Just a trick."

He looked at Thomas hopefully, but the small boy only stared at him, the foxes and chickens and grain gone from his head. He was wondering if Elton would come live with them in Dr. Nolan's big house.

After lunch Branwyn went back to the flower shop and cried. She sat on a stool at the back of the big orchid refrigerator. Thomas stood next to her and held her hand.

"What's wrong, Mommy?"

"I'm just happy, baby," she said, choking on every other word.

"You don't sound happy."

"Sometimes people cry when they're happy."

"What made you so happy?"

"Seeing you and your father together at the same table, talking and telling each other things."

"Uh-huh."

Branwyn turned to her son and looked into his eyes.

"Would you want to live with your father if you had the chance?" she asked.

"I don't know. Would he come an' stay at our house?"

"No. We'd have to move away from Minas and Eric."

"Could Eric come live with us?"

"No. He'd have to stay with his own father."

Thomas thought and thought, standing there in the refrigerated room. He thought about his new father and his brother, Eric. He thought about his mother crying and wished that she didn't have to be so happy.

"Maybe Daddy could come and visit sometimes," he said at last. "And then I could still go to school with Eric and read with Dr. Nolan."

A FEW WEEKS after Thomas had broken the greenhouse window, Eric came down with the flu. It was a bad flu, and he had a fever of 105. Minas was worried, and Ahn kept boiling eucalyptus leaves and bringing the steaming pots into the boy's room. Eric was shivering and crying all through the night. He was in pain, and only Branwyn's company would calm him. She sat up with him for most of three days. At the end of that time, Eric was laughing and playing and Branwyn was very tired, and so she went to bed.

The next afternoon, when Thomas and Eric got home from first grade, Thomas went to his mother's room and found her still in bed.

"You tired, Mama?" Thomas asked.

"Very much, baby. I sat up so long with Eric, and now all I want is to sleep."

Thomas and Eric spent many hours at her side that afternoon and evening, both of them trying to make her laugh.

She kept her eyes open as long as she could, but more and more she just slept. Minas wanted her to go to the hospital, but she refused.

"Hospital is just a death sentence," she told him. "All I need is rest."

On the third day Branwyn was not better. Eric heard his father tell Ahn that Branwyn had agreed to go to the hospital in the morning.

The blond tank rumbled up to his brother's room and said, "They're taking Mama Branwyn to the hospital in the morning. We should pick flowers for her so her room'll be pretty."

"The hospital?" Thomas said.

Thomas hated the hospital. He'd been there half a dozen times that he could remember. Twice for pneumonia that had developed after he'd come down with chest colds, twice for broken bones, once for a cut when he fell down on a broken bottle, and one time when he fainted in school for no apparent reason. Every time he went they gave him shots, and twice he'd had to spend the night. He knew that people sometimes died in the hospital, and so when he went to bed later that night, he couldn't go to sleep. He sat up remembering the stories of how his mother came every day and they looked at each other through the glass bubble. He believed that she had saved him by being there, and he wondered who would be there for her if he was at school.

Thomas went to her room after midnight. Branwyn stayed in her own bedroom when she was sick. She needed everything quiet and "no man kicking around in the bed."

He climbed up quietly on the bed and stared into his mother's face. At first he planned just to look at her as she'd told him she'd done when he was asleep in the ICU.

"Didn't you wake me up?" he asked her.

"No, baby. You needed to sleep to get better and so I just sat there, but I'm sure you knew I was there in your dreams."

Thomas planned to do the same thing, to sit so close that his mother's dreams would drink him in. But after a few minutes he worried that maybe she had died. She was so quiet, and he couldn't tell if she was breathing.

"Mama?"

She opened her eyes and said, "Yes, baby?"

"I know how to answer the story."

"What story?"

"The one Daddy said."

"What is it?"

"First you take the rooster to the other side an' leave him there. Then you come back and get the fox and bring him to the other side. Then you put the rooster back in the boat and take him back and leave him on the first side and you take the corn over to where the fox is. Now the corn and the fox are together but that's okay, and so you can go back an' get the rooster."

"You're so smart, Thomas. Your father will be very happy."

"Will you be okay now that I said it?" the boy asked.

"Why you cryin', honey?"

"Because you're sick and I don't want you to die."

Branwyn sat up. Thomas crawled up close to her and leaned against her slender shoulder.

"Are you scared 'cause I'm goin' to the hospital?"

"Uh-huh."

"It's only for some tests," she said. "Will you do what Dr. Nolan tells you while I'm gone?"

"Yes."

"And do you know that I will always be with you through rain and shine, thick and thin?"

"Yes."

"I'm not gonna die, baby. I'm gonna go in there and stay for a day or two and then I'll be back here and wide awake."

"But sometimes people die in the hospital," he insisted.

"Sometimes," she agreed. "But even when they do they don't really die."

"What happens to'em?"

"They just change. They're still here in the hearts of all the people that loved them. Your grandmother says that she talks to granddaddy every night before she goes to bed. He's still there for her whenever she gets sad.

"But you don't have to worry about that. I'm still strong and healthy. I'm just a little tired, that's all. You know that, right?"

"I guess."

"Come here and lie down next to me," she said. "Sleep with me in the bed tonight."

And Thomas nestled up next to his mother, and they whispered secrets and little jokes until he finally fell asleep in her arms.

THE NEXT MORNING Thomas went to wake up Minas Nolan in his bed.

"Mama won't wake up," he told his mother's lover. "But she said that it's okay 'cause nobody never dies."

3

AHN SET up a cot in Eric's room for Thomas — not for the sake of Branwyn's son but for the doctor's boy. Eric was desolate over the death of the woman who was the only mother he ever knew. He understood that she was sick, but he never thought about her dying. Thomas, on the other hand, thought about death all the time. The dead bugs and small animals that he'd find in the garden fascinated him. And his many months of isolation in the intensive care unit had often been the topic of conversation between him and his mother.

"What would have happened if Dr. Nolan didn't say for you to take me out of there?" he'd ask.

"Then you would have stayed small and gotten smaller," Branwyn told him. "And if you stayed long enough you would have probably died."

"And then would you come to the cemetery to visit me?"

"Every day for my whole life."

At night Eric sobbed in his bed, and Thomas would come sit next to him and tell him stories about their mother.

"She was always talking about having a small house near the desert where we could grow watermelons and strawberries," Thomas said.

"Just you and me and her?" Eric asked.

"Uh-huh," Thomas replied. "And Dr. Nolan too. And maybe Ahn if we were still little."

"How come you don't call Daddy 'Daddy,' Tommy?"

"Because I have a father, and he'd be sad if I called another man that."

"Are you gonna go live with your father now that Mama Branwyn's dead?"

Thomas had never thought of this before. Would they make him go live with the man that taught him the riddle? He didn't want to go. And he couldn't see why they'd make him if he just said that he wanted to stay with his brother and Dr. Nolan and Ahn.

"I sure miss Mama Branwyn," Eric said.

Thomas put his hand on his brother's shoulder.

"She's not gone away . . . just in her body, she is. But she's still in the world lookin' at us and smilin'."

THE FUNERAL WAS three days later.

By then Eric had recovered from his deep sadness. Thomas sat up with him every night telling him all the things about Branwyn he never knew, or at least never paid attention to.

Eric was a strong boy filled with energy. He loved rough-house games and running, and though he could be very sad for short periods, he always came back laughing and running hard. So when he woke up on the morning of the funeral, he was happy again, with Branwyn's death behind him. He told Thomas that he didn't need him to sleep in his room any-more. He helped his diminutive pretend sibling carry the cot back to the attic where Ahn had gotten it.

When Thomas went back to his bedroom, he realized that

something was different. It was as if there was a film over his eyes that made everything just the slightest bit darker, like a lightbulb dimming when lightning strikes outside or a cloud coming close to the sun but not enough to make real shadows.

Thomas tried to look hard at things around him, to make them shine as they had done only a few days before, but the luster was gone. He sat down on the floor in the center of his room, looking around at the new world he inhabited. He tried to remember how things had looked before, but slowly the memories of the glitter he'd always taken for granted dissipated and all that was left was what he could see.

After a while he forgot what he was looking for. When he tried to remember why it was that he sat there, he thought of what his mother had told him: *I will always be with you through rain and shine, thick and thin.* And he thought that he was waiting for his mother to tell him more.

Sitting there on his knees on the floor, Thomas felt the world settling around him. It was completely still, but he knew that over time all things got heavier and sank into one another until they became one thing rather than many. He didn't remember where he'd learned that — whether it was from Dr. Nolan or big Ira Fontanot, his mother's friend. But he knew that it was true and that if he sat in that room long enough, his knees would bond with the floor and he'd know everything that happened in the house. And the house would become part of the ground, and he and the house would be a part of the whole world. Once this happened he would be joined with everything, and then he would know where his mother was and they could talk again.

So Thomas closed his dimmed eyes and waited for his knees to become one with the floor. He heard the wind rattle a loose pane of glass in the window and, every now and then, the hard thumps of feet through the wood. Dr. Nolan's measured pace was continual as he moved around on the distant first floor. Ahn's tapping footsteps could often be heard. The loudest footfalls were Eric's. He would run hard and then stop and maybe leap, landing with a loud thud that shook the house, if only slightly. Thomas felt that he was already becoming a part of everything. He raised his head, expecting his mother to appear to him at any moment. Then came a quick tapping and the whine of his door opening.

"Tommy," Ahn said in her clipped voice. "You not ready."

He opened his eyes and saw her. He wanted to explain that things were not the same and that he was trying to find his mother in the wide world. But he didn't have the words or the heart to try.

"Get up," she said. "Put on your clothes. We have to go say good-bye to your mother."

The nanny was wearing a one-piece black dress that buttoned down the front and went all the way to her feet. She had a boy's figure and was very short, though still taller than Thomas.

"Hurry, hurry," the nanny said.

"Did your mommy die one day, Ahn?" Thomas asked, not moving from his place on the floor.

There was a long black shawl hanging from Ahn's toothpick-thin shoulders. She came up next to the boy and descended to her knees. She put her arms around him and hugged him to her bony chest. After a while Thomas could feel her body shivering, and he knew that she was crying for his mother.

"I was born in a war, Tommy," she whispered to him. "I remember being a child. I was very frightened, and we were running down a dirt road. It was my mother and father and

43

older brother, Xi'an. There were big bombs falling, and everywhere they fell fire went up like dragons in a child's storybook. And we ran and ran, and I wondered, even when I was running, where was I coming from? Where was I going?

"And then my father fell down. I tried to reach for him, but my mother grabbed me and pushed me to run. And then my big brother fell and later my mother. And then I was running all by myself and I didn't know where I came from and I didn't know where I was going. There was blood on the American T-shirt that I wore for a dress. It was my mother's blood. I still have it in a chest in my closet, the dress that has my mother's blood on the hem."

Then Ahn took Thomas by his shoulders and brought her face up close to his.

"You are like I was," she said. "Your mother has fallen and you must go on. You have to keep on going even though you do not know where you go. It is all we can do. Do you understand me?"

Thomas understood her fingers digging into his skin and her desperate eyes still looking for her mother somewhere in his. And so he nodded and said, "Yes, Ahn. I know."

"Then put on your nice clothes and come down and go to the funeral."

The last time Thomas had worn nice things was to see his father in the hotel restaurant. He dressed himself and went downstairs. Ahn, he knew, had gone to Eric's room to help him dress. Eric didn't need her, but she always helped him anyway.

They all got into a long black car driven by a black man who wore a cap with a shiny black brim. They drove to a big church in a neighborhood where there were mostly black people like him and his mother walking up and down the street, sitting out in front of their houses laughing and talking, even delivering the mail. Not just black-skinned people but brown too — all kinds of browns. Maple-syrup colored and redbrick brown, the brown you find in every wood from pine to cherry, oak to ebony. There were people that looked as though they had deep tans and some that shone like gold and copper and bronze. *People of color.* The phrase came into Thomas's mind. He had heard it in school, and he knew that it applied to him and the people around his mother's funeral.

The church was big and cool, with a dozen stained-glass windows that had pictures of Jesus and other dignitaries from the Bible. Many a black and brown woman came up to him and called him "poor darling" and "little lamb" while he and Eric walked together, looking around at the vastness of the house of worship.

Most of the people inside the church were of color too. Thomas wondered if all these people knew his mother. Most of them he didn't recognize. But there were a few familiar faces. He saw his grandmother Madeline, and there was Ira Fontanot, whom he recognized from the Rib Joint. For a brief moment he saw his father, Elton, standing along the side of the pews.

Ahn rushed the boys along until they were sitting in the front row. There, before them, was a coffin set upon a dais under a podium on a pulpit.

"Mama Branwyn's in there," Eric whispered, an uncommon awe in his voice.

A minister in long black robes edged in red came up to the podium and said Branwyn's name and then sang a little. Then he said things about Thomas's mother that the boy didn't understand. They were nice words, but they had little to do with the mother he knew. It wasn't so much what he said but all the things he left out. He didn't say, for instance, how Branwyn was so good at seeing faces in the pitted surfaces of stones.

"You see," she'd say, "there's the nose and here's the eye."

"But he on'y got one eye," Thomas had said. "Where's the other one?"

"He's standing sideways and you can only see his left eye."

This made Thomas laugh so much that his mother called him silly.

He didn't talk about when she would pull on his toes when he was going to sleep at night, counting them — one, two, three, four, five. Or when she'd pick flowers and put them into her hair and take Dr. Nolan into her arms and dance him around the kitchen.

The minister called her a good mother and devoted daughter, but he didn't say how she'd stay up all night with him and Eric when they were sick. He made her sound like a flat picture in a book rather than his mother with her warm skin and sweet breath.

Somewhere in the middle of the long sermon, Thomas started crying. He wanted Dr. Nolan to go up there and tell everybody what his mother was really like. He wanted to go home and let his knees sink into the floor.

"Do you want to go up and say good-bye to your mother?" Minas Nolan asked Thomas when the sermon was over and the organ player had started her sad song.

"No," Thomas said.

"Are you sure? It's your last chance to see her."

"I can't," Thomas said in a high whine. "I can't."

Dr. Nolan began to cry. He picked up the boy and rushed out of the church. He brought Tommy to the long black car and got in with him in the backseat.

"To the cemetery, Dr. Nolan?" the black driver asked.

"No, no. Take us to the restaurant. I'll, I'll go see her later. Later."

Tommy buried his face in the fabric of Dr. Nolan's jacket. He closed his eyes and held his breath but nothing would stop him from crying.

When they got to the Rib Joint, Tommy and Dr. Nolan sat outside in the car until the boy could sit back and talk.

"It's okay," Dr. Nolan told him. "We're all very sad."

"How could it be okay to be so sad?"

"Because we all loved her so much."

Tommy got up on his knees and put his arms around the doctor's neck. He held tight but was no longer crying. They stayed like that, holding each other until the families began to arrive from the cemetery.

IRA FONTANOT HAD closed the restaurant that day and catered a meal for the memory of his friend Branwyn Beerman. He set out fried chicken and potato salad and a special dish of the spicy catfish that Branwyn ate every time she sat at his kitchen table for a meal.

People were talking and eating and drinking throughout the restaurant and in the backyard.

It was a bright day, and the sun made Thomas squint. He found Eric talking to a little black girl who had come with one of Branwyn's cousins. The girl's name was Robin, and she wore all yellow clothes.

"Did you look at the body?" she asked Eric.

"Sure. I had to say good-bye," he said, half proud and half sincere.

"An' you too, Tommy?" Robin asked.

Thomas felt the tears come up to his eyes, but before he could say anything, or not say anything, Eric spoke for him. "Tommy went to sleep with her the night she died. He woke up in the bed with her and came in to tell my dad that she was dead."

Robin, who was two inches shorter than Eric and two inches taller than Thomas, wrapped her arms around Branwyn's son and cried, "Poor baby!"

Adults gathered around them and commented on how kind and loving children were.

Sometime soon after Robin hugged Thomas, Elton Trueblood came up to the boy.

"I guess after the wake you'll be comin' home with me," he said with not even a word of hello.

"I have to go home with Dr. Nolan and Eric," Thomas told his father.

"Not no more," Elton told him. "You're my son, and you are coming home with me."

"I live with Dr. Nolan," Thomas said, fear gurgling in his stomach.

"Yeah," Eric added. "Tommy's my brother, and he lives with me."

"Get outta my face, white boy," Elton said. "This black child here is my blood. Mine. Maybe I couldn't do nuthin' to save his mother, but you better believe I'm gonna take care'a him."

He reached out and took Thomas by the arm. The boy didn't know what to do so he let his weight go and fell to the ground as he'd done when he was younger with his mother and Ahn. But Elton just heaved the tiny boy up in his arms and began walking toward the back door of the restaurant.

Elton hadn't counted on two things. The first was Eric's powerful lungs. The boy shouted so loudly that everyone stopped what they were doing to see what was happening. The second mistake Elton made was trying to take Branwyn's son from Ira Fontanot's place.

Elton was a big man, six feet and a little more, but Ira was six foot seven in silk socks, and he had hands like catcher's mitts and arms made (as he used to say) from four hundred years of hard labor. Ira grabbed Elton by one shoulder and squeezed so hard that the would-be mechanic went down on his knees.

"Let the boy go," Ira commanded.

"He's my son," Elton hissed through the pain.

"I don't care what he is to you; you put him down or I put you down."

Elton released Thomas. He ran to Dr. Nolan, who had just come from inside the restaurant.

Fontanot released his grip, and Elton rose to his feet, rubbing the sore shoulder.

"He's my son," Elton said again.

"Then why he live up in the doctor's house?" Ira asked. "Why the doctor pay for his clothes and food?"

"He's mine and he belongs with me."

"The courts might agree, but you can't take a boy from his mother's funeral and not even let him settle his affairs. You gotta do somethin' like that right, not like some wild fool just grab a child and run."

Elton took a step toward Ira, shouting, "You don't have the right to take my boy!"

"And you wouldn't wanna make him a orphan," Ira said softly. "Back down and do this right or I will break you in two."

Elton turned to Dr. Nolan and said, "This ain't ovah by a long shot," and then he walked away.

Thomas was holding on to Dr. Nolan's leg.

"Is it okay, Daddy?" he asked his mother's lover.

"Yes, son," Dr. Nolan replied.

4

For the next week Thomas spent all of his time on his knees in his room when he wasn't at school or eating with Dr. Nolan, Ahn, and Eric. He'd close his eyes and think about becoming a part of the house, and he'd *feel* his mother's presence. He couldn't speak to her, but somehow he knew that if he kept his eyes closed she'd be standing there next to him, smiling.

One night Eric came into his room after everyone else was asleep.

"Tommy?" the big six-year-old said into the darkness.

"Uh-huh."

"Are you awake?"

"Yeah."

"What were you doin'?" Eric asked as he climbed up onto the bed.

"I was thinkin' that Mama was standin' in the corner makin' sure that I was asleep, and so I had my eyes closed so that she would think that I was."

"Do you think that she comes into my room too?" Eric asked.

"Of course she does. You're the one never go to sleep at his bedtime anyway. She'd have to come look at you."

"But I never see her."

"That's because she only comes in after we're asleep so that she doesn't wake you and then she can kiss you good night."

"Did she kiss you tonight?"

"Not yet. She was still seein' if I was asleep."

"Do you ever see her?" Eric asked, his big eyes glittering in the nearly lightless room.

"Only if I open my eyes real quick and I see her white dress and then she's gone."

"Why doesn't she stay and talk to you?" Eric asked.

"Because she doesn't want to scare us," Thomas told his brother. "She wants to make sure that we're okay, but she knows that you're not supposed to see people after they're dead."

Eric took this in and put it away. He often didn't quite understand the things that Thomas told him, but he knew that his brother understood things that he could not and so he always listened and never made fun of him.

When they went on walks in the woods or down at the beach, Thomas would always find the most beautiful shells and stones. Eric could run faster and do almost everything better than Thomas, but the smaller boy paid closer attention to any space they entered. Often, after a day trip, Eric would come to Thomas's room and ask him about what he had seen.

"I wanted to talk to you about what happened today," Eric said, broaching the subject he had come to discuss.

"What?" Thomas asked.

"You know . . . those boys that pushed you."

Still under the spell of his mother's watchful gaze, Thomas had to concentrate to remember.

"Oh, yeah. Uh-huh," he said. "Billy Monzell."

"You don't believe what they said, do you?"

Three boys led by Billy — Young William, as Mr. Stroud, the first-grade teacher, called him — had cornered Thomas on the playground and called him nigger and pushed him down. Before Thomas could do anything, Eric had run up and pushed Billy down. Young William got up, but Eric pushed him down again.

"You leave my brother alone," Billy told all of them. He was the biggest boy in the class, and even the three bullies were afraid to take him on.

"He's a nigger so he can't be your brother," Billy said. "Black and white can't ever be brothers."

Eric hit Billy in the mouth, and Dr. Nolan had to come and take him home for the rest of the day.

"No," Thomas said. "He's just ignorant. You're my brother. Mama always said so."

"Can I stay here in your room?" Eric asked then.

"Uh-uh," Thomas said, shaking his head in the darkness. "I wanna go to sleep. But I'll come down and wake you up in the morning."

Thomas didn't want to tell him that he was afraid that if they slept in the same bed, Eric might die like their mother did. He had come to believe that he was unlucky for the people he loved.

THE NEXT MORNING Dr. Nolan kept Thomas home when Eric went off to school.

"There's something we have to do," Minas told the black child he regarded as his son.

"What, Dad?" Thomas asked.

The doctor took a deep breath and sighed.

"Your grandmother and father are coming at ten," he said. "They want you to come live with them."

"But I don't wanna."

"I don't want it either, Tommy. I told them that you want to be here with me and Eric and Ahn but Madeline says that she and your father are your closest relatives . . . and, well, they are."

"But I don't wanna live with Grandma Madeline," Tommy said again. He couldn't think of anything else to say. "Why you makin' me?"

"I spoke to a man," Nolan said, his shoulders sagging, his gaze on the floor. "A lawyer. He told me that because your mother and I never married that Madeline and your father have legal guardianship."

"But why didn't you get married?"

"I asked her, Tommy. I asked her every month. But she always said no."

Thomas thought about the lunch he had with his mother and father. Elton had kissed Branwyn on the mouth before they left. At first she seemed to be kissing him back, but then she pushed him away and after that she spent the day crying.

Looking up at Minas Nolan's sad face, Thomas knew somehow that he was the reason they could not marry. This knowledge was perfectly delineated by the dimness in his eyes.

"That's okay, Daddy. I know she loved you. She told me so."

"She did?"

"Uh-huh."

Dr. Nolan coughed and turned away.

Ahn made tea and hot chocolate and said very little. An hour later the doorbell rang. Madeline Beerman and Elton Trueblood were admitted, and everyone sat together in the downstairs living room drinking coffee and talking.

Thomas perched on the hassock in front of the big chair where Minas Nolan sat.

"Thomas is always welcome to come visit," the doctor said.

"Maybe after a while," Madeline replied. "But first he has to get used to livin' with us."

"Will you tell Eric where I am?" Thomas asked Nolan.

"Don't interrupt, Tommy," Elton told him. "Grown-ups are talkin'."

"Which one of you will Thomas be staying with?" Minas asked Madeline.

"Where Tommy lives ain't none of your business, man," Elton told him. "I should have called the police on you when you took him out of that restaurant. He's my boy. Maybe I didn't do right by Brawn, but I intend to be a father to Tommy."

"I understand how you feel, Mr. Trueblood," Minas said softly. "I have a son too. But you see, Tommy has lived in this house ever since the day after he came home from the hospital. I know that you're his father, but that doesn't mean I don't feel concern."

"You can be concerned all you want," Elton said. "But he is my son. Here you talkin' like you care so much. If you loved them so much how come you a doctor and she died right here undah yo' roof?"

"She . . . I, I wanted her to go to the hospital," Dr. Nolan whispered. "I tried to convince her."

Elton stood up and so did Madeline. Ahn kissed Thomas and whispered, "You remember what I told you about running, running."

Dr. Nolan knelt down and hugged Thomas hard.

"I love you, Tommy," he said for the first time that Thomas could remember.

"That's enough now," Elton said, and Thomas found himself being dragged from the house and out to a shiny green car that smelled like cigarettes.

They drove for a long time, with Thomas sitting in the backseat and Elton driving.

"You don't have to be scared, Tommy," Madeline said. "Elton's got a nice house too, and he's your real father."

"He don't have nuthin' to be scared about anyway," Elton complained. "He's lucky he got a real father to come and take him. You know, I don't have to do this. I could leave you up there with those white people. I didn't have to take you and make you a real home."

"The boy's scared, Elton," Madeline said. "You don't have to shout like that. He's used to that house, and he thinks about those people like family."

"More than me," Elton agreed. "Here they got their pet niggah grabbin' me by the shoulder until it almost break, an' Tommy didn't even say to let me go. Here I am his real father, and he don't even say a word when that man was crushin' my bones. If I seen somebody do *my* father like that, I'd run at him with a two-by-four."

Thomas didn't know what a "toobifor" was, but he understood that his father thought that he should have fought with Fontanot. He tried to imagine fighting the giant, but all he could think of was Eric running at him. Then he wondered what Eric would do when he found out that he was gone.

"Do you hear me?" Elton said. "Tommy!"

"What?"

"Are you listening to me?"

"I was thinking," he said.

"Thinkin'? I'm talkin' to you."

"What did you say?"

"Goddamn, the boy is retarded."

"Don't say that," Madeline chided. "He was born sick and couldn't get enough oxygen. And Branwyn was alone and did the best she could."

"That's not my fault," Elton said in a softer tone.

"An' it's not Tommy's fault either."

AFTER TAKING MADELINE to her apartment on Denker, Elton brought Tommy to his rented house on McKinley. It was a small square building with chipped white paint and a flat green roof. There was an elevated porch and a tattered screen door.

Elton carried Tommy's little suitcase to the door and pulled the screen open.

"Why the hell is the front do' unlocked?" he yelled into the house as he stomped inside. Tommy ran up to the threshold, hesitated for a moment, and then followed.

The house smelled of foods and cigarettes, something sweet and something else that made Thomas think of water.

They were standing in a sitting room, where there was a TV turned on in front of an empty black couch and a brown recliner. There was a low white coffee table between the couch and the TV, and a carpet underneath it all that was dark purple.

People on the television chattered away and the sun was bright outside, but this room would never be light. Thomas felt his new darkened vision would fit well in this dim, uneven room.

"Hi, Daddy." A woman came running out wearing pink cotton pants over a black leotard. She had dark skin and wore a blond wig of thick hair that did a flip in the back.

"Ooooo," the big curvy woman cried. "Is this li'l Tommy?"

"Why the hell was the do' open for any thief to come in here?" Elton barked.

The smile on the black blonde's face shriveled, and suddenly Thomas was afraid.

"I opened the goddamned do' when I heard yo' rattletrap car comin' down the street," she said through curled lips and bared teeth.

"But you wasn't at the do'," Elton said. "You was up in the house someplace where any niggah could'a come up in here an' steal me blind. Shit. I know people go out for a piss an' come back to find they TV gone."

"You think there's some fool out there gonna break his back for that big pile'a shit you call a TV?" The woman was getting louder. Thomas felt the threat in her voice.

"You'idn't call it no hunk'a shit when I brought it home now did ya? Did ya?" Elton's voice was also dangerous.

Thomas had trouble understanding what either one of them was saying. Their voices sounded a little like his mother's though, and he wondered if she was somehow trying to communicate through them.

"I ain't got nuthin' t'say," the woman said.

"You bettah shut up," Elton agreed. "An' as long as I'm payin' the rent you bettah keep that goddamned do' shut too."

"Talkin' 'bout the rent, Mr. Sanders came down lookin' fo' the check this mornin'. He said that if he don't have it by six they gonna kick our ass out."

Elton balled up fists and raised them to his chest.

Without thinking, Thomas fell to the floor. His heart was racing, and he thought about running out the door before they could close it.

"Look what you doin', Elton," the woman said. "You scarin' the boy."

"Get up from the flo', boy," Elton told his son. "Get up!"

Thomas tried to comply. He wanted to get up before Elton used those big scarred fists on him. But he was so frightened that he couldn't move.

"Get up!" Elton took a step toward Thomas, and the boy crawled away.

"Get up!" he cried again.

Then he grabbed Thomas by the arm and heaved him into the air. He tried to put him on his feet, but Thomas's legs turned to rubber every time his toes touched the ground. There were tears coming from his eyes, and his nose was running.

"Dammit," Elton said, curling his lip in disgust.

He let go of the boy's arm and Thomas fell with a thump onto the purple rug.

"Elton!" the blond black woman cried. "The boy's scared."

She leaned over and picked Thomas up in her arms.

"What's he got to be scared about? I'm his father. He bettah not be afraid'a me."

"If you his father then act like it," she said. "Tell him you happy to have him here. Buy him some ice cream."

"I'm his father," Elton said. "He should know I'm happy. Why the hell I take him away from them people ain't no blood to him if I didn't love him? Why I'm'a add his mouth to the ones I'm feedin' if I didn't want him?"

The woman sucked on a tooth, making a loud crackling sound.

"Don't you have sumpin' to do?" she said. "Me an' Tommy gonna get acquainted."

With that she carried the small boy back through the door she'd come from. They went down a long hall and into a large kitchen that was painted gray and lit by a bulb shining through green glass.

They heard the front door slam, and Thomas breathed a sigh of relief that his father had gone.

The woman carried Thomas to a wooden chair at a table in the center of the big room. She sat with him nestled in her lap.

Thomas liked her soft warmth and sweet odor. When she put her hand to the side of his cheek, he pressed his head against her palm.

"You a sweet boy, huh?" she said, hugging him closer. "My name is May. I used to know your mother a long time ago, before you were born."

"I thought Daddy said that you moved away?" Thomas said then, remembering the conversation at the hotel restaurant.

"He did? When did he say that?"

"When we had lunch."

"You had lunch with him before today?"

"Uh-huh. Me and my mama did."

"Elton had lunch wit' Branwyn and you?"

"Uh-huh."

For a moment Thomas thought that he'd said something wrong, but then May smiled. She had a beautiful smile, and for the first time in many days the boy forgot that he was sad.

"We don't have a proper bedroom for you yet, Tommy," May said. "But there's a cot out on the back porch, and it's gonna be pretty warm for the next little while. You wanna see it?"

Thomas nodded and put his hand against May's cheek. When he did this she swelled up, taking in a deep breath. She put him down on the floor and kissed his cheek before she stood up, and then, hand in hand, they walked through the back door and into the screened-in back porch.

The floor was made of unfinished wood planks, a few of which had spaces between them so that Thomas could see down through to the ground underneath. The porch was about twelve feet long and only five feet wide. Three of the walls were made of corroded metal screening, and the roof was layered with white aluminum slats. There was a broken lawn mower in the corner and three decomposing cardboard boxes spilling out rags and papers along the screen walls. The cot supported a bright blue-and-green vinyl-covered mattress that belonged on a chaise longue near a pool.

"I got a sheet that you can have," May said. "And there's some pillows and blankets in the cabinet in our room. An' don't you worry about Elton. He ain't mad at you. Him an' me just fight sometimes."

After that May showed Thomas her and Elton's bedroom and then her "sewing room" at the end of another long hall. They got the sheet and a blanket, a pillow and a lamp — which had a ceramic mermaid as a base — for his back-porch room. Thomas had learned to make his own bed from his mother, and so he told May that he could make up the room on his own.

She went to make a phone call, and when she got off she told Thomas that she was going out and to tell Elton, when he got back, that she was going to have dinner with August Murphy.

Thomas wasn't worried to be alone. All he could see out of his screen walls were the trees of their yard and the yards of their neighbors. Beyond the trees there was a dark area and then the houses of the people behind.

Thomas threaded the cord for his lamp through a small window that led from the kitchen to the porch. He plugged the cord into a socket near the sink. He found a small transistor radio and turned the dial until he came upon a station playing the violin music that Ahn liked to listen to when she was washing clothes.

The back porch was filled with life and death. There were spiderwebs that had dead and dying moths and flies trapped in them. And there were crawling spiders and flying gnats. There was a hornet's hive on the other side of the screen. Slow-flying yellow-and-black stingers hovered on the breeze humming their low-pitched songs.

In the crook of a tree's trunk, not five feet away from his transparent wall, Tommy spied a bird's nest. The chicks chirped and cried until their mother came with food that she forced down their gullets. Then they cried again. On the ground at the foot of the tree lay a dead chick. Three long lines of black ants led to and from the small, gray feathered corpse.

Thomas was happy with his half room at the back of the dark house. He settled down on his knees on the floor and closed his eyes, trying to imagine what it would be like to be that open-eyed, open-mouthed chick on the ground below his peeping brothers and sisters, the soft tickle of tiny ants across his body, the spiky grass growing up from underneath.

After a while Thomas forgot the dead chick. He was just there on his knees slowly becoming one with the floor, searching for his mother again among the timbers and nails and then into the ground below.

As he sat there the sun, which filtered onto the porch bringing sweet green light down, began to fade. He even forgot about his mother, being aware of only the cool evening breezes and the sonorous buzzing of hornets.

Just before it was fully night, a banging sound jarred Thomas from his ruminations. Hard footsteps through the floor made him open his eyes. And the loud "May, where are you?" brought him to his feet.

When the back door to the porch opened, he was looking up, ready to face Elton.

"Where's May?" the man asked his son.

"She's having dinner with August Murphy," the boy said.

"What?" Elton cried, the word sounding more like a threat than a question.

Thomas repeated the answer, thinking that his father must have thought that he was saying something else.

"Did she tell you to tell me that or did you hear her on the phone?"

"She was on the phone, and then she said to say it," Thomas replied.

"What the hell is this lamp doin' out here?" Elton asked then. And before Thomas could reply, "What the hell you doin' here with all the lights in the house out? If you leave the lights out then thieves think you ain't home an' come an' rob you. Didn't they tell you that at those white people's house?"

"I don't know."

"What you mean you don't know? You stupid?"

Thomas realized that there was no answer he could give that would keep Elton from getting angrier, so he didn't say anything.

"She said to tell me that she was going out to dinner with August Murphy?"

Thomas nodded.

This seemed to work. Instead of shouting, Elton went back into the house. He banged around and made noises with what sounded to Thomas like bottles and glasses. He made a phone call and did a lot of loud cursing. Then he went two rooms away to the living room, where he turned the TV up loud.

The night came on as all of this was happening. Thousands of insects fluttered up to the screen and thumped up against it in their attempt to get at the lamplight. Beyond the night bugs were a few stars and the quarter moon. Looking up there, Thomas remembered the nights when Dr. Nolan and Eric were gone to some family party. Branwyn and Thomas would go out into the flower garden in their pajamas and bare feet. Big pale-green moths flew overhead, and the boy and his mother made up stories about the stars.

"It's like a big coat on the man in the moon," Branwyn would say, "and all the stars are just the dust that fell off the sun."

"An' if he brush it off," Thomas would add, "all the dust would fall down on us, but it would be yellow diamonds and dimes."

They'd laugh and run through the garden until way after Thomas's bedtime. And when he'd go to bed finally, he'd get the giggles so bad that he couldn't go to sleep for laughing.

Lying across that hard and lumpy mattress, on Elton and May's back porch, Thomas thought about the flower garden and his mother, and he believed that somewhere she was thinking the same things. This made him very happy, and he fell asleep feeling that he wasn't alone in that screened-in room.

In his dreams he was drowsing in the big chair in the back-yard near the pool. As usual he was tired after only a little while, but Eric was still leaping from the diving board and telling everybody to look. Dr. Nolan and Branwyn were lying side by side on two lounge chairs, and Ahn was sitting near to where Eric was, just in case he got into trouble from playing too hard.

Thomas was perfectly happy and dozy in his chair.

Then a woman's loud scream brought him wide awake.

"What the fuck you mean 'out'!" Elton yelled.

Then another scream.

"Get your hands off'a me," May shouted.

"I'ma see if he been up in there," Elton said. They were in the kitchen, Thomas realized. "An' if he have been, then I'ma bust yo' head."

There was a scuffle and more screams.

Something crashed to the floor, and May let out a yell that picked Thomas up out of the bed and dragged him to the door to the kitchen. He didn't want to go into the room, but he couldn't help himself. He was drawn by the sounds of violence.

When he pushed the door open, he saw that Elton had thrown May up on the kitchen table. Her dress was hiked up to her waist, and Elton had his hand up under her red panties.

"If I feel him up there I'ma make it that you ain't nevah gonna have no babies," Elton shouted.

"I ain't done nuthin', baby," May moaned. "I just had dinnah."

"Till two in the mo'nin'?"

Elton moved his hand with a violent twist, and May screamed again.

Without thinking, Thomas rushed at Elton's leg and wrapped his arms around it.

"Stop, Daddy!" the little boy screamed. "Stop!"

"What?" Elton cried, surprised by the appearance of his son.

He looked down at Thomas as if he had never seen him before. The man's eyes were very bloodshot, and there was a crazy curl on his lips.

Just then there was a loud sound at the front of the house.

"Help!" May cried. "Help! He's tryin' to kill me!"

Four uniformed policemen rushed into the room.

"What the fuck?" Elton shouted.

"Stand down," a tall black policeman said, and then, before Elton could move, the policeman hit him across the forehead with a short black stick.

Elton fell to the floor. His arms were flailing and his eyes were wild.

"Fuckin' hell," Thomas's father said. "This my house."

He got halfway up, but another cop hit him with a night-stick and he went down again. But he wasn't unconscious. He tried once more to get up while May was gibbering and shouting behind an Asian officer near the door.

Thomas had backed up against the wall. He was more frightened of Elton now than he had ever been. He couldn't understand how someone could be hit so hard, so many times, in the head and not stay down. He now saw his father like a monster on one of those scary shows that Eric liked to watch — a monster that couldn't be killed and who came back through bombs and gunfire and killed everyone except the women and children he took to his cave, where later he would eat them.

Two of the officers had jumped on top of Elton. They were pulling his hands behind his back. Thomas was expecting to see the policemen thrown off like on TV, but instead they bound Elton's hands and dragged him to his feet. He struggled but didn't get away. He yelled, but the threats didn't hurt anyone.

"You don't have to hit him like that," May cried.

Suddenly the big woman jumped at the Asian officer, knocking him into the men trying to subdue Elton.

"Leave him the fuck alone!" May cried. "Leave him!"

"I will kill you when I get outta here," Elton warned May even though she was trying to help him. "I will kill you when I get out." And then he turned his head toward Thomas. "An' you too, you little bastid. You think you cute tellin' her about that lunch. Lyin' like I was after her. Lyin' 'bout what I said. I'ma get you too."

Then the policemen dragged Elton off. They handcuffed May and took her along too. Finally there was just Thomas and the Asian policeman left in the house.

His name was Robert Leung, and his grandparents had come from China.

"And so Mr. Trueblood is your father?" Officer Leung was asking Thomas. They were sitting on the black couch in the TV room.

"Uh-huh," Thomas replied.

"And Miss Fine is your mother?"

"No. May's Daddy's girlfriend."

"Does she live here with you?"

"I think so."

Officer Leung frowned. "Don't you know?"

Thomas explained that his mother had died and that he had just come to live with his father.

"Does your father hit you?" the policeman asked.

"No."

"Are you afraid that he's going to hit you?"

Thomas didn't know the answer and so remained silent.

The policeman took him in the squad car down to the precinct police station. There they put him into a cell and locked the door.

"I'm locking the door so nobody else can hurt you," Officer Leung said. "Child services has to come to get you, but they're all asleep and so you'll have to stay here until they get here."

"Can't I go with you?" the boy asked the cop.

"I have to go home."

Thomas couldn't understand why the policeman didn't realize that he wanted to go home with him. He thought that if Eric was there he could make the policeman understand. *Eric always makes people understand,* Thomas thought.

"Pssssт," THOMAS HEARD, when Officer Leung had left the room full of human cages.

It was a tall, light-colored man across the way, also locked up in a cell.

When Thomas looked the man said, "You ever see a man's big thing?"

Thomas thought he knew what the man meant, but he wasn't sure. This uncertainty made him shake his head slightly.

The man, who was clad all in gray, pulled down the zipper of his pants and fished out his penis. It was very long and slender.

The man laughed.

Thomas turned away from him and settled down to the floor on his knees. The man kept talking, but Thomas hummed to himself so that the words the man uttered were unintelligible. After a while the man stopped talking, and all that was left were the sounds of Thomas's own humming and the hardness of the concrete floor beneath his knees.

5

B UT WHERE'D he go?" Eric asked his father when he got
home from school and was told that Tommy had moved
away for good.

Ahn and Minas were both afraid to have Eric there when
Tommy left. They knew that he would react loudly and violently, and it would have been harder on both children.

"Tommy's father came to take him," Minas told his son.

"But you're his father," Eric argued.

"No."

"Mama Branwyn was my mother, and she's his mother
too. So you have to be his father."

"I love Tommy like a son, but Elton Trueblood is his real
father. He never married Branwyn, but Tommy is his blood
and the law says that he has to go live with him or with his
grandmother."

Eric felt the color red in his head and in his fists and feet. He
stormed out of the downstairs den, stomped up to his room,
and systematically broke every toy that he owned. He broke
the soldier action figures, the rocking horse, the colored lamp
that turned slowly, showing horses and circus clowns on his
wall at night. He shattered the screen of his television and
crushed the clay drum his father had brought back from Alge-
ria. He slung his mattress on the floor and threw his baseball

through the closed window. Then he picked up his aluminum baseball bat and beat it against the wall and furniture with the intention of breaking the bat in two. But it wouldn't break. Instead he dented his maple desk, put holes in the plaster of the wall, and made deep notches in the oak floor.

All the while Eric screamed his brother's name and shouted obscenities he'd learned from the older kids on the playground.

"Fuck damn!" he shouted.

"Shit!" he cried.

And for every curse or profanity, he broke something or struck the walls or floor with his metal bat.

When the baseball went through the window, Minas headed for the boy's room. By the time he got there, Eric was wreaking havoc with his bat.

When Minas entered the room, Eric swung at him but missed. The surgeon's hand darted out and pushed the boy down on the mattress that had been spilled off the bed.

Minas had never struck Eric before. The novelty and shock of that, plus the deep desolation he felt about losing his mother and then his brother, brought Eric to tears. He cried on the mattress and then rolled onto the floor. He caterwauled and howled, whined like a motherless cub, and shouted unintelligible sentences at the Infinite. Minas held his son, and even then, in the boy's most miserable state, his father marveled at the depth of feeling that Eric was capable of. His sorrow seemed to diminish Minas's own fears and losses. It was as if Eric was deserving of more care and consideration because he was more, much more, than other humans.

They sat there on the floor of the boy's destroyed room, Minas thinking of how much they had both lost and Eric howling like some animal faced for the first time with a giant harvest moon.

Late in the afternoon Minas drove Eric down to the beach at Malibu. The boys had always liked it there, and so the father thought it might be good for his son.

"Why did you let them take Tommy?" the child asked his father on the drive.

"I couldn't stop them, Eric. They had the law on their side."

"*You* couldn't stop them, but *I* would have," the boy said. "And you should have too. Tommy is our family. You can't let family go."

They walked down the beach on sand left wet by the receding tide. Minas was wearing a yellow shirt and dark-blue pants. His shoes were made of woven brown leather; a thick golden watch hung from his right wrist.

Eric had taken off his shoes in the car. His T-shirt was yellow like his father's pullover, but his pants were tan and rolled up past his ankles.

"Can I go visit Tommy?" the boy asked his father while scanning the waterline.

"Maybe after a while. His grandmother wants him to get used to being with them before letting us come see him."

"He's gonna be with them every day," Eric said. "He's gonna be used to them anyway."

"We'll see," Minas Nolan said to his son.

At that moment Eric gasped and ran out into the shallows of the retreating Pacific.

"Eric," Minas Nolan said, but before he could go out after his son, the boy was coming back with something wriggling in his hands.

It was a bright-green fish with brownish bumps along its back and big googly eyes that seemed somehow to contain mammalian intelligence. The tail was long and elegant, with a fin at the end shaped like a Japanese fan. The body was thick, and the fins below were so long and powerful they might have been used as legs.

"What is it?" Minas Nolan asked, forgetting his losses for a moment.

"A fish," Eric said bluntly. "It was stuck in the sand."

"But what kind?" his father asked. "I've never seen anything like that in my life. It's certainly not a California fish. Maybe it's from the tropics or the deep sea. Maybe this is some fish dredged up by an undersea storm, a fish nobody's ever seen before."

With a careless motion, Eric tossed the googly-eyed green fish back into the water, whereupon it darted away.

"I don't like fish," the boy said simply. "Let's go home, Dad."

THAT NIGHT ERIC had his father write a letter to his brother, Thomas.

Dear Tommy,

Dad told me that you had to go away with your father. I don't like it that you had to go, and I know that you want to be back here with us. I'm going to go get you as soon as I can figure out where you are and how I can get there. I will save you and bring you back here so we can play overhand catch and finish the first grade together.

Eric Tanner Nolan

p.s.

I found a green fish today that Dad said was real rare. If you were here I bet that you would have found him first.

Minas wrote the letter in bold characters that Eric could examine when he was done. They put the letter in an envelope, which Minas addressed and Ahn sent off to Madeline Beerman.

Madeline received the letter, but she never gave it to Thomas. She put it, unopened, in the bureau drawer next to her bed.

ERIC RETURNED TO his life. At school he was the most popular boy in his class. He won every game he played at recess and was always chosen by the teacher to help clean the erasers and pass out papers.

Sometimes at night he would flip a coin with Ahn. It was a simple game. He'd flip an old Indian head nickel his father had once given him, and either he or Ahn would call heads or tails before it settled on the floor.

Eric won almost every time. Ahn was astonished by this. Even though she had little formal education, she knew that he shouldn't win any more than she did. But there it was — time after time Eric would call heads and heads would turn up; Eric would call tails and tails it would be.

The nanny woke up one night from a deep sleep in which she was having a dream about flipping the coin with Eric. In the dream her faceless father was standing above her and the big blond boy. She and Eric were the same size in the dream. Ahn had lost sixty-three flips in a row when her father said, "One more loss and you will die, my daughter."

That's when Ahn awoke with a start.

"Every time he wins someone else loses," she said to herself.

She gasped and suddenly saw her charge as some kind of monster.

"He killed his mother," Ahn said to no one. "He killed Miss Branwyn."

She lay back in her bed thinking of little Thomas.

"Maybe he's safer away from Eric," she thought. "Maybe Eric will destroy everyone he touches."

THE DAYS AND months and years passed in the Nolan household. Everyone wanted to be Eric's best friend. Every girl wanted to be his girlfriend. The teachers loved him, and the sun illuminated his path.

He skipped the sixth grade because he knew all the subjects by grade five. It wasn't hard for him to enter junior high school early because he was much bigger than his classmates anyway. He had natural agility and strength. And he was more mature than many adults at this early age.

And Eric was fearless. Nothing bad ever happened to him. He and another boy, Lester Corning, were once playing with fireworks when Lester's parents were out. They were both leaning over the same Roman candle when instead of firing a flaming ball into the air, the rocket exploded. Lester took the full blast on the left side of his face, but Eric went unharmed. His hair wasn't even singed. This was lucky for Lester, who was in so much pain that all he could do was roll on the grass of his backyard and scream.

Eric ran to the house and dialed 911. He explained the problem to the man on the other end of the line, and the ambulance came there in time to save Lester's eyesight.

Eric was not only unhurt but seen as a hero by everyone. The ambulance attendants praised him for keeping Lester from touching his severely burned face. Lester's parents thanked Eric for having the presence of mind to call for help. (Lester admitted that playing with the fireworks was his idea and that Eric didn't even want to.)

That night Dr. Nolan took his son, then ten years old, aside and did the fatherly thing by explaining how risky it was to allow other children to persuade him to do something dangerous.

"You could have been burned just as easily as Lester," Minas told his son.

"But why wasn't I burned, Dad?" the boy asked. "We were holding the Roman candle between us. It was just as close to me as it was to him."

"That's what you call *serendipity,*" Minas replied. "Sometimes something terrible happens to one man and leaves another alone.

"When I was a boy in Kansas, a tornado hit a neighborhood in my town. The twister set down at the beginning of the two-hundred block of Orchard Street. It knocked down four houses in a row, veered around the fifth, and then came back with a vengeance, destroying every other house on that side of the block. I suppose that there's some scientific explanation for what happened, but for the people in house number five it was just good fortune."

Eric went up to his room pondering the word *serendipity.* He often wondered why so many good things happened to him. He never counted on his luck, but things always seemed to go right. He was lying in his bed in the dark, in Thomas's old room, thinking about Lester and the accident, when there came a knock on the door.

"Come in."

The door opened, and Ahn shuffled in.

Eric had known Ahn his entire life. She was no longer his nanny. Now she was Dr. Nolan's housekeeper and the family cook. Eric would have never said that he loved Ahn. He did love his father, but it wasn't a very strong feeling.

"You have to be careful," Ahn said to Eric.

"You mean about the fireworks?" the boy asked. "Dad already told me that I could have been burned too."

"No. I mean, yes, you shouldn't play with danger because you will hurt others."

"Not me?"

"You are dangerous," Ahn said.

Eric tried to decipher what the Vietnamese servant meant. Many times when they talked, she would say things like "you are dangerous," really meaning that he was in danger.

"You mean I'm in danger?"

"No. You are the reason that boy is burned," she said. "You are never hurt, but he is not lucky. Be careful with your friends. Do not put them in trouble."

Ahn's black eyes stared into Eric's great blue orbs.

The boy wondered about what she was saying. Sometimes he felt like that, that he was lucky.

The housekeeper turned away.

"Ahn."

"Yes?"

"Have you heard anything about Tommy?"

"Nobody ever answers your letters, but they don't come back," she replied. "I am not finding Mr. Trueblood in the phone book, and his grandmother says that Tommy is with him."

"But he must be somewhere."

"I don't know. Maybe they left Los Angeles."

"They have to be somewhere."

"He is safe," she said, and then turned away again.

Eric was angry at what she said. He knew that she meant Tommy was safe from him. But he would never hurt his brother. He loved Tommy. Always had. Tommy and Branwyn were the only people he'd ever felt passion for.

The door closed behind Ahn, and Eric was once again in darkness. He sat there worrying that maybe Ahn was right. Maybe he drove Tommy away.

That night Eric didn't go to sleep. Instead he stayed awake thinking about his real mother, dead for so long, and Mama Branwyn, who was the perfect woman in his eyes. He thought about Tommy, whom he hadn't seen or heard from in more than four years.

After Tommy had left, Eric's father went back to working long hours. He was quiet at the dinner table, and they hadn't taken a vacation, or even a weekend holiday, in all that time.

Eric still missed his brother every day. Now and then he made friends at school or summer camp, but he'd never met another soul who saw the world the way Tommy did. Tommy saw faces in rocks, and he laughed at big, broad things like fat trees and passing images in clouds. He knew Branwyn better than anyone and never got mad at Eric for needing her love too.

Eric didn't feel close to Ahn. When he was smaller she was just always there — to dress him, feed him, make sure that he was in the right place at the right time. He played games with her after Tommy was gone, but he didn't care about her.

Eric realized that he didn't care about much. He had fun and was befriended by almost everyone, but he never minded having to go home or when someone he saw every day left for good.

No, he wasn't close to Ahn, but he remembered one day sitting outside the pool area in a health spa in Palm Springs. He and Tommy were five, and the smaller boy wanted to sit on the brick wall and wait to see if a roadrunner, the fleet-footed bird, might pass by.

Eric got bored and started asking Tommy questions.

He asked how it felt to break a bone. (Tommy had broken

his finger, an ankle, his right leg, and his collarbone in falls.) He wanted to know what Branwyn wore when she went to bed. He asked Tommy if he ever wished that he and Branwyn were white like everybody else that they knew.

Tommy answered every question in his soft and slow voice.

"When my ankle broke it hurt so bad that I had to think that I was in another room from my foot," Tommy said.

His mother wore a white cotton slip to bed, and he didn't care what color they were.

Finally Eric asked Tommy, "Why do you think Ahn's crazy?"

For a long time Tommy stared out into the desert between the cholla cacti and Joshua trees. After a while Eric thought that his brother had forgotten the question.

Then Tommy started talking in a voice so soft that he was in the middle of his answer before Eric realized that he was being addressed.

"An' she's been in the places where everybody's sad all the time," Tommy was saying.

"Who?" Eric asked.

"Ahn. She comes from far away in a war, my mom says. She's always lookin' to see bad things comin', and that's why Dr. Nolan hired her, so she could see trouble before it gets here."

Remembering these words in the bed, Eric sat up and turned the lamp on. *She sees bad things coming,* he thought.

Eric believed that Tommy understood things. Even now, after years, he listened to his brother's words. Ahn knew what she was talking about. It was her job to see trouble coming.

With the sun rising over his dead mother's garden, Eric decided that he would stay out of trouble as much as he could and that he would never put anybody in danger again.

6

THE MORNING AFTER Elton and May were arrested, and Thomas was put in the holding cell, Madeline Beerman came to retrieve her grandson. She brought him home to her fourth-floor apartment on Denker and served him cornflakes for lunch. Thomas didn't mind the breakfast food. He hadn't eaten since the afternoon before because May and Elton were away at dinnertime and there was nothing he could eat in the refrigerator or the cupboards.

"I don't want you thinking bad about your father because of what happened last night," Madeline told him at the pine dining table that was crowded into her tiny studio apartment.

"Uh-huh," Thomas replied, gulping down cereal.

"It's really that May that's the problem," Madeline continued. "She's been a bad seed ever since a long time ago when she was friends with Branwyn. She wants every man she sees."

"Uh-huh."

"I went to visit Elton in jail. He'll be out in a few days. He says he wants you to come back and live with him and that he's showing May the door."

Thomas stopped eating and turned his eyes to Madeline. He wondered what violent act occurred when you were shown the door, and he knew that he didn't want to go back to live with his brutal father. But he understood that he couldn't say what he wanted. Whatever he said would cause trouble, and so he kept his mouth shut.

It was just as well that he did so. After three days in Madeline's house, Thomas would have gone to live anywhere else. There was only that one room besides the kitchen and toilet. Madeline slept on the sofa, and Thomas was given a mat on the floor. Madeline watched television day and night, and the boy couldn't get to sleep or look for his mother with his eyes closed because there was always somebody talking on the tinny TV speaker.

Madeline even kept the TV on when she was asleep.

"I use it for my sleeping pill," she told Thomas on the first night. "I leave it on and it drowses me."

When Elton came on the fourth morning, Thomas was actually happy to see him.

Elton wore his mechanic's overalls. There was a bump on his right temple, and two fingers on his left hand were bandaged together.

"You ret to go, boy?" Elton asked.

Thomas stood up from his chair and nodded. He'd hardly slept in the past three days, and he hadn't left the apartment at all because Madeline said the streets were full of hoodlums. So he was ready to go anywhere.

In the car Thomas sat in the passenger's seat and was barely tall enough to peek out of the window.

"I'm sorry about what happened with that bitch," Elton said.

Thomas giggled to hear a man say a curse word that the bad kids used on the playground.

"I didn't mean to get so upset on your first night there. But you know she made me mad goin' out with her old boyfriend an' tellin' me through you. But I got my head together ovah that shit. I was gonna leave May for your mother anyway. I sure was."

Thomas got up on his knees and looked out at Central Avenue. He liked this street more than Wilshire or Sunset, near to where Dr. Nolan's house was. The stores looked more inviting, with bright colors and chairs outside. There were children playing on the street too. And almost all of the people were brown or black like him and his mother.

"Watch it!" Elton cried.

A boy on a skateboard had veered out in front of the car. Elton hit the brakes, and Thomas's face slammed into the dashboard. He felt the pain mainly in his nose. It was like a bright red flame in the center of his face.

His eyes were closed, but he heard Elton open his door and then scream, "What the fuck is wrong with you, boy? You almost got killed!"

He yelled for a while, and Thomas held his nose trying to keep the blood from spilling out onto Elton's car seats. He knew that his father would not want blood in his car.

"What happened to you?" Elton cried when he tired of screaming at the skateboarder and came back to the car. "You bleedin'?"

AT THE EMERGENCY room the nurse asked Thomas if somebody had hit him.

"No, ma'am," the boy answered. "I wanted to look out the window, so I sat up on my knees instead of putting on my seat belt."

The nurse's name was Stella. She was sand-colored and had

straight black hair. She had big breasts, and Thomas wished that she would let him sit on her lap so that he could lie back against her and close his eyes.

ON THE RIDE home Elton complained about the two hundred thirty-seven dollars and sixty-two cents that the emergency room visit cost.

"Why you got to go an' break your nose, boy?" he asked. "That was our spendin' money for the next three weeks."

By now Thomas knew that Elton didn't expect an answer. He only wanted to complain about whatever there was in front of him. So the boy simply held the ice pack to his nose and closed his eyes, thinking himself around the pain.

This was another trick Thomas had learned — to concentrate on some part of his body that wasn't hurting when he was in pain. If his head hurt he thought about his hands and how they worked. He looked at his hands, grabbed things with them, anything to keep his mind off the place that hurt.

At home Elton gave Thomas a pill that made him dizzy. So he went out into the back porch and lay down with the ice pack on his face. He couldn't sit on his knees, but he could lie on his back and listen to the baby chicks and the murmuring drone of hornets. Every now and then a bird would cry or a dog would bark. Cats in heat battled in the yards, and people talked and laughed, called out to one another and played music.

Thomas felt good about his new home. He wasn't afraid of Elton anymore. The big car mechanic just needed to be left alone to complain and shout.

That was on a Wednesday.

On Thursday and Friday, Saturday and Sunday, Thomas

stayed in the house mainly and ate peanut butter and tuna fish. He went through the porch screen door into the back-yard and found out that there was an abandoned road, an alley really, on the other side of the chain-link fence at the back of the property. Across the alley there were the backyards of other houses and buildings, some of them abandoned.

Thomas didn't try to go into the alley because there was enough to see in the yard. There were weeds and proper plants, a wild rosebush that had small golden flowers. A gopher had pushed up half a dozen mounds of earth here and there, and a striped red cat passed through now and then, alternately crying and hissing at Thomas.

The boy didn't try to climb the tree because he often fell. But he did sit underneath it listening to the crying chicks. Hornets hovered above him, but he wasn't afraid of their stings. He'd been stung many times and had no fear of the pain.

From under the tree he scanned the skies and listened for traces of his mother in the world. He missed Eric, his brother, but he knew that Eric and Ahn and Dr. Nolan would all be fine. And he was about to go to school.

Elton had enrolled Thomas in Carson Elementary, only a block and a half away from the house. On Monday morning he would walk there with Elton, and then he'd finish the first grade.

Thomas liked school. There were so many people with so many different kinds of voices. And there were books and sometimes pictures of animals, and teachers who wore nice clothes and smelled good.

Thomas wasn't afraid of the new place. He had not often felt fear. He couldn't fight and he couldn't run very well, but he'd learned to skirt around pain and bullies and anger.

So he looked forward to the new school.

* * *

It was a big salmon-pink building with red and dirty green unglazed tiles for a roof. When he was led into Mr. Meyers's first-grade class, the children were all laughing at something, and the bald-headed teacher was trying to make them quiet down.

"Everyone be quiet. Back to your seat, Maryanne," the teacher was saying when Miss Andrews from the Registrar's Office brought Thomas through the back door of the classroom.

The children got louder.

Miss Andrews waved at Meyers. He pointed at an empty chair, and she said, "Sit here, Tommy. Mr. Meyers will introduce you later."

And so he entered the first-grade class with no one noticing, no one but the boy who sat in the other chair at the two-student table.

"I'm Bruno," the husky boy said. He stuck out a chubby hand, and Thomas shook it.

"I'm Tommy. I just moved here last week. Why's everybody laughing?"

"You talk funny," Bruno said.

At first Tommy thought Bruno was saying that the class was laughing at him, but, he thought, they couldn't be because they were laughing before he got there.

"Mr. Meyers farted," Bruno said then.

He giggled.

Thomas giggled.

Then they were friends.

Thomas gazed around the room filled with laughing black children. One girl jumped up out of her chair and ran from one desk to another while waving her arms in the air, all the time laughing. A boy made a farting sound with his mouth, and the whole class broke down. Several kids rolled out of their chairs and laughed on the floor.

There was a chalkboard with the letters *A, B, C,* and *D* written upon it. There was a carpeted corner filled with toys and books.

The children were laughing and the sun was shining in, and for some reason Thomas began to weep. He put his head down into his arms, and the tears flowed onto his hands and then the desk.

If someone had asked him at that moment why he was crying, Thomas wouldn't have known, not exactly. It had something to do with one new room too many and the sun shining in and all the children laughing at a joke he hadn't heard.

"Shut up!" Mr. Meyers shouted in a deep, masculine voice.

The children all stopped in an instant. Now that the rest of the class was silent, Thomas's soft weeping was the only sound.

"Yo, man," Bruno whispered. "They could hear you."

"Who's that?" a girl asked.

"Why he cryin'?" another girl added.

Thomas wanted to stop but he couldn't.

A shadow fell over Thomas, and the deep voice said, "Stop that."

Didn't he know that you can stop laughing but not crying?

"You, boy," the voice said.

A hand pulled his shoulder, and the sun lanced Thomas's eyes. The tears ran down, and he cried out from the attempt to stop crying.

"Who are you?" short, pudgy Mr. Meyers asked.

"Thomas Beerman," the boy said, but nobody understood him because of his sobbing.

"Do you know this boy?" Meyers asked Bruno.

"That's Tommy, Mr. Meyers," Bruno said proudly.

"Take him down to the nurse's office, Mr. Forman."

Thomas felt Bruno's hands on his shoulders. He got to his feet and, blinded by tears, allowed his new friend to guide him into the darker hallway.

Thomas breathed in the darkness, and the sadness in his chest subsided.

"I'm okay now," he told his burly friend.

"Yeh," Bruno said, "but now we got the hall pass."

He held up a wooden board that was about a foot long and half that in width. It was painted bright orange, with the number *12* written on it in iridescent blue.

"That means we don't have to go back to class," Bruno said. "We could go to the nurse's office an' hang out."

Thomas didn't want to go back to the room of sunlight and laughter.

"Do we have to go outside?" he asked.

"Naw," Bruno replied, and then he ran up the hall.

Thomas ran after him. Even though Bruno was big and slow, he got to the end of the hall before Thomas.

"Why you breathin' so hard?" Bruno asked his new friend.

"I was in a glass bubble when I was a baby. 'Cause of a hole in my chest. Ever since then I get tired easy."

"AND WHAT'S WRONG with you?" Mrs. Turner, the school nurse, asked Thomas.

The boy just looked up at her thinking that she had the same skin color as his mother but her voice and face were different.

"Well?" the nurse asked.

"He was cryin'," Bruno, who stood beside the seated Thomas, said.

"Crying about what?" Mrs. Turner asked Bruno.

"How should I know?" the fat boy replied, folding his arms over his chest.

The nurse smiled instead of getting angry at Bruno's impudence.

"Why were you crying, Tommy?" she asked.

"They were laughin' and the sun was too bright — it, it pained me."

Bruno giggled, and Mrs. Turner cocked her head to the side.

"It hurt?" she asked.

"In my heart," the boy said, "where I had to heed."

Thomas touched the center of his chest.

The nurse gasped and touched herself in the same place.

Bruno had stopped his laughing. Now he was staring goggle-eyed and astonished at his new friend.

"Would you like to take a nap, Tommy?" Mrs. Turner asked in a most gentle voice.

Thomas nodded.

"Can Bruno take one too?"

"No. He has to go back to class."

"Dog," Forman complained.

After Bruno left, the nurse led Thomas to a small room that smelled slightly of disinfectant. There were built-in glass-doored cabinets on the right side and there was a small cot against the opposite wall. When she pulled the shade down, Thomas realized that it was made from clear green plastic so the sun still shone in but not so brightly like in Mr. Meyers's classroom.

Thomas took off his shoes and put them under the cot. Then he got into the bed, and Mrs. Turner pulled the thin blanket over him.

"What happened to your nose?" the school nurse asked.

"My dad put on the brakes so he didn't hit this kid on a skateboard." Tommy liked it when she put the flat of her hand on his chest.

"Is this your first day at school, Tommy?" Mrs. Turner asked the boy.

"Uh-huh."

"Where is your family from?"

"My dad lives down the street."

"But then why is this your first day?"

Thomas told the nurse the story about his mother dying and his father coming to take him. He told her about the police and his grandmother's TV and Eric, his white brother who lived in Beverly Hills.

"I'm so sorry about your mother," Mrs. Turner said.

"She looks over me," Thomas replied, and the nurse gasped again.

Nurse Turner shared her lunch with Thomas. After that he returned to Mr. Meyers's class. The sun still bothered him, but he kept from crying by looking at the floor.

Toward the end of the day, Mr. Meyers called on a tall black girl named Shauna Jones. He pointed to the letter R, written in dusty yellow on the dark-green chalkboard.

"Are," Mr. Meyers said clearly.

"Ara," Shauna repeated.

"Are."

"Ara."

"Are."

"Arar."

"Thank you, Miss Jones," Meyers said. "New boy. Your turn."

Shauna sat down, showing no sign that she had failed the white teacher's test.

Thomas tried to stand up, but somehow his feet got tangled and he tripped and fell.

The children all laughed, except for Bruno, who helped his new friend to his feet.

"Shut up!"

Thomas turned to face the angry teacher.

"Are," Meyers said.

"Are," Thomas repeated, raising his voice and using the same angry tone.

"Are."

"Are."

Meyers stared at the boy suspiciously. It was almost as if he thought that this slender black child was pulling a joke on him.

"Constantinople," the first-grade teacher said, suddenly jutting his head forward like a striking snake.

"Wha'?" Shauna said.

"Constantinople," Thomas said easily.

"Sit down," Meyers said.

As Thomas did so he noticed that many of the children were staring at him with the same concentrated frown that the teacher had on his face.

"You talk funny," Bruno whispered.

AFTER THE FINAL bell Bruno showed Thomas where the big front door was. But when the new boy got out in front of

the school, he found himself in the midst of a thousand running and shouting children. In all that confusion he didn't
know which way to go.

"Where you live at?" Bruno asked him.

"I don't know."

"You'ont know where you live at?"

"My dad walked me here today," Thomas said. "He was
tellin' me how I shouldn't be in trouble and I didn't look."

"Where you near?" Bruno asked.

Bigger children were pushing by them. They were laughing and yelling, and the sun shone down from the western
sky. Thomas felt his heart beating, and he clenched his jaw to
stem the onset of tears.

"There's a gas station that's closed," he said. "It's got a horse
with wings in front of a big *A*."

"I know where that's at," Bruno said with a reassuring
smile. "You go on down that street there."

Thomas looked in the direction that Bruno was pointing.
There were dozens of children that they had to get through
to get to the crosswalk. There stood an old black man with a
red handheld stop sign.

"You sure is lucky," Bruno was saying.

"What?"

"The nurse let you stay an' you wasn't even sick."

Thomas giggled.

"See ya, Bruno," he said.

"See ya, Lucky."

HALFWAY DOWN THE block to Elton's house, Thomas ran
into a knot of four boys. They were all dark-skinned like him

but a year or two older. None of them smiled, and they all walked with exaggerated limps.

"Who you, mothahfuckah?" one of the boys asked.

He was moving his head from side to side and wore black jeans and a white T-shirt that was at least three sizes too big.

Hearing the anger in the boy's tone, Thomas didn't answer, only stared.

"Don't you heah me talkin' to you, mothahfuckah?" the boy said, and then he slapped Thomas — hard.

Thomas tried to run, but after only three steps, he felt a fist in his back. One more step and something hit him in the right calf. Thomas fell and the boys set on him. He put his hands up around his ears, and with nothing else he could do, he counted the blows.

One, two in the back. Three on the ear. Four, five, six on his shoulder. Seven was his head bumping the concrete.

And then it was over. No more hitting or cursing. Thomas looked up and saw the four boys limping away from the battle scene. The smallest one (who was still much larger than Thomas) looked back. Thomas ducked his head, not wanting to make eye contact.

When he got home he had a bloody scrape on the side of his head and pains in his back and leg. His pants were torn at the knees, and his injured nose throbbed.

Elton got home at seven.

"What you mean them boys beat up on you?" he asked his son. "Did you hit'em back? Did you?"

"No."

"Well then how you evah expect them to respect you if you don't fight back? An' look at yo' pants. I cain't go out an' buy you new clothes every time you a coward."

The whine in Elton's voice made it seem as if he was pleading with Thomas, begging him not to make him treat him like a coward.

Thomas didn't want to talk about his day at school or the bullies that beat him. He didn't want new pants or respect.

Elton brought home pizza, but Thomas had already eaten tuna on slightly moldy whole-wheat bread with Miracle Whip and a glass of Tang.

He got away from his angry father as soon as he could, going out to his bedroom porch. He moved around on the mattress until none of his bruises or scrapes hurt. He had to breathe through his mouth because his nose was stuffy from the swelling, but he didn't mind. In a short while he was asleep.

And in that rest he finally found what he'd been looking for all the days since his mother had died next to him in the bed.

He was hunkered down in a room that he'd never been in before. There was no furniture at all, no paintings on the white walls or carpeting on the dusty, dark wood floor. There was a doorway with no door in it that revealed nothing but an outer hallway and a real door that Thomas knew somehow opened onto a closet. He was squatting in the middle of the room, but he didn't know how he got there.

"I'm just sittin' here," he said aloud to himself.

Very slowly, the closet door opened. And then Branwyn stuck her head out, smiling at her son. He stayed perfectly still and silent so as not to scare her away. She moved her head around, looking to see if there was anyone else there.

"You alone?" she asked.

She came out of the closet wearing her white slip and the cream-colored satin slippers that Dr. Nolan had bought her in Chinatown.

Smiling broadly, she knelt down in front of her son and ran her fingertips along his brow.

"What have they done to you, baby?" she asked.

Thomas began crying again, as he had in Mr. Meyers's room. Branwyn sat in the dust and took him on her lap. They rocked there in the middle of the floor, both crying in separate sadness and combined joy. After a long time the mother lifted her boy's chin and looked deeply into his eyes.

"The birds and crickets and hornets and spiders have all been telling me that they see you looking for me."

Thomas nodded and kissed her hand.

"You don't have to look so far, honey," she said. "I'm right here in your heart whenever you want me. Just whisper my name and then listen and I will be there."

Thomas raised his head to kiss his mother's lips and came awake in the bed kissing the air.

Ribbet, came the call of a frog.

Ribbet.

It was late in the night. The house was dark. The neighborhood was dark. And two sociable frogs were talking about their day.

Thomas took their calls for proof that his mother had been there and that she would always be there with him — inside, where no one could ever take her away again.

"No I will not walk you to school," Elton told him the next morning.

They were sitting at the kitchen table having breakfast. Thomas was eating Frosted Flakes and toasted English muffins with strawberry jam. Elton had instant coffee while he smoked a menthol cigarette.

"It's not that I don't have the time neither," Thomas's father continued. "I could walk ya if I wanted to, but you got to learn to stand up for yo'self."

Slowly, Thomas made his way toward the front of the house.

"Tommy," his father said before he entered the long hallway that led from the kitchen to the front room.

"Yes, Dad?"

"Come here."

Thomas obeyed. He walked up to his father's chair and stood before him, looking down at the floor.

"Look at me."

Thomas raised his head, afraid for a moment that his father was going to hit him.

Elton did reach out, but it was only to put a hand on his boy's shoulder.

"You don't have to flinch from me, boy," he said. "I love you. Do you know that?"

Thomas stared at his father, trying to understand.

"I know you mad that I took you outta that white family's house. I know you want me to walk you to school. But you have to understand that everything I'm doin', I'm doin' for you. You need to be with your own blood. You got to learn to stand up for yo'self. Do you understand that?"

"I don't know," Thomas said. "I'm scared."

"I'm scared too," Elton replied.

"You?"

"Scared to death every day I climb out the bed," he said. "You know, a black man out here in these streets got a thousand enemies. Men want his money, his woman, his life, and he don't even know who they are. That's why I took you, Tommy. I want you to learn what I know. Do you understand what I'm sayin' to you?"

"If a rabbit sees a lion he gets scared and runs," Thomas said, remembering a story that Ahn had told him.

"What's that?"

"If a rabbit sees a lion he gets scared and runs," the boy said again. "But then if a lion sees a elephant he runs 'cause the elephant could step on him an' break his back."

"The lion is the king of the jungle," Elton said, his tone angry and not angry at the same time.

"I know. But he's still afraid of the elephant."

Father and son stared into each other's eyes for a moment. Elton had the feeling that he'd missed something, but he had no idea what that something was.

"Go on to school now, boy," he said at last.

ON THE FRONT step of the shabby box-shaped house, Thomas looked both ways, watching for the big boys that he'd run into the day before. He didn't see anyone except an old woman across the street sweeping the sidewalk in front of her house. Thomas hurried down the pavement, almost running on his way to school.

Three houses down a hidden dog jumped out, lunging at him. The dog growled and snapped, but the chain around its neck stopped him from getting at the boy.

Thomas froze, thinking that the dog would get away somehow and chase him down. But the restraint held.

Thomas sighed. He took three steps toward school.

"Hey you, mothahfuckah," a familiar voice called from behind.

They surrounded him quickly. Three of them were dressed in signature white T-shirt and jeans. One boy wore a jean jacket and black pants. All of their tennis shoes were white.

Thomas noticed these things, categorizing, listing, and hoping somehow the knowledge would save him from another beating, still knowing that nothing would save him. Nothing ever would.

"You got money in yo' pocket, suckah?" the tall eight-year-old leader asked.

Thomas breathed in through his mouth and shook his head — no.

The backhand stung his left cheek. He felt a trickle of blood come out of his left nostril.

"Empty yo' pockets, man," another boy said.

Thomas looked at all eight eyes staring angrily at him. Years later he would wake up from a nightmare about those eyes, not in fear of violence but from the sad memory of their hatred.

Fight 'em back, he heard his father say. And then he turned to run. But his feet got tangled up, and he fell right there in front of his enemies.

"Kick his ass!" a boy shouted.

Thomas rolled up like the gray-shelled pill bugs he would watch in the garden. He closed his eyes and made ready to count the blows, but instead he heard a girl shouting. He wondered if the boys had attacked somebody else, somebody behind him.

He opened his eyes and raised his head.

A very large black girl (who looked somehow familiar) was punching the ringleader of the gang in the face. The other boys rushed at her, but she slapped one, punched another, and kicked the third, one, two, three times. The first boy she hit was crying. Thomas hadn't believed that those mean boys *could* cry. The other three were running.

"Git!" the big girl yelled, and stamped her foot on the concrete.

The crying boy let out howling.

"You show'em, girl," the old woman from across the street called. "Show them li'l niggahs a thing or two."

The girl turned her head toward Thomas, and the boy quailed. He thought that she would destroy him now with her fists and feet and loud shouts. But instead Bruno ran up from nowhere and held out his hand.

"Come on, Lucky," the jolly first-grader said. "Git up."

The girl reached down too. For a moment Thomas felt weightless, and then he was standing on his feet.

"This Monique," Bruno said in the way of an introduction. "My sister. She's twelve, in junior high."

"Hi," the big girl said. She smiled. "That li'l Alvin Johnson need somebody to kick his butt ev'ry mornin'. That's the on'y way he evah gonna do right."

"I told Monique about you, Lucky. I told her you talked funny but you might get lost on the way to school. So she walked me ovah here."

Thomas was very happy. He laughed, and big Monique smiled down on him.

"Don't you know the secret way to school?" she asked him. He shook his head.

"Com'on," Monique said, and with a wave of her hand she led them down the driveway of the house with the leashed dog.

When it barked at her, she got down on her knees and held out her hand. The dog growled, then sniffed, then licked her fingers.

Thomas knew that if he tried that the dog would bite his whole hand off.

Behind the house was a fence with a hole in it that led to the blocked-off alley behind Elton's house. Back there sapling trees grew in profusion and birds sang and small creatures scuttled. There were pools of water with bright-green algae growing over them and an old redbrick incinerator that housed a large rodentlike creature.

"This alley was blocked off a long time ago," Monique was explaining. "An' it go all the way to the end of the block. All you got to do is climb through the fence next to the church and cut through the back'a there an' you across the street from the school. Not so many other kids do it 'cause the hole is too small."

"Thank you, Monique."

"What's your real name?" she asked.

"My name is Tommy, but everybody calls me Lucky."

"You right, Bruno," Monique said. "He do talk funny."

7

EIGHT YEARS after Thomas met Monique, a fourteen-year-old Eric Nolan was getting ready to play a match on a public tennis court above Santa Monica Boulevard in Beverly Hills. He was set to play against an older boy from his school, Hensley High, which was known as the Yale of private high schools. The boy, Drew Peters, was a seventeen-year-old twelfth-grader who had already been accepted to three Ivy League schools for the following year.

Drew had called Eric's class a bunch of pussies, and then he pushed around Limon, a delicate Peruvian boy who was also in the tenth grade. Eric told Drew that he couldn't even play tennis and challenged him to a match. Eric agreed that if he lost he'd pay Drew a hundred dollars and carry him around the track on his back. But if Drew lost he'd have to go down on his knees and ask Limon to forgive him.

Both classes showed up for the match, which took place at 4:00 p.m. on a cloudy Saturday afternoon. The upperclassmen came into the bleachers all cool and superior. The sophomore class was loud and cheering. And even though Eric was a year younger than most of his classmates, he was the best of them, and they loved him for daring to challenge a boy who was almost four years older. Drew was in the California Junior Tennis League and had placed second in the statewide tournament.

In the front row of the senior side of the bleachers sat Christie Sadler, whose father, it was said, owned a riverfront block in Paris. Christie was the prettiest girl in any class at Hensley. She looked like a woman already, tall and lithe with violet eyes and skin that defied comparison. Mr. Mantel, the English teacher, had been fired midyear for suggesting to Christie that she would get the grade she was looking for if they could go out on a date.

Christie and Drew were the perfect couple at school. They'd be king and queen of the prom. They were definitely having sex.

Eric wasn't thinking about any of that when he came out onto the court. He liked playing tennis. It was a sport where he didn't need clumsy teammates who competed with one another. He liked things one on one or, even better, sports where he could excel without competition, like diving or running.

But Drew had roughed up Limon, and Limon was the clos-est thing to a friend that Eric had. Not that they were really friends. Limon talked too much, and he always wanted advice about how to be more popular and better in school. He wasn't satisfied with his life, and Eric looked down on that.

Don't you mind it when you lose at tic-tac-toe? Eric had asked Thomas sometime before his brother disappeared forever.

Nuh-uh.

Why not?

I'ont know, Thomas said. *I guess it's just fun to play. And any-way, if you win and you're my brother, then in a way I win too.*

The day of the match was cloudy and cool. So was Drew, with his light-gray tennis clothes and serious brow.

Drew's father had offered to judge the match. Mr. Peters

was hale and tall. He had red hair everywhere and skin that had seen a lot of sun. The Peters family made their money in construction. He was a hard man, and Eric was confident that he wouldn't cheat to favor his son.

But even if he did, Eric expected to win the match anyway. He always won when it was important. He was, as his Episcopalian minister, Uncle Louis, always said, "born in the circle of light."

Eric hadn't told his father about the match. He never wanted Minas or Ahn to be anywhere where he was the center of attention. Something about that talk with Ahn the night after Lester Corning was scarred had made him leery of the trouble he might cause. For the next few weeks after the accident, Eric asked about his real mother and what had happened.

She succumbed after childbirth, Minas had said in simple doctorese.

Having me, Eric said.

It wasn't you who killed her.

But having me killed her.

But . . . Minas couldn't say any more.

Eric could tell that his father blamed him, not angrily, not wishing that his son had died instead, but simply knowing that Eric's being born had killed Joanne. Between mother and son Eric had won the coin toss.

While Eric was thinking about his luck, Mr. Peters cried, "Heads up."

Drew served, and Eric returned with an easy backhand. He felt weightless on his toes out there, predicting where every volley would land. He watched Drew's effortless movements and saw that this was a kindred spirit on the court. Here they both ruled. Who cared who won? They were one, the same side of the coin. And while Eric watched Drew, Christie found that her gaze, more and more, drifted toward the sophomore Adonis.

She noticed his strong legs first and then the careless precision with which he returned each volley. Where Drew had an angry, snorting demeanor, Eric was neither angry nor glad. The sophomore moved freely, not worrying when he lost a point or even a set. He flipped his blond hair out of his face naturally, with no posing or apparent knowledge of his beauty. He only got serious when he saw a hole in Drew's defenses. Then he came down on the ball like a predatory feline clamping down on the throat of a fawn.

Christie felt her heart skip when she thought that Eric might miss a return. She found herself, for no reason that she could name, hoping that Eric won the game — or, at least, that he didn't lose. She clutched her hands and watched the carefree youth make her boyfriend run back and forth like a gerbil cornered by the devil-pawed tomcat that lived on her family farm in Santa Barbara.

No one knew what the high school beauty was thinking. The match was very close. No matter who was receiving there was something to worry about.

On Eric's final match point, Drew lobbed the ball to the back of the court when Eric was playing the net. Christie gasped loudly as Eric ran toward the foul line swinging at the ball with his back turned. He connected, but the ball flew high and slow. The exertion made Eric stumble and fall. The senior class let out a loud whoop (except for Christie, who was inexplicably near tears). At that moment the clouds parted, and a shaft of concentrated sunlight shone in Drew's eyes. He swung wildly, hitting the ball so hard that it flew off the court and into the park beyond.

"Game!" shouted Mr. Peters.

"No!" screamed his son.

The tenth-graders leaped and hollered for their hero. Even some of the seniors applauded the incredible play.

The only incident that scarred the game was Drew's rage at the sun. He was so angry that instead of going to the net to shake Eric's hand, he threw his racket at the victor. But Eric merely held up his own racket, deflecting the force of the missile, then catching it handily by the haft.

Eric walked to the net, holding out the racket as if Drew had merely dropped it.

"Take it," Drew's father commanded.

The audience had gone quiet.

Christie felt a tremor between her legs that her boyfriend had never made her feel.

Drew was taken off the court by his father. The sophomore class put Eric on their shoulders and carried him three blocks to the Beanery, the coffeehouse that, until that day, only the senior class inhabited.

As Christie watched him float away on the shoulders of his class, she felt an ache inside her that she feared might never completely subside.

"ERIC?" MINAS SAID outside the boy's half-open door.

"Yeah, Dad?"

"Phone."

"Who is it?"

"A girl."

Girls called sometimes, but they soon gave up because Eric had become a loner in his teenage years. He learned how to dance but never went to parties. He'd gone out now and then, but found kissing in the backseats of cars and on porches unexciting. It's not that he didn't think about sex. He dreamed about naked women every night, often waking with an enormous erection.

Don't you want somebody to love you? Limon once asked him when the conversation drifted to girls.

No, Eric replied. *Not really. I like being alone.*

"What's her name?" Eric asked his father.

"I'm not your secretary, son. Ask her yourself."

Dr. Nolan pushed the door open and threw the cordless phone onto the bed.

"Hello," Eric said into the receiver.

"Eric?"

"Who's this?"

"Christie. Christie Sadler."

"Oh. Hi."

"I'm just calling to apologize for what Drew did today. I mean, he shouldn't have thrown that racket at you."

"He was just mad," Eric said. "He should have nailed me on that last shot, but the sun got in his eyes."

"But he's a senior. He should be more gracious. I bet you wouldn't have thrown anything at him."

"I don't know," Eric said. "I mean, I was thinking how hard it must be on him because he always does the best. But you can see that he's doing it for his father."

"What do you mean?"

"His father's all big and strong and sure of himself. Drew just wants to make him proud, and so losing to me like that means that everything else doesn't matter at all."

"How do you know all that?"

"You can see it in the way his father talks to him and the

way he's so serious. He makes Drew nervous. I bet if his father wasn't there, he would have beat me easy."

"And would you care?"

"Sure. I'd have to carry him around the track on my back."

Christie laughed. Her voice sounded like chimes to Eric. His erection came on without him knowing it.

"Whenever we go out he's real worried about how I look," Christie whispered into the phone as if it were a big secret. "I can't ever wear loafers or jeans when we're on a date, even if it's only at the pier."

"Wow. That wouldn't bother me. You'd look good in an overcoat and brogans."

There were a few moments of silence then. Eric realized that there was something different in the way he felt. His mind wasn't wandering away from the conversation. His attention was fully concentrated on Christie.

"Do you want to go get something to eat?" the senior asked.

"When?"

"Now."

"I don't have a license. I'm only fourteen, you know."

"I have a car."

"What about your boyfriend?"

"You won the match," she said, and for the first time since Branwyn lived in the house with them, Eric felt his heart stutter.

AT THE PANCAKE House Eric asked Christie about her aspirations for college. She'd been accepted to all the schools that Drew had and was making up her mind whether to go to the same school or one that was driving distance away.

He wanted to know what she planned to study. Her strength was in science, but she loved poetry. T. S. Eliot was her favorite, "The Waste Land" in particular, but she worried that it might not be responsible to want to be a poet.

"Most kids in school never know what they want to be," Eric said. "I read an article once that the average college student changes majors three times, and a lot of them still take jobs in different fields from the ones they majored in."

"You read that?"

"Yeah. In the *Times.* I like reading the paper in the morning . . . with my father."

"Are you close to your father?"

Eric didn't know what to say. He sat with Minas reading the paper every morning because his father liked the time together. The boy's heart was thumping because of those violet eyes staring so intently at him.

"You want to take a drive with me?" Christie asked before Eric could formulate an answer about his father.

THEY STARTED KISSING as soon as Christie parked at the lookout point in Topanga Canyon. Eric knew that he had never really kissed before that night. Christie told him that she loved Drew and so all they could do was kiss, but a moment later she was unzipping his pants. Eric thought of reminding her about just kissing, but instead, when he felt her cool fingers on his erection, all that came out was a deep, very masculine sigh. Christie echoed him in a higher register, and their kissing became more urgent.

She leaned back at one point and said, "Drew asked me to marry him and I said yes."

Eric nodded to show that he understood, but at the same time he thrust his pelvis forward, putting the straining erection near to her lips. She took it in her mouth and they both hummed.

When the boy came he roared out her name. She stared into his eyes, seeing both pain and gratitude. Her grip tightened until she worried that she might be hurting him, but she didn't ease up or slow down.

After the tremors subsided, Christie lay down on top of Eric in the front seat.

"I've never met a guy like you, Eric Nolan," she said, kissing the tip of his nose.

"Was that okay?" he asked.

"What?"

"I mean about Drew. You said we should just kiss."

"That was like kissing," she said. "I mean, we didn't do it or anything."

Eric noticed their breath misting chilly air.

"I think you should be a poet," he said then. "I mean, people need poetry just as much as they need chemicals."

Christie kissed him and reached down.

"You're still hard," she said, only slightly in awe.

"Let's get in the backseat."

She took her time rolling the condom down on his erection. He kissed the side of her neck and the cleft between her breasts while she did so. Eric felt awkward at first, but Christie didn't seem to mind. She told him to be careful because she hadn't had a lover so well endowed as he. When they came for the fourth time, they still shuddered as violently as the first.

"We shouldn't do that again," Christie told Eric the next night on the phone.

"Okay," he said, still feeling spent from the night before.

"That's all you have to say?"

"Isn't that what you want me to say?"

"I don't want you thinking I'm a slut who would do something like that with just anybody."

"That was my first time," Eric confessed. "I never even knew how wonderful it could be."

"Oh. I didn't know . . . you seemed like . . . I don't know . . . experienced."

"But we could see each other, right?" Eric asked. "I mean, we don't have to do that. You know, I could ride my bike over."

"Um . . . I think it would be better if we didn't. You know, guys get kinda possessive after their first time."

"Okay," Eric said.

Christie didn't reproach him this time.

"Well . . . I guess we should go," she said.

"All right. Bye."

FOR THE NEXT four nights Eric lay on his back in the bed for hours with his heart pounding and his mind on Christie. He'd seen her in school three times. She always turned away when their eyes met. He didn't know what he wanted more than to hold her again and to feel the release she gave him. He didn't think he was in love. It was something else. Love for Eric had always been about smiling and swooning, about people who couldn't live without each other. He lived without his mother and Branwyn too. He survived even when they took his brother away without a word of warning. He didn't need anybody, but he sure wanted Christie.

That Friday, on the lunch court, Drew Peters confronted Eric.

"I'm not apologizing to that little faggot because you didn't really win," the brooding boy said. Drew was a head taller than Eric and twenty pounds heavier, but the sophomore didn't draw back.

"That's your decision," he said.

"It's true," Drew yowled. "The sun shined in my eyes."

Eric noticed Christie on the other side of the court looking at him with a worried expression on her face. It was in that moment that his sleepless nights crystallized into knowledge. He could see that she was worried about him, not Drew. His heart began to race, and Eric took a deep breath to slow it down.

"The dog ate my homework," Eric said, mimicking Drew's whining. "My hand slipped. I didn't do anything."

The quiver of the senior's lower lip warned Eric. He was already ducking down when Drew threw the first punch. Missing completely, the senior stumbled. Eric's blow connected with Drew's chest. Then Drew hit Eric on top of the head. Eric heard the finger snap and the cry of pain from the upperclassman. Then they fell into each other's arms, wrestling and punching.

A sudden fear entered Eric's mind. He didn't want to be fighting. It wasn't that he was afraid of being hurt but of the harm that might come from their fight. A moment later, Mr. Lo, the gym teacher, was pulling them apart. Drew clutched his broken finger. Christie was looking directly at Eric.

She called his house at four.

"Do you want to get together?" she asked.

"What about your boyfriend?"

"I'm still going to marry him."

They made love in Branwyn's old room, which had been left

untouched since her death. Ahn was always away on Friday evenings, and Minas got home later every year. So they were alone from five that afternoon until late. Eric kissed Christie everywhere. She complimented his physique and his loving nature.

"No man has ever made me feel like this," she said.

She confessed that she'd flirted with Mr. Mantel, the fired English teacher. Eric told her that Mantel was a grown man and should have known better than to proposition a student.

"How do you know so much?" she asked him.

"I don't know a thing compared to you," the fourteen-year-old said.

Christie put her hands over her breasts and said, "I'm still marrying Drew."

"Can I still see you?"

"I don't know," she said, and he kissed her covering hands. She uncovered one nipple.

"You can't tell anybody about us," she said.

"That's easy. I don't know anybody."

"You're crazy. The whole class carried you off on their shoulders."

Eric took the free hand and placed it on his erection. They both shuddered.

"Every time you call me I'm here," he said. "I don't talk to anybody but Limon, and nobody talks to him either."

"But why don't you have friends?" she asked. "You're really handsome and friendly and smart."

"I don't know why," he lied. "But I'm happy now because I never knew I could feel like this."

At nine they went to dinner down in Santa Monica.

Over roasted chicken and lasagna, Christie told Eric that Drew had broken his finger and that the school suspended him for picking a fight with a sophomore.

"They said that he'd be expelled unless he apologized to you."

"Really? What did he say?"

"That he wouldn't."

"That's stupid. He'll lose his place in all those schools if he doesn't."

"His father won't let him leave the house until he does."

"That's why you can be here with me?"

For some reason this embarrassed Christie. She ducked her head.

"You should call Drew and tell him that you talked to me and I said that he could tell the school that he apologized. If they ask me I'll tell them he did."

"You'd do that?"

"I don't want your future husband to be a dishwasher."

CHRISTIE AND ERIC saw each other at least twice a week until the end of the semester. All that time she warned him that she was going to marry Drew and live with him in the East. Eric didn't mind. Now that he had experienced sex, he was aware of all the girls at school who wanted to be with him. When Christie left, he knew he would find somebody else.

And so he was surprised in the late summer when Christie came to his house crying.

They went out in the overgrown flower garden and sat on the marble bench there.

"What's wrong?" Eric asked.

"I told Drew."

"About us?"

"No. I told him that I wasn't going to Yale with him."

"Really? You're not going to the East Coast?"

"No. I can't leave you," she said.

"But what are you going to do?"

"I'll get a job at my father's office and rent an apartment. Then we can spend more time together. I know you're still in high school and you might not even want me, but I can't go with Drew. I don't love him. I haven't since I saw you on the tennis court that day."

Christie had on a small cranberry-colored dress. She stood up and took it off, revealing that she wore nothing underneath. It was four in the afternoon on a Friday. The sun was bright, and they were the only ones there. As they made love on the marble bench, Christie moaned and cried, dug her nails deep into Eric's back, and begged him please, please, please.

"I'm yours," she said at the door that evening, "if you want me."

She drove off leaving Eric to think about the past semester. He wondered not about Christie but about Drew. The darkly handsome senior had everything before they tangled over Limon. Eric had borne no animosity toward the older boy. He hadn't meant to take his girl away. On the school yard the boys had been civil. Drew appreciated Eric not making him apologize.

A week after his first night with Christie, she'd told him that Drew had seen a semen stain that Eric had made on the inside roof of the car.

"I told him that he made it, but you know his never shot out like yours does."

Eric had felt embarrassed for Drew. He wasn't competing. He just couldn't say no to Christie's surrender. He still couldn't.

"Mine," Eric said to himself, watching the red lights of Christie's Honda recede down the street.

8

FOR THREE days six-year-old Thomas made his way to school using the abandoned alleyway. The gang of third-graders didn't bother him anymore, and he loved the green, dewy wilderness of the walk. Going to school and coming home on the secret path were the highlights of his day.

But school itself was no better than on that first morning. The light in Mr. Meyers's classroom still made him weep. He managed to keep everybody except Bruno from noticing. But the other children all thought that he was different, that he "talked like white people," and that he was strange in other ways too.

Thomas had rarely watched television, not even very much with Eric. He never watched at all at his father's house. He preferred looking at bugs and insects, and he fell a lot and lost his lunch money all the time and never completely understood what people were saying to him. And, worst of all, he seemed to have spells. On the playground at recess, he would sit by himself and close his eyes and talk even though there was nobody there.

"He talks to dead people," Bruno said, sticking up for his friend.

But this only made the children more wary of the odd new "bug boy" that acted so weird.

The big boys picked on him, and the girls often screamed and ran if he came near. Mr. Meyers was bothered by the way he answered questions in class. The only good thing about school was Bruno and sometimes his sister, Monique, when she came to walk Bruno home after school.

Once in a while at lunchtime and recess, Bruno and Thomas would go to a far corner and talk about comic books. Bruno knew everything about the Fantastic Four. He studied them from old reprints and new comics that came out each month. At the library they had big hardback books that compiled the first issues released in the early sixties.

Bruno knew everything about them. Johnny Storm, the high-flying Human Torch; bashful Benjamin Grimm; Stretcho; and Suzie, the Invisible Woman. Every day he'd tell Thomas another story about their battles with Doctor Doom or the Mole Man. Bruno couldn't read all the words, but his sister helped him sometimes. He told Thomas that in the old comics you didn't need the words because the pictures told the story.

The worst thing about school was the sunlight in the first-grade classroom. He told Mr. Meyers that it hurt his eyes, but the teacher didn't know what to do.

"We can't put down the shades, Lucky," he said. "Children need light."

"You could get those green shades like the nurse has," Thomas suggested.

"I'm lucky if I get a budget for pencils," Meyers replied.

The sadness he experienced in that bright room became so unbearable that on Thursday Thomas "Lucky" Beerman made a decision.

"I'm not comin' to school tomorrow," he told Bruno.

"How come?"

"I'm not coming back anymore. I don't like it here."

"But where you gonna go?"

"Nowhere. Daddy goes to work every morning and doesn't come back till late. He always goes out, and he doesn't care 'bout what I'm doing."

"But what if he stays home sometimes?"

"I'll just go out in the back alley," Thomas said. "I'll stay back there."

"Okay," Bruno said as if the final decision was his. "An' I'll tell Mr. Meyers that your mother come and took you away. An' if they send a letter to your house from the school, we could get Monique t'read it and then th'ow it away."

THE NEXT MORNING Thomas went out the front door and then through the hole in the fence a few houses down. That's where his journey both ended and began. He climbed around the broken chunks of concrete in the middle of the road directly behind his house, and then he went through the thick bushes that had grown up along the sides. The alley was lower than the yards that abutted it, and so it was always wet from people watering their gardens and lawns.

On the first day Thomas saw lizards and a garden snake, three mice, one rat, and a family of opossums living in the incinerator. He saw crows, redbirds, one soaring hawk, and a bright-green parrot that had escaped from some cage, no doubt. The parrot made his home in an oak tree half in and half out of Thomas's little valley.

"No man," the bird would say now and then. "No man."

Thomas felt that the bird, which he called No Man, was announcing that this was their home and not a place for grown-ups.

The alley valley was overgrown with sapling trees and other vegetation. Thomas could stay under a roof of leaves that modulated the light and made him calm.

That first day he explored the length and width of his new home. It was a long block, twenty backyards on either side. At its widest it was twenty-eight boy-sized paces from one fence to the other. There was asphalt and concrete and dirt that made up the various terrains, mostly flowerless trees and bushes. There was a lot of trash too: bits of paper, crumbling cardboard pallets that the occasional homeless person had used to sleep on. There were soda and beer cans, plastics of all kinds, and even old machinery and chunks of metal that people had discarded over the years. But there were few other visitors that Thomas saw in those first few months. That was because it was hard for anyone much larger than Thomas to get back there. The stone wall of the church had a chink big enough for only the little boy to squeeze through, and the rest was fenced off from the private backyards of houses.

Many of these yards had dogs that barked and growled at Thomas, but he stayed out of their way and soon they got used to him.

It was his paradise. The only stable respite his childhood would know. He spent that first Friday laughing and thinking that maybe the name Lucky fit him.

"What you smilin' 'bout, boy?" Elton asked at the dinner table that night.

They were eating meat loaf, mustard greens, and watery mashed potatoes from a take-out restaurant three blocks away.

"Here I am workin' my butt off to pay the rent and for yo' breakfast, lunch, an' dinnah, an' all you could do is smile. Life

is serious, Tommy. You cain't be goin' through yo' day grin-
nin' like some fool. You got to get serious an' work hard like
me. You think I keep us in house an' home walkin' down the
street smilin'?"

"I'm sorry," the boy said, even though he wasn't.

"Damn right you sorry. Now eat your damn meat."

"It makes my stomach hurt."

They ate food from the mom-and-pop takeout at least
three nights a week. Thomas had trouble digesting meat with
a lot of fat in it. Ahn used to trim all the fat from his portions.

"Hurt your stomach. You should try not eatin'. That's
what hurts."

Thomas took a bite of meat loaf to placate Elton. Then he
worked on the mashed potatoes and greens.

The boy didn't want his piece of lemon meringue pie, and
so Elton gobbled it down to teach his spoiled son a lesson, he
said.

THAT WEEKEND BRUNO came over. Thomas didn't invite
his jolly friend into his valley. He wanted to keep that paradise
for himself. Instead he and Bruno walked the four blocks to
Bruno's house, where together they read a very old, very
beat-up comic book about the Fantastic Four and their journey to the planet of the Skrulls.

The Skrulls were born shape-shifters who could become
any creature or thing they could imagine. They could be birds
or monkeys or even giant bugs. They had the ability to make
themselves look human and pass among men with no one
knowing the difference.

"If you could turn into anything you wanted, what would
it be?" Bruno asked his new and best friend.

Thomas had never thought about being different before that day. It was a novel idea, and he found no words to answer.

"I'd turn into a white man," Bruno said, impatient with his friend's deliberation. "No, no, no. First I'd turn into Lana McKinney and look up under my shirt at them fine titties. Then I'd turn into a white man. You know why?"

Thomas shook his head, still trying to find an answer to the first question.

"'Cause if I was a white dude I could be all up there in Beverly Hills and Hollywood and on the cowboy ranches an' shit like that. An' they wouldn't even know that some niggah be all up in they business, so they'd all act natural and then I'd get'em."

Thomas was lost in Bruno's sea of words. What would he be? And titties and white men and Hollywood and cowboys.

"I think I'd be a snake," Thomas said haltingly. "Yeah. A snake."

"A rattlesnake? Then you could bite Alvin Johnson and kill him, but nobody'd ever know it was you."

"I don't care what kind of snake," Thomas said. "I just wanna be a snake 'cause then I could go all the places I want."

"Like what?" Bruno asked.

"A snake can climb trees and go real high, and he could go in a hole down in the ground. And he could get through any fence or thornbush and see everything."

"But a snake don't have no hands. How would you eat?"

"Like snakes do."

"Not me. If I was a animal it'a be a tiger or a eagle."

That afternoon Bruno got tired and had to go to bed. Monique walked Thomas back home so that Alvin Johnson and his gang didn't beat him up.

"How come you're wearin' them tore-up pants?" Monique asked as they walked.

" 'Cause my daddy says that I have to wear'em because I let those boys beat me up."

"You didn't let'em. They bigger than you. Don't he know that?"

"He doesn't care about that," little Lucky replied.

"Why you so different from other little boys?" Monique asked.

"I didn't know that I was different."

"Yeah you is," Monique assured him. They were walking down Central Avenue under a too-bright sun. "You talk half like a niggah an' half like somebody white. An' you don't know nuthin' on TV, an' you always lookin' at stuff real close like you crazy or sumpin'. An' if somebody tell you what to do, you just do it like you they slave, but if you don't wanna talk you mouth be shet like a clam."

"I like you, Monique," Thomas said.

"There you go again bein' different. I'm tellin' you how weird you is an' then you tell me how much you like me."

"But I do," the boy said. "You're nice to me, an' Bruno too."

Elton met Thomas and Monique at the front door.

"Where's the fat boy?" Thomas's blood-father asked.

"Bruno's sleep," Thomas said.

"And who are you?" Elton asked Monique.

"Bruno's sistah. I walked Lucky heah 'cause I'm going t'see my auntie ovah on Fi'ty-second Street."

Thomas pulled on Monique's arm until she bent over enough for him to kiss her cheek.

She grinned at him and said, "Stupid," in not an angry way at all.

In the house Elton asked him, "Why you kiss that girl?"

"I don't know. 'Cause she walked me home."

"I don't want her doin' that no mo'," Elton said. "No son'a mine's gonna be protected by a girl."

ON SUNDAY THOMAS left the house because Elton was sleeping and left strict orders that he was not to be awakened for anything or anyone.

So Thomas went into his valley and studied the landscape. There were a few breaks in the fence. One was the oak tree where the green parrot No Man lived. Another was an old, old brick apartment building that had all of its windows and doors barricaded by cinder blocks. There was a metal cellar door, however, that could be bent up enough for a small boy to squeeze through. Thomas stuck his head inside, but it was too dark in there, even for his eyes, and so he decided to come back during the week with candles and a flashlight.

At the stone fence behind the church, Thomas was looking for snakes when he heard the organ sound.

A choir began to sing.

Pressing through the chink in the wall, Thomas cut his cheek. He knew from many, many cuts and scrapes that he had to put pressure on the gash. And so he entered the double door of Holy Baptist Congregational pressing his fingers against the bloody cut, with a crooked nose and pants torn at both knees revealing the scabs from his recent falls.

He sat at the back of what seemed to him a huge room. There he looked up at the black men and women dressed in off-white satin gowns singing about Jesus and his Word. The stained glass and dark woods reminded him of the church where they'd had his mother's funeral. He felt that the singers both in the choir and among the parishioners were offering hymns for his mother, and so he hummed along with them. He didn't notice that the well-dressed church members were looking at him sitting there, with his broken nose and bloody face, his sockless feet in muddy shoes, and his torn pants.

A tall, white-gloved deacon came up to him and asked, "Where are your parents, boy?"

"My dad's asleep and my mother's dead," he said.

"They have to be members of the congregation for you to be here," the man told him.

It took Thomas a few moments to realize that he was being asked to leave. He went out the front door and sat on the concrete stairs listening to the chants and sermons under the shadow of the eaves.

THAT WAS THOMAS'S life for the next few years. He spent his weekdays in the alley valley and Saturdays at Bruno's house. On Sundays while Elton slept he perched in a tree behind the church where he could listen to the beautiful songs, which were, in his opinion, about his mother.

He made his way into the old brick apartment building. There he set out candles to use when it was raining or too cold outside.

Mr. Meyers took Bruno at his word and struck Thomas Beerman from the class roll. Somehow the registration office also overlooked Thomas, and so he nearly ceased to exist in the files of the school system. The cut he got on the church wall turned into a scar, and though his body stayed small his hands became large and callused as a result of the work he took on.

Thomas decided that he would clean up his alley valley.

And so he brought an old broom from the back porch and plastic trash bags from the bathroom to begin that task. He swept and picked up the papers, cans, and man-made items that had been thrown over the fence. The first place he cleaned was directly behind his father's rented house.

THE DAYS WENT by peacefully for the next few weeks. Thomas explored and cleaned his little Eden. He left bread crumbs for the opossums and salvaged discarded furniture from various apartments in the abandoned building. In the dark, on the second floor, Thomas would get on his knees and feel himself sinking into the floor. He loved this feeling and would sometimes stay like that for hours. Once he stayed too long, and Elton was already home and angry that Thomas was so late from school.

"Where were you, boy?"

"I went to play at Bruno's house."

"I don't want you seein' that fat boy no mo'. Hear me?"

Thomas nodded, but he didn't worry. Elton had other things on his mind. He wasn't concerned about Thomas unless he was late for dinner.

The next day, Thomas had a conversation with his mother.

"Why's Daddy so mad at me, Mama?" Thomas asked in his normal voice.

Then in a deeper, more musical register he replied, "Because when he was a boy he didn't have anybody to be nice to him."

"Like you are to me?"

"That's right, honey," Branwyn said. "And now you have to be nice to him and let him be mad. Don't worry, I won't let him hurt you."

"Do you mind it that I don't go to school, Mama?"

"You know I want you to be in school and to get smart like your brother and Dr. Nolan."

"But I hate it, an' it hurts my eyes."

"Sometimes we have to do things we don't like, Tommy."

"I know. But I go to Bruno's house after school sometimes and on Saturdays, and we do his homework together a little bit."

"Well, okay," Branwyn replied after a meditative silence. "For now. But later on you have to go back to school."

"I promise."

THOMAS WORKED HARD to clean up his alley paradise. Along the edges of the fence, he'd come upon small patches of wild strawberry plants. He loved eating them with the peanut butter sandwiches he'd make when he'd sneak into his father's house in the middle of the day for lunch and other supplies.

When he wasn't talking to his mother, he'd go to the oak tree and call to No Man. He'd put bread crumbs on the ground at his feet, and after some days the parrot would fly up and eat, croaking "no man" now and again. After a while the parrot would follow Thomas around looking for food and maybe, Thomas thought, a little company.

One late morning when going up to the house, Thomas found May sitting on the porch with her head on her knees, crying.

"Hi, May," Thomas said.

When she looked up Thomas could see the ruined makeup running down her dark face.

"Hi, baby. What you doin' here? Ain't you supposed to be in school?"

"They let me come home for lunch," he lied. "Why you cryin'?"

"Because I'm so stupid," she said, sobbing. "Because I had to go play around and get your father mad at me. Now I'm miserable, and he changed the locks and his phone numbah. An' I need to tell him that I'm sorry."

The tears flowed down, and Thomas felt her pain. He reached out to touch her wet face.

"I could let you in," Thomas offered. "But . . ."

"But what?"

"You can't tell Daddy that I come home sometimes. He don't know I do that, an' he'd get mad."

May wiped her eyes and she was beautiful again. Her smile warmed little Thomas, who had been chilled from picking up dirty, wet tin cans all morning.

"How long you gonna be here?" May asked.

"About a hour, I guess."

"I'ma run to the store an' get food to make for dinner."

She ran down the porch stairs, and Thomas went up into the house. Since May had been gone neither Elton nor Thomas had even picked a pair of socks up off the floor. There were beer cans and dirty dishes scattered everywhere, with roaches sifting in and out of the debris. There were unopened letters and bills strewn across the coffee table, and the kitchen was a total mess. The sink was piled with dishes soaking in cold, gray water. There were clothes all down the hallway, and even May's sewing room was turned upside down from Elton going in there now and then to look for a pair of scissors or some papers he needed.

The only room that hadn't suffered was Thomas's back porch. Elton had offered Thomas May's room, but the boy demurred. He said he liked his room.

Sour Elton said, "Suit yourself, fool."

May came back with three bags of groceries, and Thomas let her in.

"What is that smell?" she asked as soon as she walked in the door.

Thomas hadn't noticed it.

"You just go on to school," she said. "And when you get home I will have a good meal for you."

THOMAS WENT UP to the roof of his abandoned clubhouse because it was a cloudy day and he wanted to hear the school bell so that he could get home and into his room before Elton returned.

He unlatched the roof door and pushed it open. He'd been up there a few times to look out over the neighborhood, but he usually stayed inside where he could be sure that nobody would see him.

But that day he found another surprise. Sitting at the edge of the roof smoking a cigarette was an olive-skinned, wavy-haired teenager. Thomas froze when he saw the boy, but it was already too late to run.

The teenager turned and said, "Hey, bro," with a sing to his voice. "What you doin'?"

Thomas was shocked by the boy's eyes. They were bright, light gray, like Thomas's mother's eyes.

"Nuthin'," Thomas said. "What you doin' here?"

"Run away from the foster home they had me in." The boy slapped the beat-up brown suitcase that sat at his feet. "I climbed up the fire escape. You got the key to that door?"

"It's just a latch on the inside," Thomas said. "This is my clubhouse."

"You think you could let me stay in your club awhile, little man?"

Thomas realized that the sing in the boy's voice was close to the accent that he heard when Mexicans spoke to him in English.

"What's your name?" Thomas asked.

"Pedro."

"Why you look like that?"

"Like what?"

"I don't know."

"My mother's a beaner," Pedro said then. "And my father's a spook. I don't know where I got the eyes though. All I know is that the kids beat me up an' down the street."

"What's a foster home?" Thomas asked.

"It's where they put you when you ain't got no mother and father."

"But you have."

"Not no more," Pedro said. He took a long drag on his cigarette. "My mom died, and my dad live down on Figueroa. He sells smack and some coke down there, and he don't wanna know about me."

"If you stay here," Thomas said, "you can't tell anybody else, okay?"

"Sure, man. I ain't gonna stay too long anyway. I got a sister up in Seattle. I'ma go up an' live with her just as soon as I get the thirty-five dollars for a Greyhound."

Thomas brought Pedro down into the building and gave him candles that he'd taken from his father's house.

"There rats in here?" Pedro asked, looking around suspiciously at the shadowy corners.

"Naw," said Thomas. "There's nuthin' for rats to eat in

here. As long as you don't have any food there's no rats or roaches. Just some spiders and moths and stuff."

They settled in, and Pedro told Thomas about his sad life. His mother's family, who didn't like his father, and his father, who was a good guy when he wasn't high. And all the people who hated Pedro because he was a half-breed.

Thomas felt akin to the boy. He gave him a peanut butter sandwich that he'd made in his house. They talked for hours, until the school bell rang and Thomas had to go.

"When you coming back, Lucky?" Pedro asked his host.

"Not till tomorrow morning." And he was off.

WHEN THOMAS GOT home, his house smelled of cooking.

"I'm makin' chicken an' dumplin's," May told him. "That's your father's favorite."

The kitchen was spotless, and so were the living room and the hallway, Elton's bedroom and May's room too. She had picked up, swept, vacuumed, and scrubbed the whole house in the time Thomas was gone.

The cleanliness somehow elated the boy. He laughed and capered.

Later on May gave him string cheese and black cherry jam on dense pumpernickel bread. Then she made some not-too-sweet hot chocolate, and they sat at the table in the kitchen with her apologizing to him for the night she and Elton fought.

"You should never blame your father for that," she said. "It was all my fault. A man can't bear to hear about his woman bein' off with another man. He got to do somethin'. He got to get mad."

Thomas was sitting on May's lap when she told him this.

Then the front door could be heard banging open, followed by a man's voice saying, "What the hell?"

Thomas leaped from May's lap and ran to the back porch. He jumped in the bed and hid his head under the pillow so as not to hear the yelling and crashing. He counted up to fifteen, and then he counted again. When he reached thirty and hadn't heard a thing, he became even more anxious. He remembered his mother dying there next to him without even a sound to warn him. Maybe May was dying somehow, he thought. And so he climbed out of the bed and crawled to the door.

He pushed the door open and saw that Elton had May on the kitchen table again. But this time they were kissing. Elton had his hand up under May's dress again. But she was holding his head and smiling when he wasn't kissing her.

"The boy," May said wistfully.

"What about him?" Elton said in a husky voice.

"He's right back there, Elton."

"He got to learn sometime. Anyway, he probably just a little faggot."

"No, baby. Let's go to our room."

Elton picked May up off the table and stumbled out of the room, straining under the weight.

Later on Thomas heard her hollering from their bedroom. He worried that maybe they were fighting again and that the police would come and that he'd be put in a cell with some man taking out his thing.

But the screaming stopped and the police never came.

Later still May came and got him, and they all ate a late-night dinner of chicken and dumplings in the clean-smelling house.

9

YEARS AFTER Thomas was gone from May and Elton's home, Eric skipped the eleventh grade. He had done the core course work over the summer, spending the evenings with Christie. She got an apartment near the beach in Santa Monica, where he spent most afternoons doing his homework, surfing, and making love to her.

At first Drew called every day. He'd leave long, tearful messages asking Christie to come back East. She told him again and again that she couldn't, that she needed time to think about things.

One day, while Eric waxed his surfboard on the couch across from her, Christie answered the phone, frowned, and said, "Oh, hi, Drew."

He had called to tell her that he'd made the decision to come home midyear and go to UCLA.

"But you wanted to graduate from Yale," she said.

"I want you."

"I've met another man," she said in a clear, emotionless voice. "And I love him."

Eric could hear Drew crying.

"You can come back, but I'm with him now."

She listened to him cry and tried to make him feel better. But there was no caring in her voice, no love left over for him.

When she hung up the phone, she said to Eric, "Come fuck me."

Eric's embarrassment for Drew, combined with his admiration for Christie's brazen request, caused him to become very excited. They went at it so powerfully that Eric broke the condom when he came.

"It's okay," she told him. "I just finished my period yesterday."

And so they made love again, and again, without protection.

Eric called Ahn and told her that he was spending the night in Santa Monica.

"Be careful," Ahn told him.

Christie cried and then they made love. She laughed and they made love.

"I dropped him," she said, surprised at her own resolve.

"You didn't love him," Eric explained.

"I do love him. I want to marry him. I want to go to school in the East and be with him every weekend."

"Then why don't you?" Eric asked.

"I tried, but I can't go."

"Why not?"

They were sitting side by side in Christie's single bed. She'd been fired from her father's company when he found out that she was spending all her time with a fifteen-year-old boy. Now she worked for a design agency that had offices in the Third Street Mall. Her father took back the company car and disowned her.

The rent was due, and she was a hundred dollars short. Eric could help her this month, but he wondered how long she could live like that.

"I can't even be away from you for more than two days, Eric," she said. "When you stay home on the weekends, sometimes I cry until you're back again."

"Because you miss me?" he asked.

"Because it hurts," she said. "It hurts inside me. Sometimes I don't even like you. I look at you and think how great my life was before we met. I even hate you for not caring about anything. And then you get up just to go to the toilet and I get scared that I might not ever see you again."

Eric remembered the times when she came into the bathroom while he was taking a piss. She'd come up behind him, shivering against him, and hold his penis while he urinated.

"Do you understand?" she asked.

"Do you love me? Is that it?"

"It's not that at all. I love Drew. Sometimes I think about him, how sweet he was trying to be tough, trying to be the best at everything. Sometimes when we'd get together, he'd tell me about how scared he was that he wouldn't get into Yale or that he wouldn't be able to make it from nothing like his father did. That's when I loved him the most. I protected him."

Eric realized that Christie was telling him something that he'd always suspected but never really knew because he found it so hard to understand. He still didn't completely grasp what it was that people felt about him. But at least Christie opened the door.

"So you don't love me?" he asked.

"It's not about that."

"What do you mean?"

"The first time I saw you I wanted to get down on my knees," the young woman said with anger and some fear in her voice. "It scared me, and I went home and took a bath. But that didn't help. I went to my room and closed the door, and then I started thinking about dying."

"Dying? Why?"

"That's how you made me feel." She was weeping now. "I knew that either I was going to call you or that I'd die."

"Really die?"

"I don't know. I think that I might have. But even if I didn't there would have been something missing from the rest of my life. I tried not to call you. I put down the phone ten times before I dialed the number. But once I talked to you I couldn't stop myself. I couldn't."

"But you love Drew."

"Every night when you go home I want to call him. I miss his jokes and his trying to show off. I used to help him rewrite his papers. I was better at school than he was."

"Better than me too," Eric said. He put a hand on her thigh, but she pulled away.

"But you don't care. If I told you that I was going to Yale tomorrow you'd just say good-bye. You wouldn't even miss me."

Eric had missed Branwyn; he'd missed her terribly. And when Tommy left his heart hurt so bad that he still felt the pain. He had the capacity to feel loss.

"You see?" she said. "You won't even lie to me."

Eric would have missed her, but he wasn't thinking about that. He was trying to understand what Christie was telling him. He felt that she was somehow the mouthpiece of a much greater force, some insubstantial being breaking through to the material world, to him.

"Do you love me, Eric?"

"Yes, I do," he lied.

He said the words quickly, before he could consider them. This was an instinctual response. It was only later the next day, when he had time to think about it, that he realized why.

Christie wasn't responsible for what had happened between them. Neither was he for that matter. But their coming together brought out a need in her that she couldn't control. Years later he would be able to see it coming, to recognize when women, and men, felt so drawn to him that they were willing to leave everything to see if maybe he could satisfy a yearning in their hearts. Then he would stop the attraction, avoid their lavish offers and intense praise. But with Christie he couldn't say no. She offered him something that he needed, and so he told her that he loved her because it was the right thing to do.

"You do?"

"Yes. Yes, yes, yes," and he kissed her. Holding her, he asked, "But what can we do about Drew?"

"That's why I told him I was with someone," she said. "Now he can find somebody else and we can be together."

"But will you be happy with me?" Eric asked. "You love him."

"But I need you."

"Is that good?" Eric asked her. "I mean, it doesn't sound like you'll be happy with me."

Instead of answering him she stroked his cock and bit his nipple through his thin T-shirt.

ERIC KEPT SEEING Christie even though they didn't love each other. Her need and his guilt made a bond stronger than any consensual, reasonable, affectionate love.

But Eric also began seeing other girls at school. He'd call them up and ask them out, bring them to his house when no one was there, and have sex in Branwyn's old room. Patricia

Leonard and Kai Lin, Gina Maxim and Star Bennet and Vivian Bright, Estrella Alvarez and BobbiAnne Getz. Some of the girls had steady boyfriends, others did not. But they all gave in to his attentions — all of them, every one. And whenever Christie got wind of one of his affairs, she yelled and threw pots at him. But when he'd walk out the door, she'd always run after and grab on to him and not let go.

In the meanwhile Eric's grades were perfect. He joined the California Junior Tennis League and won nearly every game. Colleges began to woo him.

"You have a charmed life," Mrs. McCabe, the art teacher, told him one day after class.

She'd asked him to stay behind to talk to him about a drawing he'd done. It was supposed to be a self-portrait to be drawn at home on the previous weekend. All of the other students had drawn fairly realistic pictures of themselves. Most of these were of their faces; one or two included the rest of the body with some interesting clothes. Star Bennet had done a nude self-portrait, which she later gave to Eric.

But Eric's attempt was different. His painting was him, face forward with his eyes hollow and his forehead a cave. In his left eye was a drawing of Branwyn's profile, and in the right was a drawing of Thomas, as well as he could remember him. In the cave he'd rendered a scene of a man standing in a fire, with naked men and women dancing in a circle around him. The dancers moved in wild abandon. The man in the fire stood taller, head and shoulders above all the rest.

"What is this, Eric?" Mrs. McCabe asked.

"Me."

"Who are these people in your eyes?"

"My mother and brother."

"Why are they black?"

"Because they are."

"And this tableau in your head?"

"The man in the fire is me," he said. "The dancers are everybody else."

"What does it mean?"

"Nothing," the teenager replied.

"I find it hard to understand," Mrs. McCabe said. "You've led a charmed life, but this painting makes you seem so un-happy."

HE AWOKE AT three the next morning remembering the conversation. He had started the drawing in a straightforward fashion at first. It was just a sketch of his face. But as he looked at the eyes, he thought that they should be a reflection of what he saw. What was he looking at? Why, himself, of course. But then the idea of the mind's eye came to him. In his mind he often visualized Branwyn and Tommy. After expanding and rendering his internal visions, Eric looked at the forehead as a kind of blank screen. What was going on in there? The image came quickly with little or no deliberation. He was being burned up by the love of the world; his eyes saw lost love, and his mind was hollow and on fire, like the first man set upon by Prometheus and his promise of wisdom.

The cell phone on his nightstand sighed a sad rag tune a moment after he opened his eyes. Eric wondered if it was his phone that had awakened him from his sleeping thought or if it was just a coincidence that it rang.

"Hello?" he said sleepily.

She tried to speak, but all she could do was sob and gasp.

"Christie?"

Again the unintelligible moaning and cries, with only a few words shot through.

"What is it, honey?"

"I, I, I didn't want to call you," she cried. "I didn't. I wasn't going to. Really, I wasn't ever going to tell you."

"What?"

"I, I can't," she said, and then the connection was broken.

In the dark of the room Eric wondered what to do. Should he call her back or just wait until morning? Should he tell her that she'd be better off with Drew, whom she loved and who both loved and needed her?

The cell phone moaned again.

"Hello."

"I'm pregnant," she said in a controlled voice. "I told the doctor that I'd only had unprotected sex a day after my period, and he said that sometimes healthy sperm lives on for a week or more waiting for ovulation."

"Why wouldn't you tell me?" he asked, biding for time.

"I called Drew. I asked him what I should do."

"What did he say?"

"He said to come out to Connecticut, that we could get married and he'd raise the baby as his." She wailed then, crying so loudly that Eric had to hold the phone away from his ear.

It was nine months from Eric's sixteenth birthday. He would graduate from high school before then. And he would soon be a father. The graduation, his child's birth — he imagined both of these scenes in the hollow skull of his drawing.

"Eric?"

"Will your baby need you to love its father?" he asked.

"What?"

"A baby needs love, right?" Eric said. "He needs his

mother to love him and his father, and he needs his mother and father to love each other."

"I'll die if you leave me, Eric."

"Then why did you call Drew?"

"I'm scared," she said. "I'm scared and that's something you don't understand. I can't explain it to you because you're never afraid. Drew understands because he always is."

Eric realized that the emotion he felt the most often with Christie was shame. He was ashamed because she was like a used textbook for him, something to learn from but not to keep. She studied him so closely that she saw things in him that he never considered. And she shared her knowledge without holding back. She was selfless and transparent, almost invisible to him.

Like air, he thought.

"What are you afraid of?" he asked.

"I don't know," she moaned. "Having a baby with no money and no husband. Loving Drew and needing you so deep inside. Do you want me to give the baby up?"

"For adoption?"

"Abortion."

Eric remembered what Branwyn had said about Elton, Tommy's father: *Elton had the choice to be with me or not and Tommy didn't. I couldn't ask Tommy if he minded if I didn't have him and if he didn't have a life to live. No sunshine or sandy beaches. Tommy didn't even know what a sandy beach was.*

"No," Eric said. "You shouldn't do that. I mean, the baby needs a life, and Drew wants to love both you and the baby."

"What about you?" Christie asked.

"I don't know."

"I want to have this baby with you," she said.

"Then we'll have our baby and raise him to be a man."

"Or a woman," Christie added. Her voice was now bright and filled with hope.

Eric wondered what Drew would think when he realized that he was the backup just in case Eric said no.

"Go to sleep, Christie," Eric said. "I'll come over in the morning."

"When?"

"At nine."

"What about school?"

"I'll skip it for one day. We can go to the doctor together. And talk about having our baby."

"I love you," she said.

"And I love both of you."

BY THAT TIME Minas Nolan was leaving for work at ten to seven every morning. He rarely made it home before eleven. He was sleeping four hours a night and did not take vacations or even weekends off. The only time that he and Eric saw each other was between six and ten to seven, when they'd have breakfast together and share the *New York Times*. It was a day-old paper, but they didn't mind. Reading together was their ritual; the news had little to do with it.

Ahn would also get up to make and serve their breakfast. Minas had rye toast and marmalade with a poached egg and air-dried German beef. Eric had oatmeal with toasted almonds, golden raisins, brown sugar, and cream. Most of their time together was spent eating and reading. Now and then Minas would mention something he found fascinating in the paper or an anecdote from the previous day at work. Eric, for his part, listened or, at most, asked for clarification on a detail or a word. He never tried to have a full-blown conversation because when the clock on the wall said 6:50, Minas Nolan stood up, bussed his dishes, took his brief-case from the floor next to the door, and left no matter what was happening at breakfast or in the world according to the *Times*.

But that day was different.

Eric couldn't go back to sleep after his talk with Christie. He restrung his fiberglass tennis racket in the garage and then looked over his school papers. Eric was an excellent student. His comprehension of math was pure and intuitional; his memory for facts was a point of pride for his teachers. He didn't need to check his work, but he had to do something.

"Did you love my mother?" Eric asked Minas at six forty-two.

"Of course I did," Minas replied. The once-handsome man was now graying and haggard. "I loved her very much."

"What about Mama Branwyn?"

Minas's throat constricted, and his mind traveled back to the night she asked him for a kiss. He folded his newspaper, reached to place it on the table, but he wasn't looking and so dropped the *Times* to the floor.

"Branwyn," he said.

They had not discussed the mother of Eric's heart since before the day Eric found that green fish on the beach at Malibu.

Eric placed his hands palms down on the table. All of the manliness and beauty that was once his father's had now been absorbed into the boy's features.

Ahn walked in with their final cup of tea. She could see the confrontation in their eyes, so she silently placed the solid silver platter between them and then left to eavesdrop from the pantry.

"Branwyn," Dr. Nolan said again. "Yes . . . yes, I loved her very, very much. She saved me when your mother died."

"Did she love you, Dad?"

"I . . . I don't think she loved me the way I loved her," he said. "But that didn't ever seem to matter. The way Branwyn felt about people, she could give everything inside her to you even if you weren't her first choice or even somebody she could love."

"Were we people she loved?" Eric asked. He'd forgotten about Christie by then.

"I think so," his father said. "It wasn't hard with Branwyn like it was with other women."

"What do you mean?" Eric asked softly.

"Other women I'd known wanted something you couldn't see or touch or even say. They called it love, but it was more like a game the way I saw it. One night I asked Branwyn if she loved me, and she said that she fell in love with me every night that I carried her up the stairs to our room. When she said that, I felt like a kid. I kissed her and she laughed at me . . ." Minas got lost in the memory.

"What is it, Dad?"

"I asked her to marry me, but she said no. I asked her all the time, but the answer was always the same."

"You think that was because she didn't love you?"

"No. It had to do with Tommy," Minas said. "Tommy's father was alive, and she didn't want her boy to feel his loss with our marriage."

It was time for Minas to leave.

"Have I neglected you, Eric?"

In his mind Eric saw his father rising up and walking toward the door. He was supposed to be leaving, but he was not.

Behind the pantry door Ahn was thinking the same thing. She feared that something terrible was about to happen.

"No," Eric said.

"It's just that," Minas continued as if his son had not spoken at all, "you've never seemed to need help. All we ever had to do was contain you, hold you back from eating all the Christmas fruitcake or from jumping off the roof to fly with the sparrows.

"You never complained about anything. If I told you something, you just listened to me. Children are supposed to fight with their parents. Sons are supposed to want to push their fathers aside. But I always felt that you were trying to protect me instead of the other way around.

"But now that you're asking about your mothers, I see that I haven't been there for you."

Eric was staring at his father's face, imagining that he had his sketch pad before him. He would paint the portrait of his father many years later, but this was the sitting for that canvas. The drained blue eyes and graying blond hair, the gaunt jowls and dry lips.

Mothers, Eric thought. *Mothers.* Other children only had one mother, but he had two and both of them had died for him to survive.

"Would you like to go down to Malibu this morning, son?" Minas asked.

"I have to do something, Dad."

"What's that?"

"Christie's going to the doctor. I told her that I'd go with."

"You're still with her?"

Eric had seen Christie almost every day for a year. "Yeah, Dad."

It was 7:05, and Minas dawdled at the table.

141

"I could come home early," the doctor offered.

"Sure, Dad."

AHN CAME OUT of the storeroom moments after Minas left. She stood near the door staring at Eric.

"Hi, Ahn," the young man said.

She came up to the table and sat in the doctor's chair.

Ahn was the only person that Eric had ever been afraid of. It was long ago that he'd first felt this fear, before he was twelve and after Thomas had been taken away. He would find Ahn standing somewhere, staring at him. When he'd ask her why, she wouldn't say anything, just wander away only to return later, still staring silently.

"The only thing I remember," she began, "before I ran to the refugee camp, was a story that a very old man said to me. I don't know who he was. Maybe my grandfather, maybe some elder in the village where we work in rice paddies.

"He told me the story about a young woman who fell in love with a tiger. The woman go to her mother and tell her that she is in love with the tiger that lived in the north jungle.

"At night he calls outside my window and asks me to come away with him, the girl said. *And when I look out I see him in moonlight. Mother, he is so beautiful and handsome, and his deep voice makes me tremble inside.*

"But, my daughter, the mother said. *He is a tiger, a man-eater, a monster.*

"For you, Mother, I know that he is a beast. But for me he has nothing but love. He takes me riding on his back through the jungle under golden moonlight, and all the creatures there bow down to me as consort to their king.

"It is true, the mother said, *that the tiger is a king. He is better*

*than any man you would find in our poor village. But he is still a
tiger, something apart. And even if he believes that he loves you,
sooner or later you will answer to his claws.*

"The girl said nothing more to her mother about her love.
That night she disappeared from the house of her parents,
taking with her a yellow robe that many generations of her
family's women had worn on their wedding day. Three years
passed and nothing was heard about the girl until one morning an infant boy was found in the middle of the village
swaddled in a bloody yellow cloth. A beautiful boy with
tiger's eyes and a roar instead of crying. The grandmother
took in the child, and he became a great king. But he was
always heartbroken and sad because he had no true mother or
any father at all.

"And one day, while he was on a crusade to unite all his
people, he was beset by a tiger. His retainers mortally
wounded the beast, but before the tiger died the young king
looked deeply into his eyes. There he saw the truth: that his
father, the tiger, had devoured his mother, but she lived on
inside of him. The boy had found both his mother and his
father, but in finding them they were slain."

Ahn stood up and walked from the room. Eric felt the
warning in her words. He even understood the general meaning of the tale. But he didn't know what role she saw him in.
Was he the tiger or the boy? Was Christie the village girl? Was
Ahn the powerless mother? He sat there for over an hour con-
sidering the parable. He went over it again and again.

He imagined the stately tiger walking through the jungle
with the golden apparition of the village girl astride his back.
In his jaws the tiger carried a bloodied yellow cloth in which
the royal baby was wrapped. The image made his breath
come fast. It was beautiful and very sad.

"The tiger and the village girl had no choice," Eric declared to an empty kitchen. "They were meant to be. And the boy, the boy can't help himself either. They're all just waiting for their parts to play."

He took the bus down to Santa Monica, seeing himself as a pawn and satisfied to release himself to fate.

10

For most of those first three years away from the Nolan household, Thomas was more or less happy. He hadn't seen the inside of a classroom since the first week, but he could hear the school bell from the clubhouse/apartment building that he shared with the morose Pedro. Every day at the lunch bell he went to talk to May. She'd make him a hot lunch and talk about her life. May didn't need any response from the boy, and he loved to hear her talk because she seemed happy to be getting things off her chest. That happiness filled Thomas's own heart.

Not that May lived a happy life. Elton was very jealous of her. Sometimes at night he would come home and want to know where she'd been and who she'd been with. He'd slapped her on a few occasions; once he'd even blackened her eye.

But May, by her own account, never cheated on Elton. Twice she had to "do things" with Mr. Sanders, the landlord, because they were short on the rent for more than two months. But she did that to help Elton, even though she could never tell him because he would kill both her and Sanders if he knew. But she didn't like it with Sanders like she did with Thomas's father.

The only times that she had ever been bad were when she was either drunk or high.

"You should never do any drugs, Lucky," May had said. "It's the devil in them."

That was what had happened one day when Thomas came home to find May and a man called Wolf wrestling in the nude on the living room floor. When Thomas opened the door, Wolf jumped up and stood there with his big erection standing stiff and straight. The man was breathing hard, and his eyes were wild and very white against his black skin.

"That's just Lucky, Wolf," May said in a deep voice. "Go wait in the kitchen, Tommy. I'll be in in a few minutes."

But she didn't come in. She and Wolf made noises for a long time, and finally Thomas went out through the back porch to his alley valley.

The next day when Thomas mentioned the man May was with the day before, she said, "How you know about Wolf?"

Somehow she had forgotten even seeing Thomas. He told her about them being naked and wrestling, and asked if his peeny was going to get like Wolf's.

"You can't ever tell Elton about Wolf," she said. And then she told him that he should never do drugs.

"Drugs make you crazy like me an' Wolf," she said.

Wolf brought her drugs, and after she took them they took off their clothes and did that. And the drugs also made her forget about Thomas. She promised not to do drugs anymore, and he said okay and they went on for a long time as if that day with Wolf had never happened.

But May had other problems too. Elton was the source of many of them. Mostly it was because he never made enough money, and because of that he was mad all the time. And when he got mad he drank. And when he drank he got mean. And then he'd go out and get in fights, and when he got home May and Thomas had to hide from him.

Thomas listened to his father complain about the money he had to spend on the food that Thomas ate, including the dollar for his school lunch.

Thomas would have given up the lunch money except for Skully.

Skully was a mutt puppy that Thomas found on their doorstep one morning on his way to work. (Thomas referred to going to his alley as going to work because he spent most of his time cleaning the abandoned street and fixing up his clubhouse.)

Skully was a whining, licking ball of fur that Thomas immediately fell in love with. He brought the puppy back into the alley and fed him his peanut butter sandwich. That afternoon he went down to the corner store (after three so as not to be caught by the truant officer) and bought cheap dog food for his pet.

He named the dog Skully because of his mispronunciation of the foes of the Fantastic Four, the shape-shifting Skrulls. Thomas pretended that Skully was a Skrull prince that changed into a puppy and now couldn't change back, and it was Thomas's job to feed and protect him until his people came and brought him back home to his castle.

Over the last three years he had made a home for himself among his family and friends. Besides May and Elton, he had his grandmother, Madeline, whom he stayed with one week-end a month. (He persuaded Madeline to let him sleep on the floor in the kitchen, where the hum of the refrigerator's motor drowned out the all-night TV.) Then there was Bruno, who had been diagnosed with leukemia and juvenile dia-betes. Bruno had managed to go to school through the sec-ond grade, but now he was homebound and the school sent a tutor to visit him on Tuesdays and Wednesdays. Thomas dropped by to visit Bruno, and his pixilated Aunt Till, at least one day during the week and also on Saturdays, when May and Elton stayed in bed until noon.

Pedro always talked about going to Seattle to live with his sister, but whenever he got any money, he spent it on pizzas for himself and Thomas — only Thomas couldn't eat pizza because of the grease. But he was happy that Pedro stayed in the clubhouse. The black Chicano didn't spend much time in the alley. He was sensitive to mosquito bites, and he didn't like all the plants.

These were some of the happiest days of Thomas's young life. He had parents and friends, a pet, and even a grandmother — and then there was Alicia.

Now and then people other than Pedro or Thomas climbed the fence to get into the alley. But they never stayed around too long. The fence was high and crowned with dense razor wire; there were few places to sit, and the alley was damp and full of bugs. Pedro had put a lock on the cellar door to their clubhouse, and only he and Thomas had keys. Thomas hid from any strangers in the dense foliage on the north side of the alley. He'd move through the leaves and watch junkies smoke or shoot up and young lovers kissing and sucking on each other.

One Thursday morning, when he'd just arrived, he saw a young black woman sleeping. Skully yapped at the girl and butted her cheek with his nose.

"Come here, Skully," Thomas said.

The young dog ran to his master, always expecting food when he heard his voice. No Man landed on a tree above the young woman and squawked.

Thomas thought the noise would cause the girl to get up, but it didn't. She had on an orange skirt but no top. Her breasts were small, not like May's or Madeline's, and she had a tattoo of a heart on the left one. The heart had the name *Ralphie* written across it.

Her eyes were open, and there was blood on her lips.

When Thomas saw an ant walk across her eye, he knew the girl was dead. He ran and got Pedro.

"Shit, man. This some trouble here. Cops gonna take away all our toys."

"You mean the clubhouse?" Thomas asked.

"Clubhouse, alley. They send me back to juvy and, and maybe you too."

"What if we don't tell nobody?" Thomas asked.

"Somebody bound to find a dead body. You know, they stink after a while."

"But what if we hide her?"

"How?"

"We could take those extra cinder blocks from the basement and stack'em around her and then put'em over the top. Then it would be like a coffin."

Thomas was thinking about the casket that sat in front of the church, the casket that held his mother. He'd always been ashamed that he hadn't looked at her to say good-bye even though she'd told him in his dreams that it was okay.

Pedro spent the next two hours hauling cinder blocks out of the apartment building to the lonely corner where Alicia (Thomas had already named her) lay. Together the boys lined four of the cement bricks down either side of her small and slender body, then placed one at her head and another at her feet. Then they bridged more blocks over her. When they were done, they had constructed a long cement-colored pyramid over the dead girl.

"May you go to heaven and meet your maker," Thomas

said, paraphrasing words he'd heard his grandmother saying about her friends that died.

"Amen," Pedro chimed. "Man, I'm tired after all that. You think you could get me a peanut butter sandwich?"

Later that day Thomas covered the coffin with leaves and branches so that nobody would see it. He put a small crate near the mound so that he could sit next to Alicia's make-shift tomb and talk to her. At these times his mother's voice would come to him, and they would all talk about living and dying.

Thomas doubled his efforts at cleaning up the alley because he didn't want Alicia's graveyard to be littered. This was a lot of work because many of the neighbors threw cans and bags of garbage over the fence. For them it was their private junk-yard, not a holy place meant to house the dead.

Whenever Thomas filled up a trash bag with garbage, he'd climb up into his "church tree" and drop the bag into their open Dumpster.

AGES SIX, SEVEN, and eight were good for Thomas, but nine was not so great.

The first thing that happened came out of a conversation he'd had with Pedro. They'd been talking about how Pedro's family hated him. And he hated them too. Thomas said that he loved his family. He started talking about his mother, and then about Eric and Ahn and Dr. Nolan. He told Pedro how much he missed them.

"Why don't you call 'em?" the bright-eyed boy suggested. "You know his name is Nolan and that he's a doctor and he lives in Beverly Hills. All you got to do is call information."

Thomas tried this when May was out one weekday morning. He got the number and scrawled it on an unopened gas bill.

After many nervous moments, he decided to call.

"Hello?" a woman's voice said cautiously.

"Ahn?" Thomas said, his heart quailing.

"Who this?"

"It's Tommy."

Silence.

"It's Tommy, Ahn. Don't you remember me?"

"What do you want?" she asked in a slow, metered voice.

Thomas didn't know what to say. He wanted so much: his mother back alive, his brother living on the floor below, the elementary school where he knew everybody from kinder-garten and where the sun wasn't too bright. He wanted to sit with Dr. Nolan and talk about the heart and blood vessels and muscle and blood. Thomas wanted his room back and the floor where he learned to be quiet and to feel the world become one with him.

"Don't call here anymore, Tommy," Ahn said. "It's not good for you. You stay where you are and things are better."

Then she hung up.

Thomas cried for the first time since he could remember. He had dreamed for years about being reunited with Eric and Ahn, but now all of that was over. They didn't want him even to call. He blubbered there on the couch next to the pink phone. He was crying when May came home.

"What's wrong, baby?"

"They don't love me," the boy cried. "They told me not to call."

May thought that he was talking about some friends at school. She took him in her arms and assured him that she and Elton loved him very much. And so did Madeline and lots of other people too.

But Thomas would not be consoled. He had lost something that day that could never be replaced. He was sorry that he'd called. At least if he hadn't he never would have known the truth.

Ahn was also desolate over Thomas's call. She sat in her small room, at the back of the big empty house, wringing the blood-spattered T-shirt that she'd kept from childhood. She didn't want to hurt Thomas — she loved the little boy — but by now she was certain that Eric was cursed. He was a danger to anyone who threatened him or loved him. Thomas was safer where he was.

Three days after the phone call to the Nolan household, Elton came home in the middle of the day. May and Thomas were sitting in the kitchen.

"May!" Elton yelled.

They could tell by the way he slammed the door that he was in a bad mood. His father's heavy footfalls down the hall brought Thomas to his feet. If he'd had a moment more, the boy would have ducked into the back porch.

"What the hell are you doing here, Lucky?" Elton said when he came in.

"He's sick, Elton," May said, thinking quickly. "They send him home."

"Huh. That's me too. They send me home too. Said I cracked the block on that fool's Cadillac. I'idn't do shit, but now I'm fired wit' no references. Three years an' now it's like I never even had a job. Get me some gotdamn beer."

Elton was drunk for the next three weeks. Thomas couldn't come back home at noon anymore, and there were fights every night. Some nights he would sneak out of the house and go to stay with Pedro so he didn't have to hear the yelling and crying.

One moonlit evening, while Elton broke furniture and called May a whore, Thomas went out to sit by Alicia's tomb.

There were crickets and frogs singing all around him. He delighted in the moon shining on his hands and feet, and spoke softly to the girl.

"Are you lonely, Alicia?" he asked. "I know you must be, and I'm sorry if I don't come talk to you enough. But I been real busy tryin' to keep it cleaned up around here. An' sometimes it's better to be alone. Sometimes people jus' scream an' watch TV an' tell you they don't like you."

Thomas climbed up on the makeshift tomb and lay down. He slept for a while, and when he awoke the moon filled not only his eyes but all of his senses. He tasted it and heard its rich music. He felt the light on his skin like golden oil soothing him. In his mind the moon was speaking to him, telling him that everything was all right. He fell back to sleep on the rock-rough crypt smiling at his good fortune.

The next day Pedro's father was killed in a shoot-out on Slauson.

Alfonso Middleman was shot dead on the street. People told Pedro that it was kids trying to take his drug money. No one knew where Pedro's mother's family lived, and the father's family wouldn't even let him in the door.

"I went to his mother's house," the gray-eyed teenager said. "But they said that my mother lied and they were no blood to me. I don't even know where they're burying him. I can't even go to his funeral."

Pedro got a job selling crack out of an alley six blocks east of Thomas's Eden. He made enough money and then bought a pistol from the people he dealt for.

"I'm gonna kill them suckahs murdered my dad," he told Thomas one night. "Kill 'em all. And then they can put me in jail. I don't even care. But I'm not gonna let 'em get away with that shit."

Thomas spent seven nights with Pedro in the clubhouse. The bigger boy was despondent over the death of a father he hadn't talked to in eight years. He hungered for revenge.

Thomas didn't have to worry about getting in trouble at home. Elton had a night job at an assembly plant by then, and May was seeing Wolf again. Many nights she wasn't home, and even when she was there, she was too high to miss Thomas.

It wasn't until about a month later that everything went completely wrong.

Thomas was asleep in his back-porch bedroom. In his dream his mother was showing him how to fly. Wolf had been arrested the week before for drug dealing and implication in the murder of a man in Compton. That night May had promised Thomas that she wouldn't see Wolf again and that she'd stop getting high. The boy had not asked her to stop, but he was happy that she wanted to.

He came awake suddenly with fear clutching his heart. He didn't know why.

He hurried out of the house and across his valley into the clubhouse and up to the roof. There he found Pedro sitting on the rusted-out fire escape with the muzzle of his pistol shoved in his mouth. Pedro was crying. Thomas screamed and ran at his friend.

"Stop!" Thomas shouted as he leaped onto the metal basket.

The gun fired before Thomas could grab his friend. But he couldn't stop, and when he fell upon Pedro, the metal wrenched away from the wall and crashed the four floors to the ground.

For long moments all Thomas knew was pain.

When he could finally think a bit, he crawled over his wide-eyed dead friend to the hole in the fence and back home. He made it to the street and up to the front door. There he collapsed.

Elton found him in the morning when he was coming home from work.

"Lucky."

"I fell," the boy said.

"Don't worry, boy," Elton said in an unusually kind voice. Thomas was happy to hear his father's gentle tone.

He woke up in the hospital with May and Elton standing over him. There was a white woman wearing a brown dress suit standing there too, and a doctor and a nurse and a police-man in uniform.

"I want to speak to him alone," the white woman in the suit said.

"Why?" Elton complained. "You think we did somethin' to him? I'm not leavin'. I'm not."

"I can have you arrested right now, Mr. Trueblood. Right now."

Thomas didn't understand what the woman wanted. He was feeling kindly toward Elton because he obviously cared about what happened to him. After all, he had brought him to the hospital even though it was bound to cost a lot of money.

Thomas felt dizzy, and somewhere beyond that his hip hurt. But he wasn't worried about the pain.

The room cleared out except for the nurse in white and the white woman in the brown suit.

"My name is Mary," the woman said. "You're Tommy, right?"

"Yes."

"How did you get hurt, Tommy?"

"Fell."

"Did anybody push you?"

"No."

"Did anybody hit you?"

"No."

"Were you alone when you fell down?"

"No."

"Was your father there?"

"No."

"Was your mother there?"

"My mother's dead."

"Oh," the woman said. Thomas could see the sad kindness in her face even though she wore lots of makeup. "I mean your father's friend, Miss Fine. Was she there?"

"May wasn't there either. It was just me an' Pedro. He was sad about his father, and he had a gun that he was gonna use to shoot the boys that killed his father, but then he was on the roof and he shot the gun and I jumped out to save him but we fell."

"Where is Pedro now?" The woman was frowning.

"Dead, I think."

AFTER THAT THINGS were not the same. Thomas told the woman about the clubhouse but not the alley. She left and he went to sleep. Neither his father nor May ever came back to visit him, and every time he woke up he was in a different room with different nurses talking to him and smiling. One day he woke up feeling lots of pain in his hip. He reached down, finding something hard there instead of flesh.

"It's in a cast," a smiling black nurse said. "They operated on your broken bone and now it has to heal."

"Can I walk?"

"Not now, but later on you'll be able to."

Thomas lived in the hospital for six months after his operation. He had to use crutches at first, and later he walked with difficulty. He was told by the doctor that he might have a slight limp afterward but, if he did the right exercises and went to rehabilitation, that it would go away.

May and Elton had been put in jail and held over for trial. That's what the social worker, Mr. Hardy, said.

"Why didn't you go to school, Lucky?" he asked.

"Because the light hurt my eyes."

"Did your parents know that you weren't there?"

"No."

"Didn't they ask for your report cards?"

"I just told them that they didn't have report cards no more."

"Did they believe that?"

"No. Daddy said that he was gonna go talk to'em about it, but he was always workin', and then after they fired him he was asleep all day. How long is he gonna be in jail?"

"Soon you'll be leaving the hospital," Mr. Hardy said. "There's a family that wants you to come stay with them."

"But what about my dad and May?"

"The Rickerts will make a very nice home for you, Thomas," Hardy said. He had pink skin, short gray and black hairs on his head and chin, and glistening droplets of sweat across his forehead like a netting of glass beads.

157

"Do I have to?" Thomas asked.

"It's what's best," the social worker told him. "They'll send you to school and be home every night. And they have three other boys in their care, so you'll have brothers to play with."

THREE DAYS LATER, Thomas was driven to the Rickerts' house by the social worker. Thomas's limp had become permanent by then, but he didn't mind. He was much more worried about the family he had come to live with.

Robert Rickert was thin as a rail and the color of a green olive that's turning brown. Melba, his wife, was deep brown and as broad as the doorway. The husband was silent and sour, but his wife was mean.

Thomas's foster brothers had names, but he never learned them. They were all about the same age, and the first night they told him about the gang they were in at school.

"Nobody messes with us," the biggest boy with the silver tooth said. "'Cause they know that it's all'a us then."

"You wit' us?" the smaller, darker boy asked. "'Cause if you ain't, we gonna mess you up bad."

The first night at the Rickert house, Thomas was sent to bed without dessert because he didn't answer half of the questions Melba asked. He didn't want the sherbet anyway, but he knew that she wanted to hurt his feelings by depriving him.

The George Washington Carver School classroom for slow third-graders was loud, and the teacher (whose name Thomas also forgot) didn't teach very much. Thomas got into two fights the first day. Instead of going home he wandered away; then, after asking directions, he headed toward Central. When he got to his old block, he climbed under the fence and into his blessed valley.

Skully was gone. Thomas hoped that the puppy had found a home with children that loved him.

No Man was still there. He had taken a mate to live with, another green parrot, and together they built a nest in the top branches of the oak tree.

After two days, Thomas went to the alley where Pedro had sold drugs. The older boy had told him that little kids like Thomas could make good money delivering for the drug dealers there.

"Li'l kids can't get into trouble if they get busted by the cops," Pedro had told him. "So they pay you good money just to walk down the street."

In the alley Thomas met a boy named Chilly. Chilly was even smaller than Thomas, and he had an oval-shaped head and freckles on his nose. He wore a gray hat with a brim and green sunglasses. Chilly told him about the main man — Tremont. Tremont was a tall man with wide shoulders, big muscles, and a scar that started at the left side of his forehead and went in an arc down the center of his face all the way to the chin.

"You wanna run fo' me, li'l man?"

"Yes, sir."

"Where's your mama?"

"Dead."

"Where's yo' daddy?"

"In jail."

"Where you livin'?"

"With my friend Bruno sometime, an' with May," he lied.

Tremont squatted down so that he could look Thomas in the eye.

"How old are you, li'l man?"

"Nine and a half."

"Who told you about this place?"

"Pedro. He used to work here."

"If I give you work an' you tell I will kill you. Do you understand that?"

"I won't tell. I swear."

THE FIRST JOB Tremont gave Thomas was to carry a small paper bag to an address four blocks away. A lovely brown woman in a violet dressing gown answered the door.

"Are you Lucky?" she asked.

She knelt down and put her hands on his sides. This tickled, and Thomas giggled.

"Aren't you cute," the woman said.

She picked him up and hugged him.

"My name is Cilla," she said. "I'm Tremont's girl."

She carried Thomas down a dark and narrow hallway into a small yellow kitchen. There she sat the boy at a table and fed him half a ham sandwich and part of a pomegranate.

While he ate she took the paper bag and opened it. She took out a wad of money and counted it — twice.

"Tremont send you to me to make sure you could do the job," Cilla told him. "He told you not to look in the bag, and he put a tape on the inside so that I could see that you didn't. He wanna know that you can be trusted. How old are you?"

"Nine."

"You look younger."

Thomas kicked his feet and ate his sandwich.

"How come you limpin'?"

"I fell off a buildin' an' broke my hip."

Thomas smacked his lips after eating the sandwich. He hadn't had a meal in a few days.

"You're so cute." Cilla leaned over and gave Thomas a slow kiss on his mouth.

He closed his eyes and hugged his shoulder with his chin because the kiss both tickled and excited him.

AFTER THAT HE worked every afternoon for Tremont. Mostly he took white packages, which he kept in his underpants, to people's houses and apartments between four and seven, after other little kids were out of school. Once a week Tremont would send Thomas to Cilla's, where the boy would take a bath and wash his clothes in a small washing machine in the kitchen.

Thomas made twenty dollars a day, and nobody molested him on the streets because people had seen him limping down the sidewalks with Chilly, and everybody knew that Chilly was with Tremont. And nobody messed with Tremont's peeps.

After four weeks Thomas went to Bruno's house. His friend's elderly aunt Till answered the door.

"Hello, young man," she said, with eyes that held no memory of him.

"Is Bruno home, Aunt Till?"

"No," she said, looking as if someone had just kicked her in the stomach. "Bruno died."

"No. From what?"

"It's the leukemia got him. He was in so much pain."

"Hi, Lucky," Monique said. She had come up from behind the bent-over older woman.

"Hi, Monique," came Thomas's joyless greeting.

The older woman turned away, and Thomas could see Monique's big belly.

"Come on in," the young woman said.

She took Thomas into the kitchen and served him a glass of lime-flavored Kool-Aid.

"I thought the county took you away, Lucky," Monique said after lowering herself into the kitchen chair.

"I runned away from them."

"When?"

"Long time ago."

"Where you livin'?"

"With a woman named Cilla," he said. Thomas didn't want to tell her that the police hadn't changed the lock to the cellar at the back of his clubhouse. He found the key where he'd left it — under the crate next to Alicia's hidden tomb.

"An' what you doin'?" the girl asked.

"Nuthin'. What about you?"

She put her hand on her belly. "I'm havin' a baby. It's Tony Williams's boy, but he got shot. We got a studio 'partment ovah on Hooper, but now I'm there by myself. But I cain't hardly pay no rent so I guess I'ma be in the street."

"Why don't you stay here?"

"I could but they wanna treat me like a baby, an' here I'm havin' a child'a my own."

"I got three hundred dollars," the boy said to the big girl, now made bigger by her pregnancy.

"You do?"

"I could give it to you," he said. "I mean, I was gonna go out wit' Bruno an' buy a whole lotta Fantastic Fours with it. But I bet he would want me t'give it to you."

MONIQUE'S APARTMENT WAS just a room. One wall had a stove against it, and there was a big footed bathtub next to the window on the opposite wall. Between these was the bed. Thomas slept in the bed with Monique that night and every night after for the next three years.

With the money he made from drug dealing, he paid the rent and bought the groceries. During most days he'd leave Monique to stay in his alley and on the roof of his apartment building. There he'd visit with Alicia and commemorate his friend Pedro. In the afternoon he went to work for Tremont delivering ecstasy, cocaine, crack, and sometimes heroin.

TWO MONTHS AFTER he and Monique had moved in together, Thomas came home to find that Monique's mother had come over and helped deliver Monique's daughter — Lily. Thomas loved the little baby girl and thought of her as his baby sister. Now he had two sisters.

ONE NIGHT, TOWARD the end of his first year working for Tremont, Thomas went to a house where a big, fat black man, wearing only a ratty bathrobe, answered the door.

"Yeah?" he said.

"I brought you sumpin' from Tremont," the boy said.

The man looked around and then grabbed the boy, pulling him into the darkened apartment. He shoved Thomas into a big room where the only light came from a giant television set. The scene on the screen was like when Thomas had come in on Wolf and May. There was a laughing black man with a large erection that he was pressing into a white woman who cried out in pain.

"I'ma do you like that man doin' that woman," the large man said.

The big man opened up his bathrobe, and Thomas could see the erection rising up toward his captor's belly.

"Gimme that rock," the man said.

Thomas reached down into his underpants and handed over the package.

The man on the screen said, "Take all of it, bitch."

The woman screamed.

"Take off your pants," the man told Thomas.

The boy fumbled with the snap while the man tore open the paper.

"I gotta go bafroom," Thomas said.

"You bettah not have nuthin' on when you come out." The man already had the first rock in his glass pipe. He was lighting the match as Thomas closed the bathroom door. The boy turned the lock and jumped up on the toilet. There was a little window over the commode.

Thomas tried to open it, but it wouldn't budge.

"Hurry up in there!" the man yelled.

Thomas could see the doorknob jiggle.

"Unlock this goddamned do'!"

There was a loud thump, and the door shuddered.

"Open up!"

Thomas wondered if he should unlock the door.

The loud thump came again, and the doorjamb buckled and cracked.

Thomas found a thick green bottle of aftershave and threw it into the glass. The window shattered, and the door caved in. Thomas jumped through the window, cutting his left thigh and right forearm as he did. He could hear the man's heavy footsteps across the floor behind him. He stuck his arm out after Thomas, grabbing the boy by his shoulder.

"Let me go!" he cried.

Thomas moved from side to side, scraping the fat man's arm on the jagged glass that lined the window frame. Suddenly he was free and running down the street in his underwear and T-shirt.

When he got to the secret door in Tremont's alley, Chilly let him in.

"What the fuck you mean you ain't got my money, niggah?" Tremont bellowed. He surged up out of his chair and lifted Thomas by one arm.

"He made me take off my pants and showed me what he was gonna do to me in a movie," Thomas whined. "I had to jump out the windah."

"Where the money, li'l man?"

"He didn't pay me. He was just naked, an' his thing was big."

"I'ont care about that. I want my money."

"You know Lucky ain't stealin', Tree," Chilly said in a calm, slow voice. "All he do is what you say, man."

Thomas's right arm was bleeding, and his left was in pain from the way the powerful drug dealer held him.

"Look at him," Chilly continued. "He bleedin'. He ain't got no pants."

"RayRay cut you like that?" Tremont asked.

Thomas nodded and sniffed. The drug dealer's biceps was bigger than his head.

Tremont put Thomas down and then said, "Com'on wit' me."

They got to the door, and Tremont turned to Chilly. "Give the li'l man yo' pants," he said.

On the way Tremont promised Thomas that he'd kill him if he was lying.

"If you stealin' from me I'll kill you," he said.

Thomas knew the threat was real. Tremont had killed man and boy before.

TREMONT BANGED ON RayRay's door with the butt of his pistol. When nobody answered, he knocked the door in with his shoulder.

In the dark room the DVD was still playing. Now it was a scene of two men having sex with each other. A woman was kissing one and then the other while they groaned. When the screen got very bright, it shone on RayRay, who was sitting in a big chair, the glass pipe still in his hand. His other arm hung down at his side. Below it there was a great deal of gelatinous blood.

"Mothahfuckah daid," Tremont said, amazed. "Got so high he bleed to death an' didn't even know it."

When Tremont turned on the light, Thomas could see that the fat man's eyes were half open and sightless, as Alicia's had been.

"Mothahfuckah cut himself tryin' to grab you, but he was so fucked up that he just did more rock. Damn. I guess you ain't lyin', li'l man."

MONIQUE CLEANED AND dressed Thomas's wounds, but the next day he had a fever. By evening he was talking out of his head.

She brought him to the emergency room with a story about them being brother and sister. He had forgotten his key and locked himself out of the apartment so he broke the window but cut himself climbing in.

"I tried to clean it up, but then he come down with fever," she said.

The nurse saw her with the infant Lily in her arms and admitted Thomas without alerting social services.

The next day Thomas was weak, but Monique couldn't keep him from going off to work.

"You gotta quit," she told him.

"But who gonna pay for you an' Lily?" the ten-year-old replied. "I'm the only one."

11

IN THE next two years Thomas got stabbed twice and badly beaten once. He'd lost the use of the baby finger of his left hand after being knifed in the arm, but that didn't bother him much. "Baby finger don't do much anyway," he reasoned. He grew, but something about the damage to his hip made his limp worse. Lily was walking and talking and calling him Lucky. Monique had a job at Ralph's Market as a checkout clerk, but she could only work part-time while Thomas stayed home in the mornings and some evenings with Lily.

They all slept in the same bed, snuggled up and warm, every night. Sometimes in the day, when Monique was working, Thomas would take Lily to the alley valley he loved so much. He told her about Pedro and introduced her to Alicia's tomb.

On the morning of Thomas's twelfth birthday, he got up early to go to the toilet. When he came out, Lily giggled and said, "Look at Lucky's peepee, Mama. It stickin' out."

Thomas was embarrassed. He went back into the toilet and came out wearing a towel around his slender hips.

"You want Frosted Flakes?" Monique asked Lily to stop her from laughing.

Thomas was grateful to his friend.

That evening when he got home from drug dealing, he found Monique there alone.

"Lily spendin' the night wit' her grandmother," Monique told him.

The apartment felt funny without Lily there to greet him. But Monique said that the girl needed her grandmother and that they needed time alone sometimes.

"Come here an' I'ma show you sumpin'," Monique, now eighteen, said to her partner.

She made him take off his clothes and lie down on the bed. She took off her top. When he saw her large breasts, he became excited and turned over onto his stomach to hide his stiff thing. But Monique said, "Turn back around."

When she placed her cold hand on his erection, he giggled and sat up.

"Lay back," she said.

Bolstering the small erection from behind with her four fingers, she began rubbing the underside with her thumb.

"Wh-what you doin', Monique?"

"Givin' you a birthday present."

"What is it?" he asked.

"You know. I feel you gettin' hard in the bed when I hug you sometimes at night."

The boy put his hands to her wrist as if to hold her in place, and she moved her thumb lightly and fast. He came all at once and shouted, "Uh-oh!"

"It's okay," she said. "That's what you supposed to do. When you have a real girlfriend, you s'posed to do that in her coochy."

She kept moving her thumb, using the greasy white come as a lubricant.

"That tickle," he said, squirming now.

"It'a feel good in a minute," she assured him. "I used to do this for Tony when I was pregnant. I'ma only do it this one time for you 'cause it's your birthday an' you been so good to me an' Lily."

Thomas came three more times. Then they lay together, his head on her naked breast. He didn't know if he felt good or bad. He couldn't slow his mind down, and in the middle of the night he went to the restroom and threw up. When he got back to bed he felt calmer. On his way to sleep he thought about Lily and wished that she was home with them.

The next day the bust came down on Tremont's alley.

Police cars rolled up with their sirens blaring and their bullhorns commanding everyone to put his hands in the air. When Tremont came out shooting his Uzi, the police opened fire. Tremont went down immediately, and even though he was the only one shooting at them, the police kept firing until there were three dead, including Chilly, and another five wounded.

Thomas was hit in the chest, another hole in his lung. He was kept in the police ward of General Hospital, unconscious and near death, for more than a month. When he regained consciousness he was still very weak. Monique came to visit him only twice because now she had to work full-time and take care of Lily too.

At the trial Thomas's court-appointed lawyer, a kind old man named Sam Neiman, said that Thomas was a virtual orphan, that he'd lived by his wits since a very early age. He said that the system had failed the boy. He was illiterate and wild. There was no proof that he was firing at the police. He dealt drugs because it was the only way to survive.

The prosecutor was a young white woman, Flora Pride.

"The fact remains, Your Honor," Flora said, "that Mr. Beerman was a willing member of the Tremont gang. He has been implicated in at least one homicide, a Raymond Smith, also known as RayRay, and he dealt drugs every day for the past three years. He resisted arrest with violence and was wounded by policemen afraid for their lives."

The judge sentenced Thomas to nine years with the juvenile authority in the hope that they might rehabilitate him.

"I'm sorry, son," Mr. Neiman told him after the trial. "If you were tried as an adult, the sentence would have probably been less. But as it is, the system was against you."

Thomas thanked his lawyer for being nice to him, and then he was taken to a prison camp for boys on the outskirts of the eastern desert.

Many things happened to him there. Between the guards and the boy gang leaders and the cramped life of lockdown, Thomas suffered. He was slashed, gang-raped repeatedly, beaten, and then punished by the guards for being a troublemaker. But he learned to ignore his wounds and humiliations when he wasn't actually faced with them. At night he would sink to his knees on the stone floor and feel his mother in the earth.

He was in the worst child prison because he had been convicted of a violent crime. No one thought he belonged there, not even his torturers. After a year or so the punishments and molestations ended. He remembered how to read in the classroom he was brought to three times a week. He spent as many hours as he could in the library and fell under the protection of a bigger boy named Bo.

Bo wasn't tall, but he was the strongest boy on their floor, maybe in the whole facility. He liked to have Thomas around him on the yard, called him his "bad luck charm." And when other boys would ask him why he'd want something like that, he'd say, "Without bad luck I wouldn't have no luck at all."

At the age of fourteen, around the same time that Eric

faced off with Drew, Thomas was transferred to a minimum-security home in Los Angeles. Three days after he got there, he wandered away.

He was outside on the gray wood porch, and there was no one else there. He hadn't had a walk down a city street in so long that he said to himself that he'd just go around the block. But when he got to the end of the block, he took one left and kept on going.

For three days he traveled across the city on foot. At night he slept in alleys behind pizza restaurants that provided his dinner in their overflowing Dumpsters. He couldn't eat the cheese, but the crusts kept him from starving.

He asked directions in the daytime and finally made it to Monique's apartment. An old man lived there now so Thomas went to Bruno and Monique's old house.

Their parents told Thomas that Monique was living in Compton. After some hesitation they gave him her address.

When he made it to her street it was already evening.

She lived in a white house that had a lawn behind a wire fence and toys on the porch.

The door was open, but the screen was closed. When Thomas rang the bell, a chubby little girl came to answer.

"Hi," she said.

"Lily?"

"Uh-huh. Who are you?"

"I'm Thomas."

"Do you know Harold?"

"I know your mother," the escapee said.

"Mom!" Lily shouted, and then ran into the house.

Monique came lazily to the door wearing a big blue robe. When she saw Thomas her eyes opened wide.

"Lucky?"

"Hi, Monique."

"Lucky, what you doin' here?"

"I wanted to see you and Lily. She's big."

While Monique and Thomas talked, a shadow came up behind her.

"Who's this?" a man's voice said in a tone neither friendly nor unfriendly.

"This is Lucky, Harold," Monique said.

"What does he want?"

"He's my friend."

"He looks like a bum."

Harold was a tall man with bronze skin, a receding hairline (even though he didn't look much over thirty), and a large, powerful-looking belly. He had no eyebrows at all, small eyes, and large hands.

"He's my friend," Monique said with authority.

"What does he want?"

"Come on in, Lucky, and go have a seat in the living room."

"Oh, no," Harold said. "I ain't havin' this ratty-lookin' nig-gah sittin' on my new furniture."

Thomas held back, but Monique said, "Come on in, Lucky. Harold ain't gonna touch you if he know what's good for him."

"Monique," Harold said. That one word carried a whole chapter of information.

"Don't you 'Monique' me, Harold Portman. I put up with your thievin' sister, your drunk father, and them three friends'a yours leave my house in a shambles every other Saturday night. Your mother lived with us for six months, so either my one friend is gonna come up in here or you'n me gonna talk."

Harold turned on his heel and walked from the room.

"Wait for me in the living room, Lucky," Monique said, and then she went after Harold.

They had nice green furniture on a golden carpet. The TV was tuned to a cartoon show, but Thomas didn't watch. He sat down on a straight-backed wood chair and clasped his hands on his lap. Looking down, he could see that his hands were dirty and his light-blue pants were stained by alley grease.

The TV tinkled, and Monique's and Harold's voices boomed from somewhere in the house.

"Do I know you?" Lily asked. She was standing at a sliding-glass door that led out into the backyard.

"Do you remember me?" Thomas asked.

"How come you don't sit on the couch?" she asked then. "It's more comfortable."

"I've been walkin' so far and sleepin' outside," Thomas said. "I wouldn't want to get your fancy couch all dirty."

Lily was staring hard at Thomas.

"Did we go to a secret green park once?" she asked.

"You remember that?"

"Was there a big pile of rocks?"

"Cinder blocks," he said.

"And a secret clubhouse?" Lily's eyes were open wide at the memory.

"We would go there when your mother was at the supermarket working."

"I remember," she said. "I used to think about it, but then I would think that it was a dream."

"No," Thomas assured her. "We went there all the time when I took care of you while your mother was gone."

"An' we used to all sleep in a big bed, and there was a bathtub in the kitchen."

"You have a good memory for a little girl," Thomas said.

"I know."

Just then there was a loud yell from somewhere in the house.

"Your parents can really fight," Thomas said.

"Harold's not my dad," Lily told him. "Only my mama is my parent."

"Oh."

"Go to your room, Lily," Harold said.

The child and Thomas turned to see Harold standing in the doorway. His voice was now definitely angry.

"But Lucky used to take me to the secret green park."

"I said, go to your room."

The big man came in looking around, as if searching the golden floor around Thomas for crumbs or dirt he might have dropped.

While Harold stared, Monique came in wearing a long maroon dress. She was still big-boned and thick, but Thomas thought that she was good-looking. She stared at Harold.

"Well?" she said.

Harold turned his hateful gaze to her, but he soon looked down.

"Monique tells me," Harold said to the floor, "that you, that you put yo' life on the line feedin' her an' Lily when you was just a boy. She says that you was on the street buyin' her food an' payin' her rent."

He looked up at the skinny boy. Thomas had seen that hateful stare every day through the bars of the cells at the desert youth facility.

"An' because you did that you are welcome in this home. You can, you can . . . You are welcome to stay as long as you need to."

Lily hadn't gone to her room. She was staring with amazement at the man who was not her father. Monique had her eyes on him too.

"I'ma go out," Harold said, no longer able to bear the scrutiny.

And soon it was only Monique, Thomas, and Lily in the house.

They talked about the old days for a long time. Lily had lots of questions about half-remembered adventures she'd had all those long child-years ago.

Monique told Thomas that she met Harold when she was a checkout girl at Ralph's.

"He's a plumber an' he liked it how I worked so hard. An' I liked him because life was so normal in his world. No shootin's or drugs or tiny li'l 'partments."

"No bathtubs in'a kitchen," Lily said a little wistfully.

Monique served baked beans and white bread in their large eat-in kitchen. She poured lemonade squeezed out of fruit from their own tree.

After a while Monique said, "Do you wanna see your room, Lucky?"

They went out the back door to a pine hut that had a tar-paper roof. Inside there was a very comfortable, if small, room that had a single bed, a maple bureau, and a window that looked out on the green yard. The floor was covered by an eggshell shag carpet, and there was a radio and a door that led to a bathroom with a real bathtub.

"Harold built this for his mother whenever she wanna stay. But she's in Houston now with her new husband."

"She lived with us for six months," Lily said in an exasperated tone that Thomas recognized from his years living with Monique.

"You can stay here as long as you want, Lucky," Monique said.

She moved near to him and kissed his forehead. She moved back a bit and crinkled up her nose.

"If you put your clothes outside the door I'll wash 'em," she added. "Come on, turnip. Let's leave Lucky to wash up an' rest."

He hadn't taken a bath since the days he lived with Monique and Lily in that one-room apartment on Hooper. Thomas turned on the water and took off his clothes. He was about to step into the tub when he remembered Monique's offer to clean his soiled pants and shirt. So he went to the front door of his hut and placed the clothes outside in a neat pile. On his way back to the bath, he saw someone moving in the room and he jumped — a natural reflex for a small boy among so many predators in the juvenile criminal system.

But there was no one there. What he had seen was his own reflection in the full-length mirror that hung from the bath-room door.

Thomas couldn't remember the last time he had seen his naked image in a mirror. He knew that it had been years before, when he lived with Eric and Ahn and his mother.

Thomas was still short among boys his age. At his last visit to the infirmary he'd been told he was five foot five. He was slender and lopsided because of his shorter left leg. His face too had its abnormalities — a twice-broken nose, three scars, and a network of lines around his eyes from wincing at the light. There was the crater of flesh in the center of his chest from being shot in the drug bust, and then the various wounds he'd received in the street and at the facility. Thomas saw that his arms were long and that his hands were strong like Harold's. His ribs were visible, and his skin was near-black, with ashen patches here and there.

Thomas moved close to the silvered glass and stared deeply into his own eyes. Something about what he saw made him think that those eyes had something to teach him. He touched the mirror, outlined the contours of the face with his fingers. He kissed the cold image of his own lips and placed his hands on top of his head in surrender to a fate not of his own design.

THOMAS CAME TO stay at Monique's house at the beginning of summer. In the morning Thomas would walk Lily to the day-care center where she spent from nine to noon playing with other children and getting exercise.

It was a seven-block walk to the day-care center at Compton Elementary School. On the way, Lily was full of questions and declarations.

"I wanna be a bird when I grow up," she said to Thomas one morning.

"What kinda bird?"

"A hummingbird or a dragonfly."

"And where would you go, little bird?" he asked.

"I'd fly to the North Pole to see Santa Claus, and I'd fly to Disneyland right over the fence so I wouldn't have to pay all that money that Harold don't wanna throw away."

"That'a be fun," Thomas said.

He loved those walks with Lily. When he was in the facility he used to think about her and wonder if they'd ever see each other again.

"Why they call you Lucky, Lucky?" Lily asked. "Is that your real name?"

"No."

"What is your real name?"

"Thomas, Tommy."

"Which one is it?"

"Both, really," Thomas said. "My mother named me Thomas Beerman."

"Oh. Where would you go if you were a bird, Lucky?"

"I'd fly deep in the woods," he said without hesitation, "to the tallest tree I could find, and then I'd sit on the very highest branch and look out over the forest until it became the sea."

"And what would you look for?" the girl asked.

"What I'm always looking for."

"What's that?"

"My mother."

LATER THAT WEEK, when Lily was explaining to Thomas how she made cookies in her lightbulb-powered play oven, the topic again turned to names.

"How come if your real name is Thomas or Tommy do they call you Lucky?" Lily asked.

"Your Uncle Bruno named me that," he said. "It was the first day we met and I got to go stay at the nurse's office, and he thought that was lucky."

"Was it?"

"I don't know. Maybe if it happened to Bruno it would be. But I'm not very lucky at all. Really my name is kinda like a joke — they call me Lucky because I'm not lucky at all."

"How come?"

"I don't know. I think I was born like that. I fall down and lose things. Other people have a nice life, like you with your mother and Harold who love you. And others just end up on the street like me."

"Could you die from not bein' lucky?" she asked, worry filling her large brown eyes.

"I don't think so," Thomas said. "I've been thinking a lot about that. The main thing about being unlucky is that bad things happen to you and you feel bad. If you died, other people would feel bad, and then they would be unlucky."

HAROLD JUST DIDN'T like Thomas; most of the time the plumber ignored his houseguest, even when he sat down to dinner with the family. After the first few weeks Thomas started eating in his room at night. He didn't mind Harold's cold shoulder, but the big plumber would also fight with his wife and adopted daughter if Thomas was there.

The final straw was on a day when Thomas was supposed to have cut the lawn. Monique had baked a chicken for dinner, and she was carving it when Harold said to Thomas, "That was a piss-poor job you did on the grass today."

"I mowed it, Harold," Thomas replied. "Front lawn and back."

"But you forgot to do the edges along the path and out on the sidewalk. If you don't do the edges it's just a raggedy-ass mess."

"I thought that it looked nicer to leave the edges," Thomas said. "You know, it looked more like real grass instead of fake-like."

"Listen, niggah," Harold said, "don't lie to me about bein' lazy. You didn't do it 'cause all you want is to lie around an' live offa me instead'a gettin' a real job an' makin' something outta yourself."

When Thomas heard this he decided to stay silent. He saw that Harold was mad and found no reason to argue. Harold was a lot like Elton — angry at the world and needing to say so.

The whole thing would have blown over if Monique hadn't

driven her carving knife through the chicken, splitting the plate underneath in two and driving the blade deep into the pine dining table. The two halves of the plate leaped out from under the bird, flying off the table and shattering on the floor.

Monique's eyes were wide with rage. Only her ragged breathing seemed to be holding back the violence in her breast. When she began to speak her voice was almost a whisper.

"You don't know a damn thing, Harold Portman. You don't know how hard and how long this boy worked at a age when you was livin' up in your mama's house, eatin' her cookin' an' pickin' your nose. You never took a knife or a bullet to feed your family and you never would. You get up and go to work and come home thinkin' you did sumpin'. But you ain't done a damn thing that anybody else couldn't do. You ain't done enough to earn the right to shine Lucky's shoes."

Thomas never ate dinner with the family again. He went back to his room realizing that he couldn't stay around too long. But he didn't know where to go. The police wouldn't be looking for him, but if they stopped him and found out who he was he'd be put back in the facility. So he had to have a plan of action. He knelt down on the shag carpet and closed his eyes, hoping to find his answer in the earth.

A while later a heavy knocking came at his door. He could tell by the force of the knock that it was Harold. He didn't answer, knowing that nothing good could come from their talking.

WHEN THE SUMMER was almost over, Thomas was ready to go.

Monique had Wednesdays off from Ralph's. So, after Harold

was gone to work and Lily was at day care, she came out to bring Thomas his breakfast.

"Hi, Lucky," she said.

"Hey, Mo."

"What you doin'?"

"Thinkin'," he said.

"'Bout what?"

She sat on his bed. He was on his knees on the floor.

"'Bout how you an' me an' Lily had our own little family way back then."

"We sure did have some fun, didn't we?"

"Yeah. And it felt good too. I guess I should'a done somethin' other than carryin' for Tremont."

"You were only a child," she said. "What else could you do?"

"Yeah. The worst thing at the facility was that I wished every night that we was in that bed together. I used to feel so safe in that bed."

"Me too," Monique said with a hum.

"You did?"

"Oh, yeah. You were the onlyest man I evah knew who wanted just t'take care'a me. You went out again after that fat man cut you 'cause'a me an' Lily. You know, Harold wouldn't do that. He might figure sumpin' else out, but he's a man, a full-grown man. If he was ten he'd'a run home cryin'."

"I love you, Mo," Thomas said.

"I love you too, baby."

They were quiet for a while. Thomas closed his eyes. His mind was drifting when Monique said, "I'll leave him an' go off wit' you if you want, Lucky."

This brought Thomas out of his trance.

"But he's your husband."

"And I love him most the time. He good t'me an' Lily, an' he know how to do with money and build stuff too. But nobody evah been there for me like you have, Lucky. I will move out the house today if you tell me that's what you want."

"You don't owe me all that, Mo. I mean, I did that for you because of Bruno an' because'a the day you saved me from those boys. I didn't do nuthin' special. Anyway, nobody'd let a boy rent a 'partment alone. You made it so that I could have a home. No, you don't owe me nuthin'."

Monique got down on the floor and hugged Thomas to her breast. He let out a deep sigh and held tight to her. They stayed in that embrace for the rest of the morning — her kissing his head and him remembering the last night in his mother's bed.

In the afternoon, when Monique and Lily went food shopping, Thomas gathered up his belongings in a backpack Harold had given him. Before leaving he went into Monique's drawer, taking twenty dollars and Bruno's old social security card.

12

Eric graduated from Hensley High at the age of fifteen. He applied to UCLA, was accepted, and moved in to live with Christie. Six months later Christie bore their daughter, Mona. He got a job at the Beverly Hills Tennis Club as their youngest tennis pro and spent his spare time restringing fancy rackets for the wealthier clients. He made good money in tips, and his salary would do. He enjoyed his daughter, was rather perplexed by the deep love Christie felt for him, and drifted further and further away from his father.

He majored in economics because he liked numbers and the objective approach that dominated the department. He didn't feel overworked, and if some paper came due that he didn't have time to finish, Christie helped him by typing, reading books for him, or even writing the essays.

He didn't feel guilty taking her help — after all, he was working twenty-five hours a week, sharing the housework, and carrying a full load at school.

His father had told Eric that if he wanted to be a parent that he had to learn to support himself. The boy didn't mind. Actually he felt relieved when he was no longer expected to spend time at his father's house. Ahn still made him uncomfortable, and he felt guilty about his father's empty life.

★　★　★

ONE NIGHT ERIC and Christie were sitting in the beach-house living room, with eleven-month-old Mona rolling and crawling on the couch between them.

Christie said, "Isn't she beautiful?"

Eric thought, *Yes, she is,* though he didn't say it.

"She's so happy because we love her," Christie added.

Eric wondered about love. He felt respect for his father but not anything that he'd describe as the kind of love that he'd read about in books and saw in movies. He had more feeling for Ahn, but this too was not love — it was the remnant of fear that he felt when he was just a child. The only love that he'd ever really experienced was for Branwyn and then Thomas — who in Eric's mind was a part of Branwyn. There was something else about Thomas that Eric felt drawn to. It was a quality that Eric remembered but couldn't quite describe; Thomas was smart or clear or maybe even unafraid. He had something that Eric lacked, but the Golden Boy (a nickname they'd given him at college) couldn't ever say for sure what it was.

Looking upon his straw-headed, violet-eyed daughter, Eric realized that he felt delight but not the kind of love that he knew as a child.

Even with Christie, whom he slept with every night, there was no driving passion. He compared his life to the pleasant garden that Ahn would take Eric and Thomas to when they were small. There was a big lawn and stone animals for the boys to play on. But very soon Eric became bored with the pretty grass and the whimsical creatures. He remembered that it was only Thomas who made those days bearable.

Thomas would talk to the animals, and they would tell him

stories about what happened at night when all the people were gone. When the lawn became dark, the elephant battled the lion. Every night they fought and roared, baring claw and tusk, Thomas said in his breathless whisper, but no one could see them because no one was allowed in the children's park after sunset.

At that moment Eric could see Thomas standing there in the middle of the broad lawn while Ahn sewed on the parents' bench, chatting with the other domestics.

Eric recalled a day when he and Thomas were on top of the elephant, the largest animal in the menagerie. Thomas had raced Eric to the top, and for the first time the smaller boy won. But when he got up there he slipped on the slick head and fell to the ground below with a loud thump. Eric asked his brother if he was okay, but Thomas didn't even cry. It wasn't until the next morning that Branwyn noticed the swelling on his leg and took him to the emergency room.

"Eric. Eric," Christie was saying.

"What?"

"I was talking about Mona. Don't you care about her?"

"Sure I do. Of course."

"Then why don't you ever tell her that you love her?"

Because I want her to be safe, he thought. But he said, "I tell her all the time; it's just that I do it when we're alone."

AFTER A YEAR Eric moved his family into special university housing that UCLA initiated for their younger students with children. One day he got the letter in the mail. The school took the top three floors of one of the fancy buildings on Wilshire, the Tennyson, for this experiment. Eric was chosen.

The apartment was a seven-room penthouse that looked out

over a great part of L.A., even as far as the ocean. The rent was less though not quite enough less for Christie to quit her job.

But when the university was processing his papers for the apartment, they realized that Eric was now an independent minor no longer claimed by his father. A kindly clerk in the Student Housing Department felt sorry for the young father and passed his information along to the Financial Aid Office, where she knew there was a special stipend program for needy students with no other financial support.

Eric began to receive monthly checks instead of the rent bill, and all tuition expenses were taken on by the taxpayers of California. Christie enrolled in school, and the university provided full day care for Mona.

It was now Christie's dream to become a doctor. She enrolled as a pre-med major at UCLA.

The next three years passed without incident. Anyone looking at Eric and Christie's life together would have thought it was just about perfect. Eric rarely got sick, but whenever he did he stayed away from home, telling Christie his fear of making Mona ill. He never confessed that he was the cause of the deaths of both his mothers because of some insane fortune that allowed him to survive while others around him died.

He would usually stay in a motel down by the beach when he got ill. But during his last infection he stayed at a fellow classmate's parents' guesthouse in Bel-Air. The student was named Michael Smith. The guesthouse was rarely used, and Michael liked having Eric around because Eric was commonly acknowledged as the best undergraduate student in the Economics Department. Eric remained in isolation during the infectious period, but he promised to help Michael with his work once he'd recovered.

Eric liked Michael. He was a slender, anemic-looking young

man with brown eyes, brown hair, deeply tanned skin, and almost no apparent personality. His mother had died delivering his sister, Raela Timor. His father, Ralph, remarried and then, soon after, died because of a freak aviation accident.

The accident had to do with a sudden downdraft over the Santa Monica freeway. Ralph Smith was driving his VW Bug home when a single-engine Cessna was coming in for a landing at Santa Monica Airport. The plane was blown down upon the nearly empty highway — empty except for the elder Mr. Smith. It was three in the morning, and Ralph, as usual, had been working late. His car was clipped by the plane's right wing. The pilot survived with a broken ankle. Ralph only had a few bruises, but the hospital decided to keep him overnight. By morning the ill-fated bookkeeper was sick. The physician on duty, a heart specialist, assumed it was a heart condition. He prescribed blood-pressure inhibitors and bed rest. It wasn't until after Ralph died three days later that the autopsy revealed a blood infection that he'd probably contracted on his first night in the hospital.

Ralph's new wife, Maya, didn't think that she could raise two children and so adopted Raela, giving the child her last name, with the intention of putting Michael up for adoption if no one else in the Smith family would take him.

Maya had already entered into the adoption process when she met Kronin Stark, a wealthy businessman who had no office but instead conducted his various businesses from a small table in the lounge of the posh Cape Hotel of Beverly Hills. Stark went to the hotel every morning to meet with international businessmen of every stripe and nationality. They would talk for either minutes or hours, at the end of which time the lucky ones would be smiling and leaving with a handshake. Some people had been noticed leaving Kronin's table distraught and near tears. Once or twice his meetings had been followed by suicide a few days later.

Maya Timor had gone to the Cape Hotel looking for a job. She'd heard from friends that it was a great place to work with good benefits and some security. She left Michael at home because he was old enough to take care of himself, but she brought Raela along with her. Everybody liked the raven-haired Raela, and Maya felt that the child's presence was something like a blessing.

"I don't know, Mom," Maya once said to Jayne Henderson-Timor. "When you look in those eyes you think that she can see right into your soul. It's scary, but at the same time you can't turn away."

Jayne suggested that her daughter take the child to see a doctor. That had been the beginning of the deterioration of the grandmother-mother bond.

The hotel wasn't hiring, but before Maya found this out, Raela wandered into the lounge and saw the great bulk of Kronin Stark. She came up to the empty chair in front of him (just vacated without a handshake) and sat down.

"Who are you?" the six-year-old beauty asked.

"My name is Stark."

"It sounds like you have rocks in your throat," she said.

"That's because I'm very serious."

"It's no fun being serious all the time," the child said. "If you're too serious your mouth gets stuck in a frown and then nobody likes you."

"Raela," Maya Timor said. She was coming from the bad news at the front desk. "I'm sorry if she's bothering you, sir."

"Not at all," the humongous businessman replied. "As a matter of fact, she's done me a service. She reminded me why I'm sitting in this chair."

The big man smiled, and Maya noticed the ten-carat ruby that festooned the baby finger of his left hand.

"Raela is your name?" he asked the girl.

"Yes, it is."

"And what is your mother's name?"

"Maya," Raela and Maya said together.

Kronin told the girl that they served very good strawberry pancakes at the Cape and invited both mother and daughter to breakfast. After that they repaired to the roof, where there was an Olympic-size swimming pool. A little deal with the pool man and a swimming suit was found for the girl.

While the child swam, her long, dark hair flowing behind her like a fan, Kronin made polite conversation with Maya.

"Her father named her," Maya said, "after a fantasy princess he made up when he was a child."

"She is regal," Kronin admitted. "You say her father died?"

"Mother too. I'm in the process of adopting her. It's too bad, but I don't have the wherewithal to keep her and her brother too."

Maya was never certain if Stark kept calling because of her or her adopted daughter. But he'd call every week and take her and the children to some beach or restaurant.

Michael was in awe of Kronin — his size, his voice, the way people served him wherever they went. He traveled in a chauffeur-driven Rolls-Royce and lived in a big house in Bel-Air. Kronin didn't care about the boy, but he saw how much Raela loved him and so he asked Maya if they could keep the boy when they got married.

"You're asking me to marry you?" was her response.

"If you will have me."

Kronin was a force in the world of business. He created dynasties and destroyed men and businesses on a daily basis, rarely picking up the phone more than twice in a day. He was a giant both physically and mentally and saw the people around him as a different species somehow, lesser beings. And so when Raela appeared before him he was surprised. Something about the child's eyes, her demeanor, enchanted him. That's the reason he asked the hotel supplicant Maya to stay for breakfast — he wanted to see what made her child so fetching.

Over the weeks Kronin found himself falling in love, not with Maya but with the child. He found himself eager to leave the Cape in the evening, when he was to have a family date with Maya Timor, the nonentity Michael, and the transcendent child Raela.

He had had many women in his life: movie stars, heiresses, and divas of various ilk. And he wasn't a snob, in the ordinary way. He'd dallied with barmaids and secretaries, lady lawyers and prostitutes of all races, ages, and states of relative beauty.

The billionaire wasn't looking for companionship or sexual gratification or love. What he wanted, what he craved, was a queen: a woman that could carry his power with grace, a woman that would bear him children he wouldn't want to drown. It was plain to see that the woman he wanted was the woman Raela would one day become.

Kronin adopted Raela and not Michael, but the boy was still deeply loyal to him. The reason that he studied economics was to impress the man he wanted to be his father. He dreamed that one day Kronin would need his help, and there Michael would be, ready to comply. But he didn't have a good head for numbers, nor did he understand even the simplest part of his sister's father's business. That's why when Eric had asked him if he knew where he could stay to keep his family from catching his cold, Michael was quick to suggest Kronin's guesthouse.

Eric would sit in the small, glass-walled house reading advanced texts in economic theory and novels from the nineteenth and early twentieth centuries. He loved James and Balzac, Dumas and Eliot. He also watched tennis and boxing on a small portable TV they had out back. He ate canned soup, heated on a hot plate, and avoided all other contact until, on the morning of the fourth day of his sojourn at the Stark home, he heard a knock on the door.

He pulled back the curtain and saw a tall, dark-featured girl who was a stranger to him. Raela was fifteen then and slender. Everything about her face was perfectly proportioned, but her eyes seemed large anyway. She smiled and waved.

"Hello," Eric said through the closed glass door.

"Hi," the girl said with a grin.

"Who are you?"

"Raela," she said with a guttural roll at the back of her throat.

"I'm Eric."

"I know. Mikey says that you're afraid to get people sick so you stay out here."

"That's right," Eric said. He too was smiling, though he wasn't sure why. He found himself watching the girl's eyes, not looking into them but observing them as if they were rough gems.

"That's stupid," she said. "People get sick all the time. My father says that if you get sick that's good because it makes you stronger to fight other colds."

"Once I got sick and my mother caught it and she died," the nineteen-year-old senior said. This was also a surprise. It was the first time he had admitted to anyone this deep-rooted belief in his own guilt. But at that moment he didn't feel guilty.

Raela's face took on the sadness in Eric's heart.

"That's awful," she said, "but it doesn't mean it'll happen with me."

"How could I know that?" he asked.

"Let's flip a coin."

They settled on the rules of their game. The best out of five, but the winner had to win by at least two. Eric had never in his life lost that configuration.

They started at 10:15 a.m.

At noon she was only one flip up on him.

Eric opened the door, and the teenager came into the college man's room. They sat across from each other on sofa chairs, and she told him everything that she'd felt in her short life and he told her everything that he'd experienced. He told her about the tennis game and Christie and Mona and Thomas. When he talked about Mama Branwyn, the girl moved to sit next to him. She held his hand, listening with rapt attention and without any question of his seemingly overblown ego.

"Sometimes I wonder why people like me so much," she said. "I mean, it's not like I'm any better than anybody. Lots of people I've read about have done truly amazing things. They invented electricity or brought Christianity to Ireland. They conquered the world or made things so beautiful that people line up five thousand years later to see their works."

"Yeah," Eric said. It was a brief reply, but Raela knew that he was moved by her words. "But most people don't care about that kinda stuff. They see blue eyes or a nice body and they believe that they can get somewhere."

"Where?" Raela asked, looking into Eric's eyes.

He could see that she wasn't besotted with him. It was his knowledge she was after.

"I don't know. It's like someplace that they imagine you

come from. A room somewhere where the food is better and the TVs are bigger and then they can have anything they want."

"Yeah," Raela said with a big smile.

Raela knew in her heart that this man was meant to be hers, and he knew it too. They talked until the sun went down. In that time his chest cold cleared up, and she made him promise to be her friend.

"Raela," a man's voice called from out in the yard.

"Out here with Eric, Daddy," the innocent girl exclaimed, jumping to her feet.

He walked into the guesthouse, a rhinoceros nosing its way into a mole's den.

Eric had never met anyone like Kronin Stark. He was at least six and a half feet tall, weighing well over three hundred pounds. His black hair was too long for a man his age, and his mustache was so profuse that it overwhelmed his trim beard. He had huge hands and great black eyes made to mesmerize.

When he asked, "What's this?" Eric felt a small quelling in his heart.

"This is my new friend, Eric, Daddy," Raela said with absolute certainty.

"I thought that he was your brother's friend?"

"We can share. Eric and I flipped coins and came up even almost."

Surprise registered on the big man's face. His brow furrowed, and he began to take deeper consideration of the young man.

"I see," he said at last. "Well . . . welcome to the family, Eric."

As the billionaire turned to leave, the Golden Boy watched him, unable to speak or even to register what had just happened.

"See?" Raela said. "We will be friends forever and that's that."

The final tone of Raela's exuberance stayed with Eric, but it didn't make him at all happy. He had found the girl who would become the woman for him, but he didn't want to sink the lives of his daughter and her mother in order to have her. He feared what could happen. On the short drive home he considered deserting Christie, going to Mexico or Ghana and starting a new life far away from anyone he could hurt. He thought of telling Christie the truth: that he had to leave in order to save her more pain. Raela, he knew, would have believed him, but Christie would never understand.

Driving down Sunset Boulevard, Eric felt the trap of his fate closing in. He thought about the tiger's son who was the cause of his parents' death. In his fantasy Raela transformed into a great feline, and she stalked Mona and Christie in a dark alley. He could see them but could not stop the monster from pouncing; he couldn't because the monster was his own leaping heart.

His eyes were stinging from a sudden sweat, and his hands, also sweating, slipped and shook upon the steering wheel. He pulled to the curb and tried to think his way out of the vision that he believed was true.

People appeared to him. His father wouldn't know what to say, he knew. Ahn would agree with his assessment of the problem and shake her head fatalistically. Michael and Christie and Mona were useless. He had no other friends that could help.

All he could think of was Tommy and Mama Branwyn. But she was dead, and no matter how quickly he opened his eyes he never caught a glimpse of her as Tommy had done. And his brother was lost to him. He believed that if he found Thomas he might be saved from his own cursed luck. But there was no sign of Thomas anywhere in L.A. Even his grandmother had lost track of him.

Having lost his brother again in his mind, Eric realized and accepted that he was alone in the world. He decided that he'd never talk to Raela again. He could control his destiny. He didn't have to give in to the gravity he felt in her presence.

After all it still wasn't love that he felt. There was a *rightness* in the combination of him and Michael's sister. She was his other half in some way, his equal. She'd be immune to his providence.

But he would never see her again and his family would be safe. Mona would grow up and move away, and he and Christie would live into old age, her resenting his distance and him guarding her life.

The sweat broke and Eric laughed to himself. He felt as if he had jousted with a tiger. He'd battled an inner demon and won, with no one but himself to mark the victory.

ERIC CAME HOME to find Drew Peters sitting on the sofa, casually talking to Christie.

She seemed a little nervous, but Eric felt that that was only natural. Drew and Christie had been together, off and on, since they were twelve. There was a deep bond between them, and it must have been difficult for them to sit together when she was now with Eric.

"Hey, Drew," Eric said.

"I won that last point" were the first words out of his mouth.

"You would have," Eric agreed for the hundredth time, "if the sun hadn't come out right then."

"You better believe it," Drew added. "I had your ass."

Eric sat with them and talked about Drew's work at Yale. He went in wanting to become a physicist, but now he was interested in painting. His father was angry about the change of major, but he didn't care.

"I'm going to do what's right for me," Drew said with deep conviction and maybe even a little anger. "And I don't care what anybody thinks."

Eric had little to say about his own work. It wasn't much different than the studies he did at Hensley. Mona toddled in while they talked. She crawled up onto her father's knee and went instantly to sleep there.

Christie watched them with a frown on her face.

Drew soon excused himself, and Christie went to bed with a headache.

Eric sat on the little patio twenty-five stories above L.A. The building was also on a hill and so looked far out on the horizon. Mona woke up and said, "Daddy?"

"Yes, baby?"

"Do you love me?"

"Very much," he said.

He kissed her to cover up the lie.

13

———————

D URING THE first few years that Eric attended UCLA,
 life got very hard for his brother Thomas. The lean
escapee found a shopping cart and traveled the streets of Los
Angeles gathering things that he found beautiful and useful.
He loved blue glass and chrome, red cloth and books. He collected all kinds of books. Some he could read and others not.
He ranged all over L.A., sometimes sleeping in Griffith Park,
sometimes in the cavelike feeders to the concrete L.A. River.
He was robbed every other month or so but only raped once,
by a wild man who came upon him sleeping in an alley off
Florence, when he was thinking of going back to his alley
valley.

Once Thomas went down to Malibu and walked the
beaches where he'd gone with his brother and Dr. Nolan. He
didn't stay long because the sun on the sand was too bright.

The police stopped him all the time, but he used Bruno's
social security card as identification and claimed that he was
twenty-three. The police believed him because after all that
time living outside, Thomas's voice had become rough and
his face was quite weathered and beat-up.

He had no friends. The only people he knew were other
street people who traveled the avenues and alleys looking for
refuse that was either edible or of some value to someone

somewhere. He gathered bottles to return for the deposits and copper piping from discarded air conditioners, stoves, and refrigerators. These valuable metals he brought to recycling centers for a couple of dollars every now and then. In an old mayonnaise jar he kept the carcasses of interesting bugs that he'd find. In the day sometimes he'd dump out the bugs and investigate God's divine will manifest in their intricate designs.

While Thomas walked, he'd usually have a running dialogue with his mother, Branwyn.

"Mama, why am I like this?" he'd ask periodically. "Why am I walkin' down Pico with nowhere to go to? Why am I bein' punished? Am I so bad that I don't get to have a home like the other people in the world?"

"There's nuthin' wrong wit' you, baby," Branwyn would say in Thomas's highest voice. "You just too good for some'a these people who think poor peoples are evil. They can't see you for what you are because of your old clothes and the dirt and your shoes with the holes in 'em. If you were to get all clean with new clothes, people would see you for what you really are, and they would give you a job and an apartment and you wouldn't be so lonely and sad."

After a conversation like this, Thomas would make a pact with himself that he would find a way to get new clothes and a bath and then he would find a job and make a life and Monique and Lily could come visit and even tough-minded Harold would be proud of him.

But after a week or so of trying to get enough money, Thomas would sink once again into despair. He'd drink wine sometimes but not too often. Being drunk made him confused, and he couldn't find his place when he knelt to the earth trying to meld with the planet.

He went into the homeless shelters only rarely. The people

there were scary, and made him too afraid to sleep. In the night when he was awake, all the sad noises of the men in the bunks around him made him want to run and scream.

So he spent most of his days wandering and his nights in lonely places where wild men and the police wouldn't look.

He had a big umbrella for when it rained and a silvery, thin blanket that a young white couple had given him. The metallic coverlet was hardly thicker than tissue paper, but when the weather got cold he was always warm with the silver sheet wrapped around his skinny frame.

The years went by, and he hardly ever thought about Ahn or Dr. Nolan or Eric. Then one day he found a child's book, written in French, about a skinny blond child named Madeline Blanchet. He stared at the book for a long time thinking that the name was trying to tell him something, something about him.

Toward the end of this part of his journey, Thomas found a pair of barely chipped sunglasses. The lenses were almost black, and wearing them Thomas could walk on the sunshiniest days and never wince at all. It was like walking in the darkness even though everyone else around him was in light. This was a deep comfort to Thomas. He wore these glasses every day, was wearing them as he walked down Venice Boulevard, a little past Fairfax, thinking that he'd reach the ocean again in a day or two and wondering what that child's book was trying to say.

On the way he met a Mexican boy who was selling sacks of oranges to passing cars. When Thomas walked by, the boy broke open one of his bags and gave Thomas four large oranges.

He was thinking about how kind that boy had been and how delicious the orange was when he remembered his grandmother. Grandma Madeline. Once he remembered her name, the phone number came along with it.

★　★　★

"Niggah, what you want?" a thirteen-year-old tough standing among his posse asked. He flicked his hand out as if he intended to slap Thomas, who flinched in defense.

The six or seven boys laughed at the frail young man with the big chapped hands.

"Yeah, bum," another boy said. "Why you stinkin' up our air?"

"My grandmother," Thomas said. "I need to talk to her."

Thomas had used his last dollar three days before buying adhesive strips for his feet. His feet often bled from corns and chafing and so were in perpetual need of new bandages.

The smallest of the black boys took out a pocket knife. He picked out the blade but didn't point it at Thomas.

"I need to call my grandmother," Thomas said.

"Niggah, get away from here 'fore I cut you," the armed boy said.

Thomas shied away, knowing that the children didn't want to hurt him but they might if they blustered too much and whipped themselves into a frenzy. He'd seen it happen before. Groups of young men and boys sometimes made themselves into killers.

Thomas went north on Orange Grove wondering where he could get the quarters to call his grandmother Madeline. For many blocks in either direction the sidewalks were empty. There was an occasional person standing in his yard, but Thomas knew not to accost a person in front of his house. It was too threatening, and the person might call the police.

Four blocks from the incident with the boys, Thomas heard someone calling.

"You. Hey, you."

A boy, maybe one of the ones from before, was jogging up the street toward him. The boy was alone, and Thomas was thinking about his grandmother, and anyway, he couldn't run because of his leg, his bloody feet, and his cart and because running meant guilt. And even if the boy was alone, soon others would join him to chase Thomas down.

This child was twelve or thirteen. He had a thick neck and intense eyes.

"Hey, man," the boy said. "I'm sorry 'bout them. You know, I gotta uncle live in the street. They say he's schizo, is that's what's wrong wit' you?"

Thomas hunched his shoulders and shook his head. He didn't know.

"His name is Alfred Kwawi," the boy continued. "You know 'im?"

"No. Sorry."

"That's okay, brother," the boy said. He reached into his pocket and came out with a fistful of change. "Here you go."

As soon as the money was in Thomas's hand, the boy took off in the direction from which he had come. Thomas stood there for a moment trying to remember where he was standing and the features of the boy's face. He forgot so many things in his days on the street — he would have forgotten the incident with those boys in an hour or two — but he wanted to remember kindnesses. He collected them the way he collected blue glass. An old white woman on Wilshire that once sat next to him and shared her sandwich, a stray dog that slept up against him on a cold night before he got his silver blanket, a black man who stopped to help him pull his cart out when it had fallen into a ditch — he remembered every moment of kindness and carried them along with his cart to remember at night. He penned these events as well as he could into a bound book of blank paper he'd found behind a stationery store. Every now and then he'd copy the acts of kindness onto a new leaf in the book and admire his penmanship and the benevolence of his fellow man.

"HELLO?" SHE SAID upon answering the phone.

"Grandma?"

"Hello?"

"Grandma, it's me — Lucky. I-I mean, Tommy."

"Tommy? Tommy. Is that really you? Where are you, baby?"

"At a phone booth. I been livin' in the streets for a while now, and I, and I just thought about you and so I said to myself that I should call."

"Tommy, where have you been? I haven't heard from you in years, years. We thought you were dead."

Thomas closed his eyes and imagined the big woman in the small apartment. He could hear the TV playing in the background. He thought it was probably Oprah at this time of day. He took a deep breath and smiled.

"After I broke my hip they put me in a foster home, but the other boys didn't like me so I left. Then I lived with Monique and her baby for a while, but I got in trouble an' they put me in the facility. Now I'm just movin' around kinda. You still watch TV all the time?"

"I sure do," she said gently.

"You talk to my dad?"

"He's in Galveston," Madeline said. "He married a woman named Celia, an' they had kids and moved down to Galveston. He's a mechanic for the city down there."

"Galveston. That's pretty far, huh?"

"Yes, it is. All the way down in Texas."

"What about May? You heah about her?"

There was a long pause, and then she said, "No, not really."

"Oh. You know what, Grandma?"

"What's that, child?"

"I wish I was still small like I was. 'Cause if I was I could still sleep on the floor in your kitchen."

"I wish that too, baby. But those days are all gone. We nevah did right by you."

"You did okay. I mean, I'm fine. I ain't sick or on drugs or nuthin'. I drink some wine sometimes but not like some'a these winos out here."

Again there was silence.

"Please insert ten cents for another five minutes," a woman's recorded voice said.

Thomas dropped the dime into the slot.

"Tommy, are you still there?"

"Yes."

"Listen, baby. Maybe you should call that family you used to live with. Maybe they could help you out. You know, I don't have hardly enough to keep me goin'. Now I got somethin' in my stomach and the doctors wanna cut me open. I can't take care of you, baby."

"I called Dr. Nolan a long time ago," Thomas said. "They said not to call no more."

"You must'a not understood'em, Tommy. 'Cause that boy Eric was writin' you letters once every mont' up until about four years ago. I must'a had a hundred letters and postcards from him in my dresser."

"Do you still have'em?"

"No, baby. I did a spring cleanin' just two weeks ago and

threw them all away. I hadn't heard from you in years. I didn't know."

Thomas spoke to his grandmother until all the change ran out. He asked her if she wanted to call him back, but she said that she was behind on her phone bill and they had blocked her making any outgoing calls except for 911.

Thomas lost all direction for a while then. He wandered the streets, talking to Alicia sometimes and other times to his mother. He daydreamed about all of those letters and what they might have said. *Here in Hawaii, Tommy. The pineapples are really great,* or, *I just bought a new car and I'm driving to Frisco for the weekend.*

Thomas tried to think about what his brother looked like now that he was nineteen. But all he could imagine was a bigger version of the blond-headed boy.

Maybe there were photographs in the letters. Maybe he needed Thomas to be there for something.

Thomas knew that he was the only person that Eric ever confided in. The bigger boy was too proud to admit fear to his father, and around Branwyn he always lost his tongue. Only with Thomas, when they were alone, did Eric say how he really felt.

"I don't know why everybody thinks they like me so much," Eric once said to his brother. They were five, sitting atop the stone elephant pretending they were in India delivering spice to the English.

"They don't *think* they like you," Thomas said. "They really do."

"No. If they did they would ask me about what I liked instead of making me spell words and go to their houses. They never want you to come."

Thomas remembered the pain that his brother felt for him, and he wondered if he was still the same or if he'd changed like other boys did when they became men. Thomas hadn't changed. He was still the same, he knew. He got a little bigger, and he no longer had a clubhouse or a valley or a friend — but he was still the same.

Thinking this last thought, Thomas made up his mind to find his brother. He wouldn't be afraid that Eric wouldn't talk to him. He wouldn't be quiet. And anyway, he had found something out that he knew the old Eric would like. And if Eric was the same, he would still like it.

14

ERIC SAT up until late in the night holding his daughter and thinking about Raela. Christie loved him and so did Mona. He had fallen into this life as he had into everything else. He never made decisions — he didn't have to. Everything came to Eric.

Raela was his first real challenge — that's how he saw it. If he became friends with the child, she would own him, and his family would be destroyed. He knew this. But it didn't have to happen. All he had to do was commit himself to the life he was living. This commitment would save his girlfriend and daughter, and make him a part of the world. He would be like other people who had to deny themselves in order to survive.

At three in the morning he brought Mona inside and put her in her bed. Then he went to his bedroom and gently shook Christie by the shoulder.

She came awake with a start.

"What's wrong? What?"

"I wanted to ask you something."

"What?" she asked, the fear still deeply rooted in her voice.

"Do you still love me?"

She hesitated.

"Why are you waking me up in the middle of the night to

ask me that?" she said. Then, noticing that he was dressed, "Haven't you been to bed?"

"I've been awake," he said, "thinking about you."

"Me? What about me?"

"I want you to marry me."

Christie gasped. "What?"

"Marry me. We're already parents together. We need to work right together."

Christie slapped Eric across the face hard enough to turn his head. When he turned back, she slapped him again.

"How dare you," she said, seething.

"What? I thought you wanted this?"

"I do. I did. But I gave up. You were here, but not the way I wanted you. I loved you, and all you ever did was care in return. You never laughed out loud or ran to me or got mad and walked out. You never got jealous when men would stare. You weren't even upset when you found Drew here sitting with me after you'd been gone for days."

"You're friends," Eric said with a sheepish smile. "I didn't think women liked men to be jealous."

"But you shouldn't take us for granted," she said in a voice loud enough to fill a small auditorium.

"I do care. I love you. I want you to marry me."

Christie was fully awake now. Her violet, reddened eyes were wide with something like rage. She was shaking, but when Eric reached out to calm her she pushed him away.

"What are you?" she said. "How dare you."

"I don't understand, Christie. I'm sorry."

She would not cry. She would not.

She got up from the bed and dressed quickly in pants and a T-shirt, putting on no underwear.

"I'm going away for a while," she told Eric, holding back the rage.

"When will you be back?" he asked.

"I don't know."

"Today?"

"I don't know."

"All right. If that's what you have to do."

"It is. I'm going," she said, and she was out of the apartment in less than a minute.

CHRISTIE DROVE TOWARD the desert, finally able to cry now that she was behind the wheel and sealed in her car. She turned the radio on and then off. She took out her cell phone, entered a number, then disconnected before the call engaged. She turned on the radio again, turned it off again. She put a CD into the player. It was an old collection, one she had bought for her mother, Mary McCaslin's *Way Out West*. When the sweet, high voice began to sing her cowboy complaints, Christie calmed down enough to wend toward depression.

Drew wasn't visiting from back East. He'd dropped out of school and come back to L.A. a year before. He called her when Eric wasn't home and begged her to come back to him. Her departure from his life, it seemed, left a wound that would not heal.

She still liked Drew. She cared for him. But after months of his begging and after years of Eric's cool detachment, she couldn't take any more. So when Eric went away to keep from getting Mona sick (as if, she thought, his germs were deadlier than other people's), Christie said okay when Drew wanted to come over. She said to herself that she merely wanted company, to have her own life. Maybe they would have dinner and talk about old times, she had thought. Her mother had wanted to spend time with Mona, and so Christie packed her an overnight bag.

Drew tried to kiss her at the front door, but she pushed him away and said that if he did that again he'd have to leave. She meant that. He apologized nicely, and they sat down on separate chairs in the living room in front of the window that looked out over Santa Monica.

They started out talking about his paintings. There was a gallery in San Jose interested in showing two canvases. They were paintings of Christie the way he remembered her when they'd gone to Catalina Island for the weekend once. They were nudes. He'd love to show them to her. To him she had always been the ideal of beauty. He loved her then and he still did. He dreamed about her; he told her he dated women who looked like her. He had dropped out of school to be near her.

"I love only you," he said at last.

Her anger at Eric and the pathetic bleating of Drew came together in Christie's brow.

"It has nothing to do with you, Drew," she said, affecting a gentle tone. "It's just that . . ."

"What?"

"It's just that Eric is so wonderful." She felt a perverse satisfaction seeing the pain entering Drew's face. "It's not just that I love him, but he's got everything a woman could want in a man. That day he beat you on the tennis court I called him. We went for a drive, and I told him that I loved you and I wanted to be just friends. But he took me in the backseat and made love to me until I was completely his. I didn't even want to be with him, but he made himself my man."

The tears flowing from Drew's eyes were a balm for Christie's ragged heart. She loved hurting Drew, but at the same time she told herself that it was for his own good.

"Stop," he said.

"From that first night, we got together whenever I could get away from you," she continued. "You remember that stain on the roof of my car? That was Eric. His dick is the biggest thing I've ever seen, and when he came it was so hard that I could feel it inside."

"Stop, Christie."

"You can leave whenever you want, Drew. You're telling me how much you love me. I'm just telling you how I feel." She expected him to jump to his feet and run from the apartment. She wanted to make him run, to feel the pain that she felt. She realized that she really did blame him for not being man enough to keep her.

But when he did stand up, it was only so that he could fall to his knees and press his face against her skirted lap.

"Why are you doing this?" came his muffled cry.

"You're always calling me," she said in the same removed tone Eric used when he told her he loved her. "Telling me how you feel. But I'm not the person you think I am. That whole summer after we graduated, I fucked Eric every day. Sometimes I'd be with him and then come to be with you for a while, and then I'd go back and Eric would fuck me again. I didn't want to be with him, but I couldn't help it. I had to go. And I didn't care about what I was doing to you . . ."

As she spoke, her voice became a whisper; she leaned over him and her skirt slowly rose from the movement of him shaking his head, trying to deny her words.

"You wanted me to kiss your dick, and when I finally did you didn't know that I had been doing Eric like that since the first night in my car. He didn't ask me if I would, he just shoved it into my mouth and held my head so I couldn't move."

Drew slammed the arm of the chair with his fist.

"No!"

Christie realized that there was a new person coming out of her. She'd never talked like this, never tortured anyone like this. She felt Drew's hands on her naked thighs and she liked it.

When he looked up at her she said, "Put your head back down."

"When my parents were gone he came to my house," she continued. "When you called on the phone I was in the bed with him. When I answered sometimes I was licking his cock while you went on and on about Yale and what you would do there."

That was when Drew pushed her panties aside and pressed the flat of his tongue against her clitoris.

"Oh, yeah," she said. "Once . . . once he came in my mouth while you were asking what kind of tux you should wear to the prom."

Some of the things she told him were true, others the product of her imagination. When he tore off his clothes and fell on top of her she whispered, "And he has a really big dick and he could fuck for hours before he'd come. He'd have me coming again and again and begging him to come for me."

This last part was too much for Drew. His orgasm was a painful, wrenching thing. He pounded so hard against her that one of the legs of the chair broke. She laughed and he kept pounding. She knew that he was past feeling it but didn't ask him to stop. And he didn't stop. He kept going until he found the feeling and came again.

And when he was finished and lay beside her on the floor,

she asked, "Why didn't you do me like that when you had a chance to keep me?"

Christie called and asked her grandmother to keep Mona for the next three days.

Drew suggested that they go into the bedroom, but Christie said, "No, that's his bed," and sneered as if daring Drew to respond. He dragged her in and mounted her from behind.

"Did he do it like this?" he asked.

She nodded, half in ecstasy, and said, "Only his was much longer and thicker, and when he did it he fucked my ass."

All that night and for the next three days they made love like feral cats. Christie didn't say one kind word in the first forty-eight hours. It wasn't until the third day that she admitted that there were things she liked more about Drew than Eric. But even then she said that she was with Eric now and Drew should move on to someone new.

They slapped each other, pulled hair, and had deep orgasms that Christie never knew were possible. Drew had brought out an angry passion that fed on itself in the ex-cheerleader's secret heart. She tied him facedown to the four-poster bed with an arm and a leg attached to each corner. Then she got the Vaseline and a thick and muddy, blunt-tipped carrot from the farmer's market. He screamed when she drove half the length of the root into his rectum.

"Stop it!" he cried, flailing around, trying to get free.

She didn't remove it, only brought her lips to his ear and said, "Do you want me?"

He went still and nodded his head.

"Then you have to take it all the way," she said.

She pressed the full length in and then left the room to have her private orgasm on the couch outside.

She untied him an hour later and told him that she'd be his. They'd take Mona and move to Connecticut. Eric wouldn't mind. She really didn't think he would. He didn't love like other people did. There was something wrong with him. He couldn't get close.

BUT NOW, AS she entered the Palm Desert with the sun rising and shining through the red blooming ocotillos, Christie understood that Eric really did want her. He wanted to marry her and live together forever. He woke her in the middle of the night, as beautiful then as he had been on that tennis court years before. All of her anger disappeared in the morning, and she knew that she'd never leave Eric for Drew. All of that sweating and swearing, that wild abandon, was just a short phase, a transition, a shoehorn to help her slip into her real life.

It was on the fourth day that Eric walked in on them. Mona had gotten back that afternoon. Christie and Drew were making plans to leave. She was to meet Drew the very next day — today — at two. He would have bought tickets for her and him and Mona. They would fly to New York City, where they'd be married and begin a real life.

But Christie wouldn't be going to his house in Laurel Canyon, she knew that now. Drew had always been her backup, her second choice.

She had never let him be a man. He would never be a man while he was with her or even just thinking about her. Eric was her man. That's all there was to it.

"ERIC TANNER NOLAN," Thomas said into the receiver.

"N-O-L-A-N?" the information operator asked.

"Uh-huh."

"Yes?"

"Yes."

"I have an ET Nolan on Wilshire. Hold for that number."

After getting the number Thomas was afraid to call.

What if Eric didn't remember him or if he didn't answer the phone? What if Eric did answer and told Thomas not to call anymore?

Thomas felt that this was his last chance, that he hadn't so much been wandering as looking for his brother, his lost life. He couldn't let that hope rely on the chance of a single phone call.

The phone stall didn't have a phone book. Thomas went down street after street looking for another phone with the white pages book. It was at the sixteenth booth that he found what he wanted. He looked up ET Nolan's address on Wilshire Boulevard. It was a five-mile walk, but Thomas didn't know that — and even if he had known, it wouldn't have made a difference. He felt that he had been walking for a lifetime trying to get back to his brother: up and down his alley valley, down on his knees, walking from one drug addict to another, through the juvenile system, and finally behind this wire cart that he'd patched and repaired again and again until it resembled him — scarred and shambling down the streets of Los Angeles.

THAT WAS ON the afternoon of the day that Christie drove to the desert.

On her ride back she called Drew.

"Hello," Drew answered brightly.

"I can't go with you," she said in a rush. "I've decided that I have to make it work with Eric. Good-bye, Drew. I'm sorry."

"Wait. Wait. Don't get off."

"There's nothing to talk about, Drew. I'm sorry."

"But why? What happened? I love you."

"What we were doing wasn't love," she said. "It was pain and anger. It was trying to get a feeling back."

"I feel it," he said.

"I'm not coming."

"I bought nonrefundable tickets," he cried.

"Good-bye, Drew," Christie said. She disconnected the call and then turned off the phone.

As Thomas walked up the incline toward Wilshire, there was a strong Santa Ana wind blowing. He felt this as an invisible force pushing against him, trying to keep him from reaching his brother. He smiled, knowing that he was fighting against his own ill fortune in the attempt to reach Eric. He felt like a hero pushing that heavy cart with two dead wheels up the rough asphalt street.

The police stopped him on San Vicente.

"It's against the law to push that cart in the street, Bruno," the officer said. He was a large white man with a name tag that read PITTMAN.

"I was staying off the sidewalk, officer," Thomas replied. "Because I thought that maybe I'd get in someone's way with this big thing."

"He's right about that, Pitt," a Hispanic man, Rodriguez, said with a joking smile.

"What are you doing here, Bruno?" Pittman asked Thomas.

"I'm going to see my brother, Eric."

"He a bum too?"

"Street person," the other cop corrected with a smirk on his lips.

"He's a doctor's son," Thomas replied. "We got the same mother. I called him, and he said he'd help me out."

Officer Pittman stared at Thomas for what seemed like a long time. It was as if the policeman was trying to make up his mind about what his next action should be. He sniffed the air, and Thomas realized that he must have smelled. He knew that sometimes street people smelled bad to straights when they didn't know it. He wondered if Eric would turn up his nose and walk away.

"It's three o'clock," Rodriguez said, pointing to his wristwatch. "It'll take two hours to process this dude."

Still Pittman speculated on Thomas. Under that pale-skinned crew cut, the policeman scowled as if there was something important about this roust.

"Come on, man," Rodriguez said. "He ain't messin' with nobody."

"You got a knife in there, Bruno?"

"No, officer."

"What about pills? You got pills or pot?"

Thomas thought about the phrase *a pot to piss in,* but he didn't try to bring it to voice. He shook his head, wondering why this man was so interested in him.

"I got books," Thomas offered as if he were a salesman and Pittman a potential customer.

Something about this answer brought a sour twist to Pittman's lips. For a moment Thomas thought the man might spit on him.

"Get the fuck outta here," the peace officer said.

A minute later, cops nearly forgotten, Thomas was once again pressing against the invisible force of the wind.

An hour afterward he reached the Tennyson, the building in which the man who bore his brother's initials lived. He stopped out front, looking up at the huge edifice of glass and steel. It didn't look like a home. It didn't remind Thomas of his childhood friend and brother. Now that he was there, he didn't know what to do. There was a doorman in the lobby. He wouldn't let Thomas just walk in. And a doorman announcing his name would be even worse than a phone call.

So Thomas sat down on the curb looking up at the tower. He decided that he could wait awhile, and maybe, if he was lucky, Eric would come out of that rotating door and into his brother's arms.

PATROLMEN PITTMAN AND Rodriguez had just stopped at their favorite coffee spot. Rodriguez ordered a dark-roast coffee and Pittman a grande Frappucino made with skim milk, caramel syrup, and chocolate chips. It was their 4:45 lunch hour, and so they sat down and turned their radios to "emergency calls only."

CHRISTIE WAS AT home by then. She had told Eric that she would marry him, and they were already making plans for the wedding. The long separation from her father would be over. Minas Nolan and Ahn would certainly come. Eric had wondered if he could somehow find Thomas and share with him his new life of personal denial. Tommy would understand how much Eric was giving up. Tommy understood everything subtle and emotional.

Distraught Drew had gone to his father's house, completely lost in his grief. He'd never known such pain before. Those three days with Christie were what he'd yearned for all these years. She was his for those hours, but the moment he took his eyes off her she was lost to him again. His heart clenched into a fist, and everything he'd ever learned or loved sank into the cold ocean of his chest.

THOMAS'S THOUGHTS DRIFTED as he sat there. At first he had been nervous about seeing Eric, but now he was visited by a feeling of quiet elation. These moments that he spent waiting were exquisite in their own way — perfect weather, with birds arcing through the sky and people walking and talking up and down the boulevard. It was one of those beautiful instants that get past you if you don't look. But Thomas was looking. He had nowhere to go and everything to hope for.

While Thomas was having these thoughts, a purple Chrysler drove up and a tall young man climbed out. There was a dark cast to his face and a pained grimace in his expression.

Eric, Christie, and Mona had just gotten into the elevator on the twenty-fifth floor, going down to the street for a walk to the pizza restaurant that Mona loved.

Pittman and Rodriguez were finishing their coffees and ham sandwiches and thinking about going back on the prowl.

Drew stood not six feet from Thomas. After first glances, neither paid heed to the other.

The policemen were in the street, not a block from the Tennyson.

Eric and Christie and Mona entered the lobby. When Thomas saw Eric he stood up and smiled. He would wait patiently for his brother to come out.

Mona dashed for the revolving door, obviously ecstatic about their adventure. Christie came in the next partition, watching after the child and glowing. Eric came last. Just when he was sealed within the glass quarter section, Drew grabbed Thomas's cart and shoved it into the aperture that Christie had just left.

"Hey, man!" Thomas grabbed Drew by the shoulder, but with a sweep of his arm the tall young man knocked Thomas to the ground.

He took out his father's Lugar, and Christie screamed.

This wasn't how Drew had it planned. He didn't want to confront Christie on the street. He wanted to follow Eric to a quiet place and kill him. Kill him and maybe later he could console Christie, take her away to rest. He would be the shoulder she could cry on. But seeing her he was overcome by unexpected hatred. All those things she said that excited him so much in bed now had other meanings. She had cheated on him, made him into a fool. Made love to Eric while telling him a hundred lies.

"Drew!" Christie shouted, and he hated her even more.

The pistol rose of its own accord. Drew didn't hear the shot, only saw the young mother convulse. He fired three more times, and Christie was down.

Eric shouted and strained against the thick glass.

The child ran for her mother as Drew leveled the gun at her.

Thomas leaped through the air shouting, "Lily!" and he pulled Mona down, wrapping his skinny body around her.

The policemen were running by then.

Drew realized what he had done, but he couldn't stop his arm and hand from aiming and firing.

Thomas felt each bullet enter his back. He counted them — one, two, three. And then he heard firecrackers and yelling. The child was the loudest, shouting for her mother. Then came Eric with that booming voice Thomas remembered from childhood. And then the darkness he'd known since the death of his mother began to brighten. It got lighter and lighter until all there was was light — no details or shadows, just pure light and then nothing at all.

15

THOMAS AWOKE in a hospital room breathing in mild alcohol vapors and other medicinal scents. He tried to remember what had happened, why he was there, but it didn't come immediately. His back hurt. That brought on the memory of being shot.

Who shot me? The police? No, that was a long time ago and in the front not the back.

There was a spider tentatively making its way up the eggshell-colored nylon curtain next to the window. Thomas smiled, feeling akin to the gangly arachnid trying to survive in a place where cleanliness meant her demise.

"Are you awake?" a woman's voice asked.

Thomas looked up and saw that it was Ahn. For some reason this didn't surprise him.

"Hi," Thomas said.

"How are you?" she asked.

She put her knitting down and sat forward in the chair, touching the edge of the mattress with her fingertips.

"I'm okay, Ahn," Thomas said.

The ageless Vietnamese woman frowned and tilted her head. She looked closely at the weathered, battered, and scarred face. Then she drew back in frightened surprise.

"Tommy?"

"Yeah." The solitary word floated on the music of a life-long apology.

"What's happened to you?" Fear and guilt clouded her usually impassive face.

"Life, I guess."

Thomas could see this life imagined in her eyes — the knife wounds and roofless nights, broken bones and empty pockets. Ahn suffered for him.

"I am so sorry," she said.

"Don't cry, Ahn. It's not so bad. I'm alive."

The little woman got to her feet and touched his callused hands, hands that were so big compared to his body that they seemed swollen.

"What happened?" Thomas asked.

"You were shot," she said. "You saved Mona, but that boy shot you in the back trying to kill her."

"That was the little girl?"

"Yes. The police came and killed him before he could finish killing you."

It was as if she were talking about some story in a book or on Madeline's TV, something far away from Thomas.

"And there was a woman?" he half-asked.

"Mona's mother, Christie," Ahn said solemnly. "She died on the way to the hospital."

"I'm sorry," Thomas said. "He took my cart and shoved it into the door. I tried to stop him."

"You saved Mona, Tommy. Oh, Tommy, look at you."

"Where's Eric?"

"He's getting ready for the funeral. It's tomorrow. Dr. Nolan went with him. They asked me to come here and see about you. But, but they didn't know who you were. They said your name was Bruno."

"Why did you tell me not to call?" Thomas asked. The question had been in his heart for years. Just asking made him feel better.

Ahn couldn't answer right away. Her eyes filled up, and she slumped into her chair.

Thomas's back hurt and his breathing was shallow. He wanted to get up and comfort his old nurse but didn't have the strength.

"It's okay, Ahn. I'm here now."

"But you are so hurt. Your hands and face. Your chest. How can all this happen to a child?"

Thomas found that he could still shrug if he didn't pull his shoulders too high.

"I thought," Ahn said. "I thought that if you came back home something bad would happen to you, like your mother. Maybe you get sick. I don't know."

"Because of Eric?"

Ahn nodded.

"Eric can't hurt me, Ahn. He's my brother. He always saved me."

There was sunlight shining in through the window. Thomas realized that it didn't hurt his eyes. He smiled then and so did Ahn.

"I forgot you," she confessed.

"I never forgot you."

THOMAS SLIPPED INTO a coma that evening. Dr. Nolan and Eric came to the hospital when Ahn told them who he was. They stood over his frail body.

"He looks so peaceful," Eric said. "Just like he was taking a nap."

"There's less than a ten percent chance that he'll revive," said Dr. Bettye Freeling, the physician in charge of the ward.

"He might surprise you," Minas Nolan told her. "He's got something in him that won't let go. He might be the strongest person I've ever met."

"Do you know his family?" Freeling asked. She was a younger doctor, handsome. "I see that he's uninsured."

"I'll pay for him, Doctor," Minas said. "I owe him at least that."

MICHAEL AND RAELA came to Christie's funeral. Michael wore a medium-brown suit because that's all he owned. Raela wore an elegant black dress, flat black shoes, and a tasteful ebony tam, and carried a small black purse. When she touched Eric's forearm in sympathy, there was a loud and painful crackle of static electricity.

By then everyone knew about the tryst between Drew and Christie. Drew had told his father about the affair in their brief conversation before he stole the Luger. And the doorman of the Tennyson saw them coming in late at night and watched them groping each other through the video eye in the elevator.

Almost everyone felt sorry for Eric. He was a poor cuckold, an innocent bystander. He grieved for his dead girlfriend and held their tearful daughter in his arms. Only Ahn wondered how Eric's fateful aura had caused the hapless college dropout to murder Christie. She watched him closely. When she saw the teenage girl stand near him, she knew. It was time for him to lose his lover, Ahn thought, and so the stars conspired to kill her. The Vietnamese woman shivered under her thin silk shawl.

Christie's parents hugged Eric and kissed their sweet granddaughter. Half of Christie's class from Hensley showed up to express their sorrow.

Drew would be buried three days later. Only his parents and Eric came to that ceremony. Drew's father shook Eric's hand, thanking him for coming and apologizing for his son.

"He just never grew into a man," Mr. Peters said. "I hope that you can one day forgive him."

Eric didn't answer, but he felt no enmity toward Drew. He believed that it was his own inability to love Christie that had driven the lovers together, and then his attempt to make himself love her was what destroyed them both.

Eric moved back into his father's house so that Ahn could help with Mona. He went to the hospital every day and sat next to his comatose brother.

Thomas was surrounded by an oxygen tent that was meant to help his punctured lung heal. The doctors didn't have much hope for him, but Eric came each morning and sat for hours in silence at his brother's side.

ONE MORNING, AFTER Eric's father went to work and Ahn and Mona had gone to the stone animal park, the doorbell rang. Eric was getting ready to go to the hospital. He was on leave from his classes and had no intention of going back to school.

He opened the door to find Raela standing there. She seemed taller and more beautiful than before. It was as if she had been a child when last he saw her, Eric thought, and now she was a woman. He wondered if she had grown or if he had diminished since losing Christie.

"Hi," she said.

Eric felt his heart skip and hated himself for an instant.

"I can't know you, Raela," he said.

"It's too late for that now," she replied, her bearing both solemn and serene.

She walked into the house, and he closed the door behind her.

She went into the living room as if she had always lived there. She sat and so did he.

"We killed them," he said.

"We aren't gods," she retorted.

"I didn't love her, but I asked her to marry me."

"You had a child together. What else could you do?"

"I could have been a man and done what was right."

"What's right?" she asked him. "What can anybody do?"

"My brother did what was right," Eric said with conviction.

"Maybe. But he's special. You aren't him."

"I don't love you, Raela."

"I know that. I don't care about love. I just know that we have to be together. We have to be. You know it."

"You don't even know me."

"I do."

"What about Michael? What will happen with him?"

"He's my brother and he loves me," the raven-haired beauty answered. "Show me upstairs."

Eric and Raela became lovers that afternoon. He wasn't worried about getting into trouble. He wasn't concerned that she was too young. Staying away from her had killed Drew and Christie. Maybe even Thomas would die because of his refusal to be with her.

Raela had felt alone for her entire life. Her stepmother was more like a servant than a relative. Her brother loved her, but he couldn't comprehend what was in her heart. And Kronin was just a big bear who wanted her to pay attention to him. No one had ever gotten close to understanding her until she met Eric.

He too was alone and unable to love. His heart was as disconnected as hers. They could at least understand each other. Maybe there could be more.

In the weeks that followed, Eric found himself laughing often and intrigued by the way the woman-child thought. She beat him at swimming, though he was her master at tennis. She could sprint past him in any short race, but he could run for miles and she couldn't or wouldn't — he was never sure which.

After her last class in the afternoon, she would meet him in Thomas's hospital room, and they'd sit together holding hands and waiting.

MEANWHILE, THOMAS TRAVELED among the dead. In the depths of his coma he convened with Tremont, the drug dealer, and Bruno, his best friend. The lost puppy, Skully, scampered about at his heels while Alicia (whom he had never known in life) made them all tea and biscuits served on her tomb in the alley valley that he always thought of as his one true home. They all spoke different languages and used signs to make themselves understood. Sometimes other guests would come. RayRay shambled in one day and asked — with wordless, elaborate apologies — Thomas to forgive him. Pedro climbed down from the fire escape and handed Thomas his gun. By this he meant that he would never kill himself again.

One day Thomas said good-bye to Tremont and Bruno. Then he and Alicia started out on a walk to the far end of the alley valley. It seemed to Thomas that he had never gone to the absolute end. The valley stretched for miles and became very wide. Trees grew tall and full above them. There were strawberry fields and orange groves along the way. Skully brought them beautiful stones and fish and tools when they needed them.

Alicia and he made love in the evenings. It was the way it had been with Monique, only instead of Lily they had Skully the dog, and because they were the same age they could have sex. The sun was bright, but Thomas didn't mind it. The valley seemed endless, but neither one of them cared.

One day Thomas woke up to find that Alicia was gone. He knew that she was off taking care of her own unfinished business, something about the people that killed her and dumped her in Thomas's valley. He didn't worry about her; they would be together again.

The next day Skully didn't come when Thomas whistled. But that didn't bother him either. Traveling alone down the wide valley that started behind his father's home, Thomas knew that he was getting somewhere.

One day — after many, many days of walking — Thomas heard a strange bird cry. It was a high, burplike noise. The call intrigued him, and so he began to climb up out of the valley because that was where the birdsong came from. Climbing up the slope, he began breathing hard. He fell to his knees and struggled through the brush. The bird's odd song got louder and louder. And the louder it got, the more he wanted to see the animal that made that sound.

Maybe it wasn't a bird, he thought. Maybe it's a frog or a wolf or a man. Maybe it's some new kind of talking tree.

As he climbed the foliage became thinner and the sun

shone brighter. It got brighter and brighter, louder and louder, until Thomas was at the crest.

He opened his eyes and saw the beeping machine against the far wall of his hospital room. Next to his bed was a chair in which sat a black-haired girl.

"You're awake," she said.

"I am?"

"You've been in a coma . . . for six months."

"What's a coma?"

"Deep sleep. So deep that no one can wake you up."

"I don't feel tired now."

"I should get the doctor." The girl leaned forward, preparing to stand.

"No. Don't go away."

She smiled, and Thomas felt a tingle of happiness.

"Where have you been?" she asked him.

"In my coma?"

"No. Before. Eric said that you went away to live with your father and grandmother but ended up on the street."

Thomas felt good in his bed. He sat up, and an electric whistle began to sound. He thought about his life in terms of the girl's question, leaving the house he was raised in and then ending up on the street.

"Is Eric going to come see me?"

"Yes," she said. "He'd be here now, but he had to take Mona to the doctor for a rash on her forehead."

"Are you Eric's girlfriend?"

Raela nodded solemnly.

"Oh my God!" the nurse coming into his room exclaimed. "You're awake."

Doctors and nurses bustled around him soon after that.

They hurried the girl away and rolled Thomas into a room where they examined him from head to toe. The chief doctor probed his body with her fingers and kept asking how it felt. They looked into his eyes and ears and talked to one another, expressing surprise.

Finally the woman explained that he had experienced severe trauma to his system. He'd been in a coma for nearly six months, and it would be a while before he would be able to walk or take care of himself.

"Where's my cart?" he asked when the doctor had finished.

"I don't know what you mean."

"My shopping cart. That's where I got all my stuff."

"I don't know. Maybe the police took it after the shooting. That was a wonderful thing you did."

After a while they wheeled him back into his room. He had hoped the girl would still be there, but she wasn't.

"Would you like me to turn the TV on, hon?" a plump redheaded nurse asked while pulling the blankets up to his chest.

"No thanks. I don't like TV too much."

"I wish my kids felt like that," she said. "All they do is watch that thing. Between the one-eyed monster and video games, they don't have the sense to come in outta the rain."

When she left, Thomas thought about his books and the look in the doctor's eye when she complemented his bravery.

The room was very quiet and white. Painfully, he pulled himself to a seated position at the head of the bed. This made him a little dizzy, but it was manageable. He realized, a little sadly, that his travels in the valley were a dream.

"Maybe this is a dream too," he whispered. "Maybe everything is. Maybe it's not even me dreaming."

With these thoughts he fell into a light doze.

As he slept he tumbled down mountainsides, was attacked by feral dogs, and was raped unmercifully by boys from the desert facility whose names he had forgotten. But none of this pained him. His mother died, but she came back to console him. His brother got lost in a wilderness but still made it home in time for dinner. He found himself adrift on a tiny raft in the middle of the ocean, floating in circles and being laughed at by cruel dolphins. In this last ordeal Thomas thought that it might be time to fall over the side, allowing himself to sink under the waves. He wanted to die and be with his mother and Alicia, Chilly, Bruno, and Pedro. He could look for Eric's wife.

Eric.

When he opened his eyes again he was still sitting upright. The sun through the window had moved a good six feet across the wall. The door was open, and a moment later Eric was standing there.

"Are you a dream, Eric?" he asked.

The blue-eyed Titan came up to the bed and cupped his brother's face with both hands.

"I'm sorry I let them take you, Tommy. And for making Mama Branwyn sick."

"Ahn said that she thought you would hurt me," Thomas replied. "But I told her that you always saved me."

Eric pulled up the visitor's chair, and the brothers talked for hours. In a haphazard, rambling manner, Thomas told his story. He started out with drug dealing and Monique and Lily. Then he talked about his alley and his father's arrests.

"He isn't really a bad guy," Thomas said. "But he was just mad all the time because people were always trying to take things from him."

When Eric told his story, it started with the beached green fish that he caught with his hands and unfolded event by event until Raela came to his house and said that they were meant to be.

In the middle of his story, a nurse popped her head in to tell Eric that visiting hours were over.

"This is my brother," he said. "We haven't seen each other since we were six. I can't leave him."

The nurse, a middle-aged Chicano woman, smiled and nodded, then quietly closed the door.

Eric confessed his crimes against the people he should have loved. He killed his mother and Branwyn and Drew and Christie. He won every game he ever played that was important. He failed to bring happiness into his father's life.

"But Dad doesn't think that," Thomas stated with certainty. "All that stuff is just in your head."

Eric thought about his self-portrait and the worried look on his art teacher's face. Something fell together for him. He wasn't complaining or distraught — just feeling empty.

Thomas took Eric's hand and asked, "What about that girl? Do you love her?"

"No. I mean, she's the only one other than you or Mama Branwyn that ever made me feel something. But it's a little like I'm afraid of her, the way I used to feel about Ahn, but more."

"Because why?" Thomas asked.

Eric smiled, remembering those words from their childhood, *because why.*

"I guess I don't want anyone to know what I'm like on the inside. I feel ugly, you know? Except when I think about you or Mama Branwyn."

★ ★ ★

THEY TALKED WITHOUT holding anything back. It had
been more than a dozen years and the boys hadn't had one
thing in common since the day they were separated, but still
it was as if they'd been apart for only a day. They giggled and
awed each other; they played and vowed never to be parted
again.

"I will never let them take you away, Tommy."

"And I won't go nowhere."

ERIC DIDN'T LEAVE the hospital until Thomas was asleep,
and he was back the next morning with his father, Ahn, and
Mona.

"I'm so sorry," Minas told Branwyn's son. "I should have
done something to keep you. Or at least to find you once we
knew that you were lost."

"That's okay," Thomas said. "It's really not all that bad. I
mean, it's kinda like a dream. I'm not mad at you. And I don't
care about what happened to me. I mean, even when you get
shot it only hurts for a while. And if you don't get all upset
about it and nobody shoots at you again, then it's okay. Or if
you're hungry it's like that too. Because sooner or later you're
gonna eat, and then you're not hungry no more. Right?"

Thomas liked being with the whole family, but it wasn't
the same as his time alone with Eric. With Eric he could say
anything without thinking, but with the family it was more
like he had a part to play. He didn't mind though. He liked
the role.

"You're the man who saved me," three-year-old Mona said
during a lull in the conversation.

"That's right," Eric told her. "This is Uncle Tommy."

"T'ank you, Uncle Tommy."

"What would you like to do after you get out of here, Thomas?" Dr. Nolan asked.

"I don't know. The doctor said that they lost my cart. Everything I had was in there. I had pictures of Monique and my blank book with my writings. I'd like to find that if I could."

"But what would you like to *do?*"

"What you mean?" Tommy squinted for a moment, remembering the brightness that had driven him away from elementary school.

"Do you want a job? Do you want to go to school? Where would you like to live?"

"Could I stay with you guys for a while?"

"Of course," Dr. Nolan said. "As long as you want."

"Yaaaaaa," Mona sang.

THAT AFTERNOON THE police were dispatched with a warrant to arrest Thomas Beerman, aka Bruno Forman. They sent Pittman and Rodriguez because the officers could identify the young con-man escapee.

"Thomas Beerman," Officer Pittman announced. "You are under arrest."

"No. I didn't do anything. I, I saved the little girl's life."

"You presented yourself to the police with fraudulent identification and you escaped from the juvenile facility where you were being detained."

For Thomas the facility was a long-ago dream. He couldn't imagine that they would send him back there now that he was reunited with his family.

"No," he said.

"No," Dr. Bettye Freeling repeated. She was standing at the door to Thomas's room. "This is my patient, and he is far too weak to be moved."

"We have a warrant for his arrest, ma'am," Rodriguez said with an apology in his voice.

"I'm a doctor," she replied. "This is my patient, and you cannot take him without my permission."

"It's pretty clear-cut," Nathan Frear, the lawyer, said to Minas Nolan and his son.

They were in Frear's office at the top floor of a Westwood office highrise.

"He was convicted of assault on police officers in an attempt to keep them from their duty. It says that he was part of an organized group that opened fire on the officers trying to arrest them."

"He was twelve," Eric said. "He didn't even have a gun."

"But he was part of the group, and he was convicted under a law devised to dampen gang activity."

"But he wasn't part of a gang. He was twelve and nearly homeless. He was just trying to stay alive."

"All of that evidence was presented in court," Frear said. "The judge still found him guilty."

"What will happen if he goes to trial?" Minas asked.

"Either he'll be returned to the juvenile authority or, more likely, he will be sentenced as an adult and will serve the full term of the original sentence plus whatever else the judge might want to tack on for his further crimes."

"What crimes?" Eric asked. "All he did was save my daughter from Drew."

"He lied to the police; he escaped from custody. He committed identity theft by using a social security card that belonged to Bruno Forman. The prosecutor might even try to implicate him with the man who killed your girlfriend. After all, Drew Peters used Thomas's cart to block the door and keep you from saving your wife."

Frear was tall and extraordinarily thin. His dark-blue suit was made from the finest material, and his aqua tie had a ruby tack that held it perfectly in place.

"That's crazy," Minas said. "He's just a boy."

"He's a man," Frear corrected, "homeless and black. A convicted felon, an admitted drug dealer, an escapee from a state institution, and there's even some evidence that he was involved in the slaying of a customer of his, a Raymond 'RayRay' Smith.

"I can take the case, but it's going to be very expensive. And without remarkable luck, he's looking at anywhere from six to ten years in a maximum security prison."

BETTYE FREELING COULD keep the police from taking Thomas for three more weeks. Minas decided to retain Frear. The initial fee was fifty thousand dollars. The lawyer visited Thomas twice but received little help from his client.

"I just took a walk," Thomas said, answering Frear's question about how his escape occurred. "I just meant to go around the block, but then I kept on walking. It was such a nice day, I remember. The sky had those big white clouds that everybody likes so much."

When Frear wanted to know about the shooting, all Thomas could recall was Tremont coming out with his Uzi and the police opening fire.

"He went crazy, I think," Thomas said. "He was mad that the police wanted to be messin' with him."

"Did you know about the Uzi?"

"Sure. We all did."

"Did you know that it was against the law to have that weapon?"

"Tremont was the law in that alley," Thomas said. "That was the first time I ever saw a cop down there in the three years I worked for him."

"So you worked for him for three years?" Frear asked.

"Yeah."

Frear decided not to put Thomas on the stand.

RAELA, IN THE meanwhile, emptied a special account that Kronin had set up for her. Using her ATM card, she took out five hundred dollars a day for twenty days.

She spent the afternoons helping Eric with Thomas's physical therapy and the evenings sleeping with Eric in his childhood bed.

Her mother and father threatened to call the police, but she knew they wouldn't. Eric's father told his son that Raela was too young, but after a few dinner conversations with the dark-hued girl, he gave up his arguments.

Minas Nolan blamed himself for Christie's death because he made Eric move out. He wouldn't kick his son out again.

Raela spent long evenings talking to Ahn and Minas. She had read thousands of books since the age of eight. She was considerate and mature. She helped with the dishes and explained that she and Eric would be married one day soon.

"He needs me," she said to Minas one evening while everyone else was in bed.

"Eric doesn't need anyone," Minas replied. He was embarrassed by the mild note of contempt in his voice.

"No, Dr. Nolan," Raela said, sounding more like fifty than fifteen. "He's afraid of people. He thinks everybody is too weak and that if he isn't careful he'll hurt them. He blames himself for you losing Mama Branwyn. He even thinks that he caused Tommy to get lost."

Minas felt the weight of her words in his chest. He realized, maybe for the first time, how closely physical heart disease was connected to the emotional heart. The girl was telling him a truth that he'd always avoided. He knew that Eric had been forced to carry the weight of his broken heart. He knew that his son had lived with Christie because he hadn't wanted to hurt her.

"How do you know all this?" he asked the child.

"Because I'm just like him," she said. "Or almost. My life has been just like his, only I don't worry about people like he does."

"Why not?"

"Because."

"Because what?"

"Because you can't save anyone."

"I save people all the time," the doctor said, wondering at his need to argue with the child.

"But when people die on your operating table, do you believe that they were going to die with or without you?"

After that evening Minas could not remember if he'd answered her question. He'd lost eight patients under the knife. Eight lives that he could not save. He'd forgotten most of their names and didn't attend any of their funerals. He'd washed his hands vigorously after every failure, gone home and got into bed. He wondered how a child knew all of that.

★   ★   ★

AT THE END of three weeks Raela gave the ten thousand dollars she'd collected to Eric. The next day Ahn and Raela went with Eric to the hospital and helped Thomas down the stairs and then to the station, where the brothers boarded a train bound for Phoenix.

16

ON THE trip to Phoenix, Thomas said to his brother, "You didn't have to come with me, Eric. If you just gave me a ticket and a couple a bucks I coulda gone on my own."

"But what would you do when you got there?"

"I don't know. There's always somethin' to do. It's not that hard."

"I know, Tommy," Eric said. "But we just found each other. The only reason you would even go to jail is because you were looking for me and because you saved Mona."

"But what about her?" Thomas asked. "She needs you to be with her."

"It's not gonna take long," Eric explained. "We just need to set you up somewhere where the police won't find you. Then I'll go back home. I promise."

Thomas stopped arguing. He was happy to be able to spend time with Eric. He knew that Eric could use his help, that he was somehow lost and needed Thomas to lead him out of a dark corridor. He could tell by the way Eric looked away so often. There was even sadness in his smile.

So they took a room in a Phoenix residence hotel and began to plan for Thomas's future.

★ ★ ★

THE FIRST THING they did was go shopping for clothes. They cruised through Banana Republic buying sweaters, shirts, pants, jackets, underwear, socks, and even a hat for Thomas. The young man was amazed by the variety and cost of these things. He hadn't been to a clothes store since his days with Monique and Lily when he'd buy a new pair of pants and a T-shirt at JC Penney once every six months or so.

At the same mall they bought walking shoes and a big suitcase for the trip that Eric had planned.

"I've never been to New York," Eric told Thomas. "That means the police won't think to look for us there."

"What about Dad?" Thomas asked.

"I told him we were going and that I'd get in touch with him."

"What did he say?"

"Nothing. He just looked kinda sad and nodded, and I left."

"Why's he so sad?" Thomas asked.

They were sitting across from each other on single beds in the Laramie Extended-Stay Hotel and Residence on the outskirts of the city. Their window looked out onto a vast desert of yellows and oranges.

"He's been like that ever since Mama Branwyn died and they took you away," Eric said. "All he does is work and sleep."

"You can see it in his eyes," Thomas added. "He's got old man's eyes."

"I think it's because of me," Eric added. "When I was a kid I always made him do things for me, and I didn't even see it. And then when I got older it was already too late."

Thomas rubbed the palms of his hands over his black-cotton trousers. He thought about not being in jail or on trial.

"Maybe he could come visit after we get to New York," Thomas suggested.

* * *

THE NEXT DAY they were on an eastbound train. They sat across from each other at the front of the car and talked for eighteen hours a day.

"I took riding lessons . . ."

"I found a glass-cutter and made drinking glasses from beer bottles for a while. After I'd make'em, I sold'em on the boardwalk in Venice until the police chased me away . . ."

"After the SATs I went to UCLA to study economics. I like numbers that do things in people's pockets. It's funny . . ."

"I never had sex with a girl yet . . ."

"I've never been in love . . ."

"AND ARE YOU sad like Dad?" Thomas asked after three hundred miles were gone.

"Not like him. I'm not really sad at all. I have everything I want. Especially now."

"But you look sad," Thomas said. "You don't hardly smile, and your eyes are always movin' around like you're looking for something all the time."

"Up until now I guess I've always been looking for you. Dad tried to find you after a few years, but nobody even knew where your real father was. Finally they found him down in Texas, but by then he'd lost track of you."

THAT FIRST NIGHT on the train from Phoenix, Eric slept while Thomas sat and looked at the moon out of his window. Thomas felt safe sitting next to his brother. He didn't care about being on the train or going to New York. He wasn't afraid of the police finding him. The day Eric came to take him away, Thomas was already planning to leave. He thought he might go down to San Diego, where he'd heard a man could sleep under fruit trees and eat off their limbs for breakfast. But Thomas had a feeling of safety with Eric — between them they made something whole.

Thomas exhaled, and for a long moment he just sat there without taking air back in. The train lurched at a turn in the tracks, and he found himself breathing again, feeling deeply satisfied. For the first time that he could remember, he didn't have to worry about who was coming or when his next meal would be or where he was going to sleep.

But looking out at the lunar-lit plains, Thomas began to think that he might die soon. Death made sense to him. So many people he had known were dead: his mother and Pedro and Alicia and Tremont, Bruno and Chilly and even RayRay. He had been so close to Death for so long that he wasn't afraid of Him. But he didn't want to die, because he wanted to be with Eric. Having a brother meant he had something to live for.

"Eric," Thomas whispered in the darkness.

"Yeah?"

"You know what I worry about all the time?"

"Not having any place to live?"

"Uh-uh. There's always a place to stay or hide," Thomas said. "The thing that always scared me was if one day I went crazy and forgot about back home with you and Mama."

"Which one?" Eric asked.

"Which one what?"

"Are you afraid of going crazy or forgetting?"

"They're both the same thing."

THE NEXT MORNING, in Denver, a young black woman got on the train. The two seats next to Thomas and Eric were free, but she went to a single seat four rows down.

"She's pretty," Thomas said to Eric.

"I guess," Eric said, not really looking.

"Did you ever think that we would be together again on a train going to New York?"

"No," Eric said. "I thought that I would probably die before seeing you again."

"You?" Thomas grinned.

"What's so funny?"

"I don't know. I just don't think about you dying."

"I think about it all the time."

"Why?" Thomas asked.

A young white man moved to the seat next to the young black woman. Thomas felt that maybe he should have done that, but then he thought, no.

"I think about killing myself," Eric said seriously.

"What for? You got everything. And you said you're not that sad."

"Sometimes I think that it's because of me that other people get hurt."

"That's crazy," Thomas said. "Nobody gets hurt over you."

"I met Raela, and three days later Drew killed Christie, shot you, and the police killed him."

"And you think that it's because you wanted her?"

Sheepishly Eric nodded.

Thomas looked away a moment. He noticed the white man talking to the young woman.

"I was lookin' at the moon last night," Thomas said, "while you were asleep."

"So?"

"I remembered that I met this guy once who used to be a merchant marine, but he got a blood disease and they let him go. He said that he had enough money that he could have had a house and a car, but he found movin' around a better life. He said that livin' in a house was like spendin' your life in a tomb."

"You think he was lying?" Eric asked.

"I never thought so," Thomas said. "But I never thought about it. But he said somethin' else."

"What's that?"

Thomas thought that he heard the young black woman say something to the man next to her.

"He said," Thomas continued, "that the moon has gravity and that the ocean rises up and falls down because of that."

"Yeah," Eric said, "the moon governs the tides."

"So if that's true," Thomas said, "and if one day somebody said to you that you couldn't have what you wanted unless the tide didn't come in, what do you think would happen?"

"Of course the tide's gonna come in."

"Yeah," Thomas said. "The tide'll come in, the sun'll rise, people will live an' die, an' you can't do a thing about it."

"I could kill myself."

"But it wouldn't make no difference except to the people who love you."

"Excuse me," someone said.

The young men looked up to see the girl who had gotten on earlier.

"Can I sit with you guys? That jerk down there started talkin' shit."

"Sure," Eric said and Thomas wanted to say but didn't.

"I'm Eric and this is my brother, Tommy, I mean, Thomas."

"They call me Lucky," Thomas said.

"They do?" Eric asked.

"I thought you said you were brothers?" the young woman said, settling next to Thomas. She had a wheeled, silvery suitcase that was meant to look like metal but was made from lightweight plastic. Eric got up and put the bag in the rack above their heads.

"We were separated when we were young," the young white man explained.

"Yeah," Thomas said. "We just found each other again."

"You don't look like brothers."

Thomas and Eric told their story together, sometimes finishing each other's sentences. As they spoke, the young black woman pictured the two men as little boys and found herself smiling at their graceless affection for each other.

Her name was Clea Frank. She was a native of Denver and now was on her way to a scholarship at New York University. She was a language major and wanted to work at the UN.

The young white man had tried to "put the moves on her," and she wanted to sit with them so that he'd leave her alone. She was happy that Eric and Thomas were going all the way to New York.

"DON'T YOU FEEL funny calling him brother?" Clea asked Thomas some time after midnight as the train approached Chicago.

"That's what he is. He's the only brother I've ever had."

Eric was asleep, and Clea had just come awake after napping through the late afternoon and evening.

"But he's not your real brother — he's white," Clea said. "I mean, I don't have anything against white people, but I don't go around calling them my brother either."

Thomas liked talking to her in the darkness of the train. In a way it was like his late-night talks with his mother or Alicia, when he couldn't see them but only felt their presence.

"But we were raised together and we understand each other. He used to protect me when the big kids would pick on me, and I explain things to him."

"But he has three years of college and you don't have hardly any school. What do you explain to him? The street?"

Over the previous day and a half the three had changed trains twice and told their stories. Clea's father was a baker in Denver, and her mother was a part-time nurse in the pediatric ward of the university's teaching hospital. Clea was their fourth child. Her two brothers were high school dropouts, and her sister was a schizophrenic who lived on the street half the time and spent the rest of her life in various mental hospitals. Clea was the hope of her family, and she intended to make something of herself.

Thomas had told her about everything he'd done and about the police being after him. He didn't think that she would tell anyone, and Eric was asleep by then.

"I can see things in other things," Thomas said. "Eric's real smart, but he doesn't pay attention to everyday things like I do."

"Like what?"

"Rocks and eyes and making things up."

He chose that moment to take her hand.

"Your skin is so rough," she said.

He pulled away, but she reached out and drew the hand back.

"I thought that you were making it up about living in the street," she said. "But your hands are like a workingman's hands."

"I knew a woman that was schizo," Thomas said. "She saw things too. There was a guy named Benny who would say that she was his ho, an' he would get money from other homeless guys to have sex with her."

"And did you have sex with her?"

"No. But I'd go sit with her sometimes, and if I was really quiet she'd get still and tell me about the things she saw."

"Like what?"

"There was a big man who sometimes chased her and sometimes killed her, but then he could be nice and take her on his shoulders and show her the sea. It was a light-blue-and-pink ocean with fish that swam on top of the water and talked to the men in boats who sailed out there with them. And the moon was very close to the earth, and there wasn't any cigarettes or alcohol."

"She was crazy."

"Maybe. But I can tell you what she said and you don't call me crazy."

"What was the woman's name?" Clea asked.

"Lana."

"Did you get Lana away from Benny?"

"No. She liked him and called him her husband."

"But he was pimpin' her."

"Yeah, but she said that he never let those men hurt her."

"That's crazy. He took those men there in the first place," Clea said.

"Life's crazy," Thomas replied. "When Benny would get

money for Lana, he'd go out and buy us all pizza and a quart of root beer."

"So you lived off her too?"

"I only stayed near them for about a week. And I don't eat cheese or drink sodas. They make me sick."

Thomas couldn't have explained why he kissed Clea then. She didn't know why she let him.

Clea had her whole life planned out. She would go to college and get her degree and then work at the UN translating French, Portuguese, Italian, and other languages for the sub-Saharan African nations. She would find a young black man who was either a doctor or a lawyer and marry him and move to Montclair, New Jersey, where she would relocate her parents and her sister. Her lazy brothers could fend for themselves.

But there they were kissing passionately in the early hours, in that hurtling train. Eric awoke once and saw them. Clea had her hand on Thomas's while he kissed her neck again and again.

It was then that Eric thought about what his brother had said about the moon and tides. The Golden Boy, Eric, closed his eyes and muffled a sigh — his brother had somehow delivered him from his fear.

EIGHTEEN HOURS later the train pulled into Penn Station. The boys put Clea into a yellow taxi, and she gave them her cell number.

"Call me if you want to come down and see NYU," she'd said.

The boys met a nun collecting money for homeless children and asked her if there was an inexpensive place they could stay. She told them about a place uptown, and Eric put a twenty dollar bill in her jar.

* * *

THAT NIGHT ERIC Tanner Nolan and Thomas "Lucky" Beerman were ensconced in the men's residence at the 92nd Street YM&YWHA.

After the first few days of exploring together, the brothers started going out separately. Thomas discovered Central Park while Eric plumbed Lower Manhattan.

For the next three weeks they explored the city. Eric liked the big buildings and the Wall Street crowd. Down among the businessmen and -women he took tours, listened and learned firsthand about how the market was run. He made impromptu appointments with personnel officers, introducing himself as a UCLA senior who was looking for student programs in the stock market. He met a female stockbroker on a tour of Morgan Stanley. Her name was Constance Baker. After a fifteen-minute conversation, she took Eric under her wing.

He had told her pretty much the truth about his coming to New York. After a long separation he and his brother had come east on a holiday to have fun and get to know each other again. They were staying at the Y.

Constance was thirty-six, handsome, and in charge. She had a boyfriend named Jim Harris, who worked commodities and lived in a big house in Brooklyn. Constance had an apartment that overlooked the Hudson River in the West Village, where she slept during the week. On the weekends she stayed with Jim at his house in Brooklyn Heights.

Meanwhile, each day Thomas would walk south on Lexington until he got to 59th Street, and then he'd head west until he got to the southernmost side of the park. It was early April, and the cherry trees were filled with the white and pink blossoms of spring. There were vast lawns and horses and thousands of people wandering in the light of morning. He'd walk up the asphalt pathways each day until he got to the Metropolitan Museum of Art. Once there he'd give what money he had and then spend hours among the paintings, sculptures, and jewelry of the ages.

He walked from ancient Rome and Greece into Africa and South America. He sat for hours one day among the wooden boats of the cannibals of the South Sea Islands. He imagined himself in the cramped canoes carved from whole trees, traveling under canopies of green along rivers and then out on the cobalt sea.

He spent five days in a row surrounded by the arts of China, India, and Japan. This section of the museum didn't have many visitors, and often Thomas found himself alone, sitting on a courtesy bench in front of a great stone Buddha or in a re-created shogun's home.

Thomas loved the stillness of the paintings. He imagined that this was what his grandmother Madeline saw when she was looking at the television, but the sound and action of the TV was too much for him; just the frozen moment of men and women in motion was enough to imagine a whole world of action and life.

His favorite tableau was a doorway to the left of the entrance of the museum. It looked upon a re-created room from Pompeii. There were rose-painted walls drawn upon with pedestrian scenes and still lifes, intricately tiled floors, and a slender stone bed behind which there was the image of a window. Thomas imagined looking down from that window on the people in the street below: men in togas and women in blues and reds with no electricity or cars, no airplanes, televisions, or telephones. People like him, lopsided and broken from just living, happy among one another, next to a sea that, Eric said, was as blue as a blue crayon.

Sometimes he would have silent dialogues with his mother or Alicia while meandering through the halls of art. But not so much as before, when he was on the streets of Los Angeles. Often he found himself thinking about the afternoons when he would take the subway downtown to Washington Square Park, where every other day or so he would meet Clea Frank for coffee.

BEFORE THOMAS FIRST called her, Clea had decided not to see him or his beautiful "brother," Eric. After all, she didn't know them, and they had said that they were running from the law. But when Thomas called, he didn't ask to get together.

"I just remembered that I had your number in my pocket," the perpetual runaway said. "And I thought I'd see how you were doin' in school."

"It's really good," she said. "I like the classes, but they're big, impersonal, you know."

"How about the classrooms?" Thomas asked, remembering that awful light that drove him away.

"They're big. Sometimes there's as many as two hundred kids in the same class. But I can do the work, and the library's nice."

"Eric says that the library at UCLA is so big that you could sleep in it at night and nobody would find you . . . if you wanted to, I mean."

"How is Eric?"

"He's fine. He met a woman down on Wall Street who's showin' him about how investing works. I think he's happy. I hope so."

"Why would you worry about him?" Clea asked, forgetting that she didn't want to know the boys. "He's got everything."

"He's my brother," Thomas explained.

"Deposit another ten cents for five additional minutes," the mechanical operator said.

"I better be goin'," Thomas said. "That was my last quarter."

"What's your number?" Clea asked. "I'll call you back."

"I don't see one."

"Why don't you come down to Washington Square Park?" she said. "I could meet you under the archway at five."

The phone disconnected, and Clea wasn't sure that Thomas heard what she said. But at five she found him at the foot of Fifth Avenue and the park, sitting on the ground at the wire barrier that fenced off the crumbling arch from foot traffic.

"You made it," she said, wondering to herself why she had asked him to come. It had been a week since she'd seen him, and she'd already been out on her first date with a good-looking senior who was about to start law school at Columbia.

"Yeah," Thomas said. "I didn't have any money, so I had to walk."

"From where?"

"I was up at Ninety-second and Lexington, but that wasn't so bad. I used to walk all day long when I lived in L.A."

Clea didn't know why she looked forward to seeing Thomas. She still talked to Brad (the future lawyer) and went out with him on weekends. But Thomas made her feel comfortable, and when he kissed her he seemed to be telling her something, something dear and intimate. When Bradley kissed her it was strong, and he seemed to know what he wanted. He made her want it too, though she hadn't given in yet.

But she had agreed to go away with Bradley to Martha's Vineyard with a bunch of seniors who had rented a house for the long weekend. They would stay in the same bedroom. She told herself that she wanted to go, and her new girlfriends in the dorm agreed that she should.

THOMAS WAS WALKING across a broad green field in Central Park. The day was so beautiful that he didn't want to go into the museum just yet. He had not been so happy since he was a child. All day he walked and studied and dreamed about kissing Clea, and in the evening he got together with his brother and they talked about their day.

Eric was liking New York too. Constance had gotten him an afternoon job as an intern, and he spent four hours a day with other college students learning about high finance. But in the evenings he was happy to be quiet and listen to his brother regale him with facts about Mesopotamian cylinder seals and pre-Columbian clay whistles.

Thomas was walking across that field, thinking about asking Eric to come with him to the museum tomorrow, Saturday, when he walked into someone's chest.

"Excuse me," he said as he looked up and saw the blue uniform of the NYPD.

"Put your hands up, son," the policeman said, "up and behind your head."

CLEA'S CELL PHONE rang just when she was beginning to wonder if Thomas had somehow figured out that she was going away for the weekend with Bradley. He hadn't called about getting together, and they hadn't seen each other since

Tuesday. She still wanted to be friends with the lame man-child, but there was no future with him.

"Hello?"

"Clea, it's Eric."

"Hi. I was expecting Lucky."

"They got him in jail."

"What for?"

"Some kid mugged a woman in Central Park, and they grabbed Tommy for it."

"He wouldn't do anything like that."

"No. They found the kid who did it, but Tommy didn't have any ID and so they took him to jail as a vagrant."

"A vagrant?" Clea was amazed. Maybe he really was jinxed.

"He told'em his name was Bruno Frank, so . . ."

"Where are you?"

When Clea called Bradley his machine answered. She was relieved not to have to talk to him, and also not to be going with him to the Vineyard.

The police station was on 86th Street. The sergeant in charge asked her a dozen questions about Bruno.

"What is his birthday?"

"January 12, 1986."

"What is his middle name?"

"No one in our family has middle names."

"Why doesn't he have ID?"

"He doesn't have a license and, anyway, he lost his wallet."

Eric and Thomas had worked out all of the lies on the train ride before they got to Denver. Later on, after they had reached New York, Clea had told Thomas it was all right to use her last name. She hadn't really believed that Thomas was in such deep trouble, or that the police would just grab him off the street for no reason.

Eric posed as Clea's boyfriend from NYU.

"Your brother should really have identification," the policeman said.

"I'll get him to do it, officer," she said, relieved.

The three caught a cab a few blocks away. Eric gave the driver an address on the West Side Highway near 12th Street. There they entered a twelve-story glass apartment building. The doorman seemed leery at first, but when Eric gave him his name he handed over the key and allowed them entrance.

As he worked a key on the door of the penthouse, Clea asked, "Why are they letting us in here?"

"Connie said that I could stay here on the weekends if I wanted. She said that she'd leave my name at the desk."

"But shouldn't you knock?" Clea asked.

"She spends every weekend with her boyfriend in Brooklyn," Eric answered. "I thought we could go out in the Village this weekend. Connie said that it's a pretty big place."

The transparent walls allowed a nearly unobstructed view up and down the Hudson River. They could see the Statue of Liberty and across to Hoboken.

"I was supposed to go away with some kids to Martha's Vineyard this weekend," Clea was saying that evening after they had eaten take-out Chinese. "But I'd rather be here with you guys."

Thomas had been quiet since getting out of jail. He sat close to the future linguist and ate hardly at all.

"What's wrong, Lucky?" she asked.

"I don't like bein' in jail. But I think that's where I'm gonna end up."

"No," Eric said. "I won't let that happen."

"I didn't do nuthin' today, man. I was just walkin' in the park thinkin' about you guys an' the pictures. But those cops just grabbed me, and even though they knew I didn't do nuthin', they took me to jail. One suckah in there started beatin' on me the minute he saw me. I didn't even look at him."

There was a pronounced lump over Thomas's left eye.

"I'm sorry," Eric said.

"They just see a black man," Clea said, "and they think he did something wrong. It happens all the time."

"I never had such a good life as I do right now," Thomas said, unaffected by apologies or explanations. "I got friends and places t'sleep an' that museum. You know, I could spend every day for a year lookin' in there. I could live there. I asked them about bein' a guard, but you know you need a real social security numbah and a phone and a high school degree at least to work there. And even if you walk in the park, you could get grabbed up an' put in the Tombs."

They were sitting on a leather couch in front of a low glass coffee table. The sunset lit a fire behind New Jersey.

Without warning, the door to the hall came open and a woman walked in.

Eric jumped to his feet.

"Connie," he said.

"Hello, Eric." She had short red hair and an aggressive, angular face.

When Thomas met her eye, he thought he saw disappointment, but then she put on a bright smile.

Sharp as a hatchet. The words came into Thomas's mind.

After a moment he remembered that it was something Ahn used to say.

"I'm sorry," Eric was saying, "but I thought you said you were away on weekends."

"Don't worry," she said. "I just came back for a few things. Who are your friends?"

Eric introduced Thomas as his brother and Clea as his brother's friend. Connie smiled and asked, "Does anybody want a drink?"

Clea joined their hostess for a glass of white wine. Eric had a Coke, and Thomas took tap water without ice.

Then Constance Baker regaled them with stories about her day. It mostly concerned trading and investments. A terrorist bombing in Saudi Arabia caused a flurry because of a bus manufacturer. Only Eric seemed to understand what she was talking about.

But Constance was a good host. She asked Clea about NYU and then if Thomas was in school too.

"I wanted to go to school," Thomas said, "but it wouldn't make no difference."

"Why not?"

"It just wouldn't."

"Hm," Constance mused. "Eric, will you come into the other room for a moment please?"

They went into her bedroom, and she closed the door.

"I think she likes your brother," Clea said.

"Everybody likes Eric. When we were kids he used to go to parties all the time."

"Didn't you go?"

"Not too much. No. I coulda gone, I guess, but I liked stayin' home with my mother. We used to talk a lot."

"Is that Eric's mother too?"

"Not by blood. But she loved Eric and me."

Clea took Thomas's big hand in both of hers, and for a while they sat there looking out the window.

Then there came a low feminine moan from the bedroom.

"I was going to go away with a boy named Brad this weekend," Clea confessed.

"How come you ain't goin'?"

"Because I had to come get you outta jail."

"Oh. Sorry."

"I'm glad I didn't go anyway."

"How come?"

"He's nice and everything, but I like you. I don't want to like you, but I do anyway."

"Oh, yeah!" Connie declared loudly. "Oh my God!"

A heavy thumping began to sound through the wall.

"Why you like me?" Thomas asked.

"I think it's your big hands. At first you look so small and weak, but then when I hold your hands it's like you're the strongest person I ever knew."

Clea kissed Thomas, and Connie squealed.

"Do you have protection?" Clea asked.

"What's that?"

"You don't use a condom when you have sex with your girlfriends?"

"I never had no sex with a woman," the young man said.

The thumping got louder, and Connie cried out clearly, "Do it, do it, do it!"

"You're not serious."

"Yes, I am. I never had no girlfriend to have sex with."

"But you used to take drugs to prostitutes; you lived with a woman and her child for three years."

"But I ain't never had no sex. One time, on my twelfth birthday, Monique played with my thing. I mean, sometimes there was women who said that they would if I wanted, but I was too shy. And that was when I was livin' in the street an' I was dirty all the time. You know, it didn't sound right. And anyway . . ."

"Anyway what?"

"Nuthin'." Thomas didn't want to say that he felt that his mother was watching him and that she would have been upset to see him with some prostitute or drug addict.

"Oh, baby, yeah," Connie said through the wall.

"Do you want to sleep with me?" Clea asked. Her tone was both serious and soft.

"I'd like to try," Thomas said.

"I bet we could find some condoms in Connie's bath-room."

17

RAELA TIMOR took her place at an ebony dining table that was so large it took up almost the whole dining room, and that room was twenty feet wide and thirty long. The family of four was at the north end of the table, with Kronin Stark — still in his tailor-made suit, still wearing his red silk-and-gold tie — at the head. When Rita the maid served Raela her sliced pork roast and red cabbage, the girl thanked her but did not pick up her fork.

"You gonna eat that, sis?" Michael asked.

He hadn't been home in a week, but he could tell that there was something wrong. His court-appointed guardian, Maya, was drawn and haggard, while Kronin looked even more menacing than usual. Raela, as always, was beautiful. If anything she was even more ethereal, slighter, even closer to taking off on the slightest passing breeze.

"I'm not that hungry," she said.

"You should eat," Maya suggested, worry stitched into the words.

"Maybe later."

"Eat your food," Kronin Stark growled.

"Is that an order?"

"You damn well better believe it's an order." The master of the house spoke in his deepest, most threatening bass tone.

Michael felt a quailing in his chest.

Raela rose from her seat.

"Sit down," Kronin commanded.

"I will not stay at a table where men are cursing at me," she said.

With that the girl walked out of the room. Michael thought that she seemed a little uncertain on her feet.

"Raela," Kronin called, his voice filled with sudden grief.

But the woman-child left the room without looking back.

"What's wrong with her?" Michael asked.

"Shut up and eat your food," Kronin snapped.

LATER THAT EVENING Michael found his sister in the upstairs living room. She was knitting him a sweater made from a skein of uncolored raw silk that was specially imported from Tibet by one of Kronin's thankful business partners.

Raela was always happy to see her brother. She cared for him more than anyone, at least until she'd met Eric — and now Tommy.

"What's wrong with Stark?" Michael asked. "He's like a grizzly."

"It's nothing," she said, not interrupting her stitch count.

Though Michael was the older sibling, he knew better than to make demands of his sister. He brought out one of his economics texts and sat there vainly trying to plumb the secrets of money and how it made and destroyed men's lives.

A half an hour or so later, Kronin Stark lunged into the room. He was still wearing his suit but had discarded the tie. His feet were prone to swelling, so he wore slippers instead of shoes.

"Leave us alone, Michael," Stark said, while his eyes bored into the downcast girl.

Michael stood, and so did his sister.

"You stay," Kronin ordered.

"I'm not your damn servant," she said, barely raising her voice. "And neither is my brother. If you want to talk to me, do it with Mikey here."

Michael felt like a bug he'd once seen on the nature channel. Beneath the sand a hypersensitive subterranean snake was stalking him while from behind came the shuffle of a small rodent that had picked up his spoor. He'd die if he ran and die if he stood still. Michael had turned off the show, unable to bear it because of his identification with the insect.

"I will not be bullied by you," Kronin said to the queen of his heart.

"I'm not the bully."

"What did you do with that money?"

"It's my money, and I can do with it what I please."

"Not ten thousand dollars."

"Why not? Didn't you put it into my account? Didn't you tell me that you trusted me to make sensible decisions?"

"I don't know if I trust you anymore."

"I'm tired," Raela said then. "I'm going to bed."

"Eat something," Kronin said, no longer loud or a bully.

"I'm not hungry."

"You'll die."

"Everything dies."

Michael was beyond understanding this confrontation. He was unaware of Eric's relationship with his sister. He hadn't heard much from his friend since the funeral. Michael had called Eric, but that phone number was disconnected and he'd taken a leave from UCLA.

Raela walked out, leaving the older man seething and the younger one perplexed.

"Do you know what's going on?" Kronin asked Michael.

"No, sir."

"Why not? You brought him into this house."

"Who?"

"That Eric Nolan. He's bewitched her. She's taken all the money I gave her and given it to him."

"To Eric? Why?"

"Talk to your sister. And if you want to keep coming here you'd better make her listen to reason. The only reason you are suffered in this house is because of her."

Michael had always known that he was not a true member of the family. Maya never wanted him, and Kronin hadn't adopted him. Everyone loved his sister, not him. But no one had ever spoken these words. No one had ever told him that he was worthless. And so, even though he revered Stark and loved his life among the rich in Bel-Air, Michael went to his room and packed up his few things. He drove away from the Stark residence with no intention of returning.

Six blocks away his cell phone sounded.

"Hello?"

"Come back home, Michael," Maya said into the receiver.

It was the first time she'd called him in well over a year. He disconnected the call.

A few minutes later the phone sounded again. Michael wouldn't have answered except that it might have been his sister.

"Yes?"

Kronin Stark's voice boomed into the young man's ear. "Michael."

Again he disconnected the call.

★ ★ ★

MICHAEL DROVE FOR many miles that night, taking the same path that Christie had when she'd made her fateful decision. He couldn't have known where Christie had gone, but there he was. He stopped at a motel outside of Twentynine Palms and gave them his credit card.

"Do you have another one, son?" the silver-haired proprietor asked. "This one's being declined."

The room was only twenty-nine dollars a night, a promotional offer for the off-season. Michael had enough money to last him a week.

He went to his room, which opened onto the parking lot, and sat on the lumpy mattress, amazed that Kronin had canceled his credit card so quickly. This made Michael feel insubstantial. It was as if his whole life had been jotted down in light pencil and at any moment it could be completely erased. He had no mother or father, no one who loved him.

"Do you love me?" he had asked his sister when he was seventeen and she was eleven. He asked because he needed someone to care, and he believed that he saw his love reflected in Raela's eyes.

"I would die for you," she replied.

That night he went across the highway to the Monster Bar and ordered a beer. It was a small bungalow under the huge, looming shadow of a billboard in the shape of a Gila monster. The reptile's fat red tongue lolled lasciviously.

The woman behind the bar was named Doris Tina Warren. Her lower lip had been deeply cut from side to side, and the scar was like another, fatter lip bulging out from the first one.

"You stayin' at the hotel across the street?" she asked him.

"Yeah."

"Vacation?"

"I just got kicked out of my sister's father's house."

"You have different fathers?"

"No. We have the same father, but he died. This guy adopted her but not me."

"That's fucked up," the fake platinum blonde said. "What is he, some kind of a pervert?"

"I don't know. He gave me a credit card a long time ago, but as soon as I was gone he canceled it."

"But you have cash?"

Michael looked into the thin woman's eyes, which were two different shades of blue, and realized that she was worried that he couldn't pay.

"I got enough for this beer and the next one," he said.

Doris liked the sentence. It was the way her first boyfriend's father used to say things. The boy was a dog, but his father always made promises that he kept.

"Even after Manly dropped me, his father made him give me the car he promised," Doris was saying many hours and many beers later.

"Manly was the son?" Michael asked, a little unsteady on his bar stool.

It was three in the morning, and Doris had closed at one. She opened the tap then and refused to take any more of Michael's money.

"Yeah," she said. "Manly was the son, and Big Boy was his old man. Only Big Boy was the man, and Manly was the boy. You want another beer?"

"I don't think I could even walk across the road if I did," he said.

"You don't have to worry," she said. "I'm gonna help you to your bed."

"You are?"

"Oh, yeah," she said. "I knew that from the minute you said that you had the money for one beer and another."

They'd both been drinking.

"So your sister's just fifteen and she's with a senior in college?" she asked.

"Yeah."

"You gonna go kick his ass for robbing the cradle?"

"Huh?"

"Don't you hate him for doin' that?"

When Michael turned his head, his eyes and brain seemed to wait a second before following. He turned to look at Doris's eyes, felt a moment of fuzzy light-headedness, and then she materialized out of his confusion. This momentary hallucination seemed to have deep meaning for the young man. He touched her lip-scar with his finger.

"What did you say?" he asked.

"I said you must wanna kick his ass for molesting your sister. That's a crime, you know."

"Yeah, but I don't, I don't hate him. My sister is like, I don't know . . . she's like a woman. I mean, Eric is the smartest guy I've ever known. He can do like . . . anything. And my sister's like that too, only there's nothing holding her back. She has eyes like a snake, but I love her."

"Kiss me," Doris said.

In his desert motel bed he saw how skinny and scarred Doris was. She admitted to him that she was twenty-eight and that she drank too much. She'd slept with "more than a few men," she said.

"I've used this motel a whole lotta nights," she admitted after their first time making love. "I've fucked at least three guys in this bed."

Michael realized that this was a test of some sort. He knew

that he couldn't say that that was all right. If he said that, she'd
think that he thought she was a whore but he didn't care
because that's why he was with her. And he knew that he
couldn't say that what she had done was wrong but that he
still wanted to be with her because then he'd be looking
down on her and she'd get mad.

He knew these things, but they didn't matter. They didn't
matter to him because of how he felt.

"I'm twenty-one," he said, fingering a crescent-shaped scar
on her rib cage, just below the tattoo of the red rose on her
left breast. "And this is the first time that I've ever felt like
anybody has ever seen me. You know what I mean?"

Doris stared into his face with her mismatched blue eyes.
She wanted to speak but didn't or couldn't.

"I've never had such a long talk with anybody," he said.
"Man or woman. Not a real talk where I said things about
myself and they wanted to know what I was saying."

"I want to stop drinking," she said.

"Will you still talk to me if you do?"

"WHAT DO YOU want from me?" Kronin Stark asked Raela
five days later.

She was too weak now to get up from her bed. The giant
loomed above her. Because of the weakness of her vision, he
seemed to be shimmering.

"You know," she said. "And I want my brother back in the
house and for you to apologize to him."

"You think you can order me?"

"Leave me alone."

She closed her eyes until the shadow that covered her was
gone.

The next morning in the lounge area of the Cape Hotel in Beverly Hills, a slight man in a rumpled light-gray suit approached Kronin Stark's table. The man's name was Silas Renfield, but everyone called him Renny. Renny worked for the governor, though he had no particular job title — no official position at all. He showed up at odd hours and traveled extensively around the state and the nation. Whenever he appeared at the governor's door he was always admitted whether or not he had an appointment.

"Hello, Mr. Stark," Renny said, remaining on his feet.

"Sit," Kronin replied.

"How are you, sir?"

"I don't have time for pleasantries, Mr. Renfield. You know what I want. Are you ready to give it to me?"

"The boy was convicted of a violent crime under a state law that the governor himself pushed through the legislature. It would be . . . unseemly for him to rescind his own legislation."

"I'm not asking for him to overturn the law. All I need is for him to allow clemency for one boy, a hero."

"This boy was convicted of gang activity."

"He was abandoned by the system, left on the streets to fend for himself. He was shot down even though he was unarmed, and he saved a child's life from a mad gunman, almost dying in the process."

"I'm sorry, Mr. Stark, but the governor was quite clear with me this morning. He is not offering clemency for anyone convicted under his law."

"I understand that," Kronin replied. "A man should stick by his principles. But don't you forget that all of the resources I used to get your man elected will now be used against him."

"Mr. Stark —"

"This meeting is over."

"What about the fund-raiser at the arena this Saturday?"

"Canceled as of noon today."

"And the dinner with the Royal Family?"

"I'm rescinding the offer."

"This is a mistake, Mr. Stark."

"Yes, it is," Kronin replied. "And you and your governor are the ones making it."

AT FIRST CONSTANCE Baker thought that she only wanted Eric for a plaything. She said as much to him on that first night between their early bouts of torrid lovemaking. But she had found something in his arms that she'd never known before with a man. Maybe, she thought, it was because he was so young and sweet. But she doubted that. He spoke to her in low tones while they were in passion. He didn't whisper sweet nothings, he made declarative statements about what he was going to do. And he did everything he promised. Constance felt taken over by the young man. She wanted to make herself his.

At three in the morning she woke him to say that she had just called her Jim Harris and ended their six-year relationship.

"Why?" Eric asked.

"Because I never knew what being with a real man could be like. When you make love to me I feel like crawling out of my skin. You make me want to get down on my hands and knees. No man has ever made me feel like that."

Eric had heard words like this before from women and girls, but he was surprised at Constance. She seemed so in control of herself, so in charge. He didn't mind when she said that she wanted to sleep with him. He thought that it was just sex.

"I told the doorman to call me if you came by," she'd told him when they closed the door to her bedroom. "I told Jim that something had come up at the office and I had to go have a meeting."

Just sex, the young man thought to himself.

"But Connie," Eric said after she professed her love. "I'm just on vacation. I'll be going back to L.A. soon. I've got a girlfriend back there."

"Stay with me until you have to go," she said, giving him a coquettish smile. "Maybe I can change your mind."

"What about my brother?"

"He can stay with us. The girl can stay too if you want."

Eric stared at her face and saw Christie when the first bullet hit her in the abdomen. She had let out a terrible cry that he had heard even through the thick glass of the revolving door.

ON THAT FIRST night Thomas and Clea had found Connie's condoms and used one.

"You come like a woman," she said to him as they lay there side by side in the unlit room looking through the glass wall out on the lights of New Jersey. "I thought that you were hurting, and your eyes looked scared."

"I'm sorry," Thomas said. "I really am. It's just, it's just that I've been thinking about that for so long, and I never knew it would feel so, so . . ."

"So what?"

"I don't know. It was like you were all silk and all I ever knew was rocks. And when you looked at me and nodded I felt so powerful that I was scared that I'd hurt you. I don't know. I'm sorry."

"Don't be sorry," she said, curling around him. "It was really wonderful what you did. It was like I had your soul in my hands, like I was hurting you but it was okay."

"I don't know, Clea," Thomas said. "I never knew anything like that before. But you know, maybe you shoulda gone away with that other guy."

"I don't want to be with him."

"Yeah, but you see how it is with me. Here I can't even walk down the street without getting arrested. I don't even hardly know how to read, and you can read things in four languages."

"So? We're not getting married or anything. We're just havin' a good time."

She put her hand on his forehead the way his mother did when he was overtired and couldn't sleep.

Thomas dozed off and dreamed that he was floating on a pink-and-blue ocean with the sun all around him and fish swimming on top of the water.

THE BOYS MOVED their things out of the Y and brought them down to Connie's. Eric felt funny about it, but he had been honest with his mentor. They had a good time together, and she taught him all about Wall Street.

Two weeks went by, and Thomas learned about love from Clea as Connie did from Eric. The boys spent their afternoons together exploring the city.

One cloudy morning Eric brought Thomas to deliver one of Connie's antique watches to a watchmaker whose office was on the eighty-sixth floor of the Empire State Building. They entered the Russian's office a little after nine.

"Yes?" the burly man asked. He was frowning at Thomas.

"I brought a watch from Constance Baker," Eric told him. This took away the scowl.

"Let me see it."

It was a tiny pocket watch with gold-filled numbers and a shiny blue lacquered back.

"It's lovely," the watchmaker said.

Thomas wandered over to the window at the back of the shop. The sky outside was opaque white, pure and unfathomable.

Eric exchanged the watch for a receipt.

"Let's go, Tommy," he said.

"What's with this window?" the young black man asked.

The watchmaker, Mr. Harry Slatkin, smiled.

"Open it up," he said.

Tommy pulled the old-fashioned window wide. The dense white mass hovered outside.

"What is it?"

"The clouds," Slatkin told him. "We are in the clouds."

Thomas talked about it all the way down in the Art Deco elevator.

"We were actually in a cloud, Eric. I never did anything like that before."

"You never flew?" Eric asked.

"Where I'ma fly to? The soup kitchen?"

THEN ONE MORNING Eric got a call on a bright-red cell phone that Raela had given him.

"Hi, Eric," the raven-haired girl said into the line. Her voice was exultant.

"Hi, honey," he said.

Connie, who was lying next to him in the bed, sat straight up.

"The governor of California has commuted Thomas's sentence, and he's persuaded the district attorney to drop all the other charges," Raela said. "You can come home. Daddy's sending a plane tomorrow to pick you up at Stewart Airport."

"What time?"

"Three in the afternoon."

"We'll be there."

When he disconnected the call, Connie said, "You're leaving?"

"Uh . . . yeah."

"When?"

"Tomorrow . . . at three."

"Tomorrow?"

"I told you we were going back."

"But just one day's notice?"

"We've got to go. That's where we live. I have a daughter there."

"You're married?"

"No. But I told you about my girlfriend."

"So you take advantage of me and then walk out with hardly a good-bye?"

"Connie."

"Get out of my house."

TELLING CLEA WAS somewhat easier. She cried a little.

"Will we ever see each other again?" she asked Thomas.

"I'd come back if you want me to," he said. "I could maybe get my GED and a job at the museum. I could stay at the Y."

"Maybe I could come out to California in the summer," she said. "Then you'd have time to see your family awhile. I mean, it sounds like you haven't had a break in years."

"I love you." Thomas hadn't remembered using those words since he was a boy with Branwyn.

"Go back home, Thomas, and call me. If it's right I'll come out this summer and we'll see."

"I don't want to leave you, but I want to go home too."

"Go."

18

KRONIN STARK sent a private jet — his own personal 767, in which he had never flown — for the boys the next afternoon. Connie didn't even say good-bye to Eric. She just slammed the door after telling him that he had destroyed her life.

"I don't see how you did that, Eric," Thomas said as the jet gained altitude. "I mean, you told her that you were going back to California and that you had a girl. She's twice your age. I mean, damn — what more did she need?"

"I shouldn't have led her on."

"You didn't."

"What do you know about it, Tommy? Nobody ever threw herself at you and then fell out of a window instead."

"Maybe not. But so what? You think that means I'm too stupid to know?"

"No. Not that. But I have problems that you wouldn't understand. I have to be careful how I treat people. You have to be careful how people treat you. She said that I ruined her life."

"You didn't do nuthin' to her, man. All you did was go along for the ride. You don't know what you did to her. She don't know either."

"She knows how she feels."

"Maybe. But she broke up with that boyfriend, right?"

276

"Yeah."

"She probably needed to do that. She needed to leave him, and she told herself that she was in love with you to do it. Of course she's gonna be mad. But she's mad at her boyfriend, mad at herself for bein' with him. It don't have nuthin' to do wit' you."

Eric was once again amazed by his brother. During the years that they were separated, Eric often thought that he'd idealized Thomas, that the boy really wasn't so brilliant as he remembered. But time after time when they talked, Eric was forced to admit the rightness in Thomas's keen insights.

"How do you know that, Tommy?" Eric asked a long while later.

"What?" Thomas was looking out of the window, holding tight to the armrests of his seat. He had never been in a jet, or any other aircraft. He was elated and petrified.

"About Connie. I mean, you never even slept with anybody before Clea."

"You ever been to the carnival that come down on Fifty-fourth Place sometimes?" Thomas asked. "Down toward South Central?"

"No."

"But you ever been in a hall of mirrors like?"

"No, but I know what you mean."

"It's like a door you go in and you try to get out the other side," Thomas said, remembering when he went into that maze. "It's all glass walls and mirrors, an' you can see your reflection all ovah the place an' you see other people too. But if you go in it an' there's only you, then you see yourself a thousand times all ovah. You see the front and back, the sides. It's just you. Just you whatever way you look."

"So?" Eric said.

"That's kinda like you," Thomas told his brother. "You always been special, an' so all you see is you. Like when we was in school. It was you all the time. Teacher's helper, spelling champion, the only little boy in our class that could hit a home run."

"But that's just sports or schoolwork."

"Yeah, but everybody always knows you and is always thinkin' about you. And so it's like they're the mirrors and you look at them and see you. But I don't do that because you're my brother, and that means I don't have to care about you like they do. I know you're my friend already, and I know you feel bad. But Connie and Christie and Mr. Stroud in the first grade wanted you to see them, but you couldn't see nuthin' but what they saw — like a mirror. You see yourself makin' this one happy an' breakin' the other one's heart. I don't know exactly what I mean, but it's somethin' like that though."

"So you think that people make up how they feel about me?" Eric asked.

"Sometimes. But even if they don't, even if it's like your girlfriend who got killed. She's the one who made that man mad enough to kill her. It was what she wanted from you. I mean, if you thought about it, you'd think that everyone you meet should fall dead the minute they saw you. But you know some girls think you cute but they don't leave their boyfriends or nuthin'. You can't help it if somebody fool enough to get in trouble over you."

"But, Tommy," Eric said, "things happen with me that never happen to other people. I win games, girls fall in love; one time the sky parted just in time for me to win a game of tennis."

"That ain't nuthin' but magic tricks," Thomas said. The jet

had just entered a patch of turbulence, so he clasped his hands together and closed his eyes.

"What do you mean by that?" Eric asked, not heeding his brother's fear.

"Win a game, kiss some girl," Thomas said, his heart in his throat. "That ain't nuthin'. I got better luck than that."

"You?"

"Yeah, me."

"Tommy, you could fall down just sitting in a chair."

"Maybe so, but I was born, an' you know all those days I was walkin' on the streets, I kept thinkin' how special you got to be to get born. Nobody knows what kinda baby they gonna have or if they'll have the baby they want. Even if you're just a fly alive for a few minutes and then you run into a spider's web — even that fly is one'a the most luckiest creatures in the world. We all lucky, Eric. And the luckiest ones are the ones happy about bein' alive."

The plane dipped in the sky, and Thomas yelped.

Eric laughed and told him that there were always a few bumps in flying.

KRONIN STARK MET the brothers at the Bob Hope Airport in Burbank, California. Thomas had never seen anybody so large or powerful. He was reminded of an even larger version of Tremont, the muscle-bound drug dealer.

"Mr. Stark," Eric said. He held out his hand. "This is my brother, Thomas."

"Hello," Stark said to Thomas.

Thomas nodded but did not return the greeting. Silence gripped his throat.

"You're the reason my daughter took all her money out of the bank."

"She did it for me, Mr. Stark," Eric said. "And I plan to pay her back within six months."

"What about my influence?"

"Excuse me, sir?"

"I put pressure on the governor's office for this reprieve. What will you give me for that?"

"What do you want?" Eric asked.

Stark looked closely at Eric and then at his brother.

"Why don't you two boys come and work for me?" he said. "Work off the debt you owe."

"Sure," Eric said without hesitation. "But I thought that Mikey said that you didn't even have an office, that you just sit at a table in the Cape Hotel all day having meetings."

"Things change," Kronin said with a shrug. "I've recently been made the CEO of an investment organization — the Drumm Investment Group."

"Okay," Eric said. "But we have to figure out how much work we need to do to pay you back."

"What about you, son?" Stark asked Thomas.

"I didn't ask you to help me," Thomas said. He found himself squinting at Stark as if the huge billionaire was the sun.

"That's a bit ungrateful, isn't it?"

"I don't know about that. As a matter of fact I don't know much at all. I sure couldn't be a businessman or a doctor or nuthin', so how could I work for you an' pay off gettin' the governor to let me free? You think I could sweep enough floors to do sumpin' like that?"

"I'll work for you, Mr. Stark," Eric said. "I'll do the work for the two of us."

"I wanted both of you," Stark said, eyeing the lame Thomas.

"But why?" Thomas asked. "Why'd you do it in the first place?"

"Raela wouldn't eat until I obtained your clemency."

"Is she eatin' now?"

"Yes."

"Then you been paid," Thomas stated bluntly.

Eric was perplexed by his brother's tough attitude.

"Don't you feel at all indebted to me?" Kronin asked, still addressing Thomas.

"Why should I? I don't even know you."

Stark cocked his head like a man who has just heard a threat being issued.

"I was the one who engineered your clemency."

"I think it was Raela did that," Thomas said. "You just did what she made you do."

It was obvious to both young men that Stark expected to get his way easily. The impediment of Thomas's refusal was beginning to humor Eric.

"Why don't you let us talk about it?" Eric suggested. "I'll talk to Tommy alone."

"Why don't we discuss it on the ride back?" Stark suggested.

"We didn't know that you were coming, Mr. Stark," Eric said. "So we called my dad. He's coming to get us."

Stark glared at Thomas, who in turn squinted as if the bright light of an inquisitor was shining into his eyes.

"HOW'D YOU BOYS like New York?" Minas Nolan asked on the ride back to Beverly Hills.

"I really liked it, Dad," Eric said. He felt outgoing and effusive with his father for the first time that he could remember. "Tommy spent every day in the museum, and I was down on Wall Street. We'd get together every night for dinner though."

"How did you like it, Tommy?" Minas asked, turning momentarily toward the backseat.

"It was pretty good," the smaller boy said. "The museum was great, and we met some nice people. A lotta people talked about the World Trade Center. I think they're worried about it happening again."

"That was a terrible event," Dr. Nolan agreed.

"Yeah. There's people live in the subways, you know."

"Really?" Eric asked. "When were you in the subway?"

"Sometimes I took the Lexington line downtown, but I heard it from this homeless guy I met in the park. I guess he could tell by the way I said hi that I lived on the street before. He said that my face an' hands didn't go wit' the clothes I was wearin'. He told me that if you go down on the subway rails under Grand Central that you'd find a whole village where homeless people lived. They got everything down there, even electricity."

"That sounds like a tall tale to me," Minas Nolan said in his certain tone.

"Could be though," Thomas said. And then he told Minas about his alley valley and the apartment-building clubhouse he shared with Pedro.

"It's like when you look at someplace and say that there's not nuthin' there," Thomas concluded. "But when you look closer you see animals an' birds an' things. I met a woman who told me that there's all kindsa millions and millions'a animals too small to be seen walkin' all ovah everywhere all the time. Her daddy was a scientist, but she was crazy an' had to live in the street."

"That's terrible," Minas said.

"Yeah," Thomas replied. "But nobody know it."

ERIC AND MONA and Thomas and Minas Nolan all sat in the living room drinking a citrus punch that Ahn had made. Eric explained everything he'd learned from Constance Baker without talking about the way things ended with her. Mona sat on Thomas's lap, rubbing her hands over his fingers.

"Your fingers like sandpaper, Uncle Tommy."

"I used to spend all my time out in a park that I had."

"You had your own park?" The girl was astonished.

"Yeah. But it was real dirty because people were always throwin' trash in it. That's why I got such rough hands — throwin' all the trash away all the time."

"Oh."

Raela and her brother, Michael, came over in the afternoon. Michael was accompanied by a scarred woman named Doris. Doris wore an orange dress and had one light- and one dark-blue eye. Raela was thinner than before but just as beautiful as Thomas had remembered. After a while Eric and his friends and daughter decided to go down to the beach.

"You wanna come, Tommy?" Eric asked.

"Not today. I just wanna stay around here."

Thomas was thinking that he could go up to his mother's old room and sink to his knees. It had been a long time since he'd been home.

But Dr. Nolan wanted to talk awhile longer. Thomas didn't mind. It had been many years since he was alone with his mother's lover. When he was traveling the streets of L.A. he often thought of the talks he'd had with the doctor.

"I'm very sorry about the things that have happened," Minas said when they were alone.

"It's not your fault," Thomas replied. "The law took me away. It took me from you, then it took me from my real father, and then it put me in jail. I don't really like the law all that much. It's like no matter what I do there's some law to tell me I'm wrong."

"When you put it like that," Minas said, "it doesn't seem fair. You'd think that the law would protect young people."

"But it don't, doesn't," Thomas said, correcting his street language with the way he'd learned to speak in Minas's house years before. "All the kids I knew were in trouble or makin' trouble. And when I was livin' on the street, the cops was the last people you wanted to see."

"How did you manage to survive living like that?" Minas asked.

Thomas could see by the way the doctor winced that he was afraid of the answer.

"It was pretty much always the same," Thomas said. "You needed food and shelter mostly, and money to buy stuff like toothpaste or Band-Aids. You'd stay in one place as long as you could, but you had other places in mind in case the cops or somebody moved you out. But once you had what you needed, then you could read a book or talk to somebody or think. I liked to think."

"What would you think about?" Minas asked.

"You an' Ahn an' Eric," Thomas said, "and my mother. I used to have a blank book and I'd write in that. I wrote mostly about nice things that people did for me and some- times about why people was so mean. One man once told me that he thought that people were mean to the homeless because we were so poor. He said that people hate poor people in America . . . Oh, oh, yeah."

"What?" Minas asked.

"I just remembered what I wanted to tell Eric when I got shot."

"What's that?"

"I was lookin' at a book that had the word *America* written down on it. And I was lookin' at it, and then I saw that E-R-I-C was right in the middle of it. Eric was in the middle of America."

Minas put down his drink and lowered his head, pondering the words from his stepson.

"You want to go to the Rib Joint for dinner?" he asked.

"Yeah."

IN THE PAST six years Thomas had shambled past the restaurant from time to time. Fontanot had bought the buildings on either side of the original eatery and added a second floor to the primary structure — you could smell barbecue smoking for three blocks in any direction. But Thomas never went in to say hello. The place was too big, and he doubted that his mother's tall friend would remember him. And even if Fontanot did remember, Thomas knew that no one would let him just walk in. People dressed for street living were blocked from entering any place fancy, like restaurants or department stores.

Fontanot knew Thomas at first sight. He folded the young man in his arms and kissed his cheek.

"Boy, you are a sight for sore eyes," he bellowed. "Look just like your mother. You sure do."

They crowded into the kitchen and ate catfish and

sausages. Thomas couldn't eat too much, but he was happy at the loud entrepreneur's special table.

Ira had married a big Texan girl named Coretta.

"Got some meat on her bones," he told the doctor and his son. "But she ain't fat. No, no — just bullheaded. When she told me she wanted to live together, I said that I wasn't ready for that, so the next night when I got home she had all her stuff already moved in. I tried to th'ow her out an' she rassled me to the floor. I couldn't break her grip 'cause I was laughin' so hard. Now, you know if a girl gonna make you laugh like that then it's all ovah. We got married in Vegas the next weekend."

Thomas didn't remember ever feeling so happy or so safe as he did in Fontanot's kitchen.

"Mr. Fontanot?" Thomas said after many stories.

"Yeah?"

"Do you think you might have a job here that I could do? I have washed dishes for men's shelters before, and I know how to clean up."

"I could use a good man on my smokers," the big man said. "You know, I only put men I could trust out in the backyard."

"You can trust me."

"Then you can start tomorrow."

THAT NIGHT THOMAS was sitting on his old bed (Eric had moved back to his original bedroom) thinking about working for Fontanot. At the Rib Joint he felt that he could make a new life and maybe things would be all right. He'd have a job, and no one was looking to put him back in jail; he could get a license to drive and maybe even get a used car. That way he'd have an ID with a picture and an address. And then he could take a train back East and visit Clea at NYU when Fontanot gave him vacation. Maybe even Monique's husband would shake his hand and smile.

The knocking at his door was very soft.

"Come in," he said, knowing that it was Ahn.

The nanny-turned-housekeeper had on a boy's blue jeans and T-shirt. She also wore round wire-rimmed spectacles.

Thomas glanced at the hem of the T-shirt to see if there were old bloodstains there, but all he saw was bright white cotton.

"Hello, Tommy," she said, leaning forward slightly with just a hint of a bow.

Tommy moved toward the end of the bed, and she sat next to him.

"Are you okay?" she asked.

"Yes. I'm going to work for Mr. Fontanot. I'm gonna be a rib smoker."

"Dr. Nolan and Eric tell me that you were shot one time before," she said, frowning.

"A long time ago. I don't hardly ever even think about that."

"Was that before you called me?"

"No. I got shot later."

"I could have saved you, maybe?"

"Prob'ly not, Ahn. I was in trouble, and nobody could have got me out. You know, it's tough in the streets of L.A. I knew this guy once from down in Mexico, illegal, you know. And he told me that if he was sick he'd be better off at home because down there there was always somebody to give you some beans an'a tortilla, someplace to sleep at least."

"But I could have fed you then. But I told you not to call."

"It's okay, Ahn. Really. I always remembered what you told

me about running. No matter what happens you got to keep on movin'. You can't stop to cry or wonder why or nuthin'. I got that from you, Ahn, and that's why I stayed alive."

The small woman and Thomas hugged there on his childhood bed. She was crying. Thomas remembered all the times that he and Eric had run to Ahn with cuts and scrapes and bruises. She would always be there, ready to take care of them.

"It's okay, Ahn," Thomas whispered. "We don't have to run anymore."

WHEN AHN LEFT for her room, Thomas went down into the garden. He was barefoot and wore only his black jeans. In that way he remembered his mother and their nocturnal sojourns in the garden when Eric and Dr. Nolan were away. He expected to be alone, but he found Raela there, sitting on the stone bench.

"Hello," the teenager said.

Thomas liked this girl. She seemed to him to hold herself like ballet dancers that performed in the park in the summer. It was the way she held her head high and how her eyes took a moment to settle on you. He grinned and sat down next to her.

"What are you doing down here?" he asked.

"When Eric falls to sleep sometimes I come down to sit with the flowers," she said.

Thomas nodded.

"Eric told me that my stepfather wanted you to work for him but you said no."

He nodded again, breathing in the strong scent of far-off night-blooming jasmine.

"Why did you say no?"

"Because . . ."

"What?"

"Because he made my eyes hurt when I looked at him."

It was Raela's turn to nod.

For long minutes they sat not talking. Now and then the flutter of a nightbird or some large moth broke the silence.

"He loves me too much," the girl said after a while. "When I was a kid he'd come and watch me play. He would talk to me for hours but never even pay any attention to my brother at all."

"I knew a woman once who told me that her father made her have sex with him," Thomas said. "That's why she ran away and lived in the street. He said he'd kill her if she even went out with a boy. He had killed another daughter and put her in the basement, but she never told no one except us in the street."

"He never touched me," Raela said. "And he never made threats. But I think he hates Eric — he hates him because we're together."

"Yeah," Thomas said, nodding again. "Maybe that's why he hurts my eyes."

"I told Eric not to work for him. I told him that my step-father is like a big old stone. He just falls on top of you and stays there until you're crushed. When I was younger he would tell me about how he would sometimes just sit with a man at lunch, and by teatime the man would have lost everything it took him his whole life to make. I'd ask him why the man didn't shoot him."

"What did he say?" Thomas asked, scared as if he were being told a ghost story.

"That the way he got inside the man's soul made the man happy to be losing just his business."

Thomas thought about his lost cart then. He wondered if

Kronin Stark had ever pushed anybody out of that fancy hotel and into the street.

"Do you love Eric?" Thomas asked, still thinking about pushing that cart.

Raela turned to Thomas, taking a moment for her eyes to settle. Then her brow furrowed.

Thomas liked the way she took her time. It was as if she knew there was no hurry. Sometimes it took a while to say something.

"I don't know," she said at last. "I mean, when I see him I think, 'There's Eric. I know him from inside his core to his skin.' I think, 'I need his warmth in my bed.' Is that love?"

"Does he make you want to giggle and laugh out loud?"

"When I see him with you he does," she said with no hesitation. "Seeing you and him together makes me happy."

19

WORKING AT the Rib Joint was a joy for Thomas Beerman. Minas gave him a ride to the restaurant every morning, and Thomas took the Wilshire bus back home at night.

Smoking the ribs, sausages, slabs of beef, and other exotic meats was a seven-man job (even though three of those men were women). They had to prepare the meat by cutting it into the proper portions, marinate it for twenty-four hours, and then smoke it in the twelve big metal cans out in the yard. They smoked beef, pork, and chicken, and wild game like venison and boar. They smoked homemade, hand-stuffed sausages. Miranda Braithwaite made the sauce and marinated the meats the way Ira had taught her. Ben Tallman and Parker Todd used brushes to baste the meat and turn it from time to time. Thomas Grant and Penelope Sargent prepared the orders and prepped for the others when they weren't busy. There was a sixth man, Bishop Ladderman, who carved the meat and carried the orders into the kitchen for Ira to finish off and for the waitresses to deliver.

THREE TIMES A week Thomas talked on the phone to Clea in New York. He half expected her to start dating the law student Brad again. She did see him from time to time, she said, but only as a friend.

"He's got another girlfriend now," she said. "She's preparing to study law like him, and they're very happy."

Love flourished in the long talks they had via cell phone.

"I never knew anybody who thinks as deeply as you," she would say. "It's like you were a thousand years old and had the time to wonder about everything in the world."

Thomas liked having her to talk to. He even planned to take a flight to New York on his first three-day weekend, which would come in three months. By then he would have saved the money.

Clea had said that she loved him over the phone.

ON HIS DAYS off Thomas visited Raela and Eric at the Tennyson. They had moved in together, and he was back in school. Thomas babysat for Mona when Raela and his brother went out, and he talked late into the night with Eric when the two came home from their date.

"So you're not gonna work for Stark?" Thomas asked Eric one such late evening.

Raela was asleep with Mona in her bed because the child still had bad dreams about her mother's murder. That's why Mona liked to have Thomas babysit for her — the child was convinced that he could always save her if something bad happened.

"No," Eric said. "Raela doesn't want me to. She doesn't trust him, but I think he's just trying to keep his family together. We go over there at least once a week for dinner."

"I don't like him."

"I know. But I'm not scared. I mean, what could he do to me?"

Thomas gazed at his brother and smiled.

"What are you smilin' at?" Eric asked.

"For a while there I didn't think that anything would ever work for me," Thomas said. "I mean, I couldn't even get it together to buy a new pair of shoes. I couldn't even stop my feet from bleedin' through the holes in my soles."

"I guess we are lucky like you told me, huh?" Eric said.

"Maybe so."

ONE AFTERNOON THOMAS put on a pair of black cotton pants and a blue Hawaiian T-shirt that Raela had helped him pick out at a store in West Hollywood. He had on black sandals with no socks and a short-brimmed straw hat to keep the sun out of his eyes. Wearing this ensemble, he took four buses down to Compton and knocked on Harold and Monique's door. Lily answered.

"Uncle Lucky, is that you?"

He picked up the chunky girl and kissed her cheek. Monique came up and kissed her childhood friend on the mouth. Thomas worried that Harold would get mad about that, but he just shook Thomas's hand and said, "You look good, homeboy. Come on in."

THOMAS STARTED READING books from the shelf at Minas Nolan's house. It really didn't matter what he read: science fiction, biography, technical manuals, or general fiction — all of it served the purpose of telling him something, anything. He didn't retain much of the knowledge he perused; he didn't expect to collect ideas but merely to be exposed to them.

"What are you reading, son?" Minas would ask when he came upon Thomas in the library hunched over some book.

"Gray's Anatomy," he said one day.

"Are you interested in human anatomy?"

"It's so pretty," Thomas replied. "I saw this guy cut open once in Tremont's alley. He stole from Tremont and got his arm cut open. I could see the muscles hangin' outta his arm. They didn't look all neat like they do here in this book. In this book it looks nice and, and pretty."

"Those experiences you had must have been awful," Minas said.

"It must have been," Thomas agreed. "But it's like somebody else's life when I think about it. I mean, I know that I was there, but it feels like I always been here and those things I did are like a book."

Thomas held up the anatomy text and shook his head.

Minas wondered if he understood what the boy was saying. Later that night, when he went to bed, he decided that Thomas had become as deep and unfathomable as his mother.

BISHOP LADDERMAN WAS offered a job as an assistant chef in a fancy Brentwood restaurant, and so he left the Rib Joint. It was quite a surprise. Bishop wasn't looking for a job, but one day he got a call from Chez Vivienne's owner, Raoul Mantou. Mr. Mantou said that he'd heard a lot about Bishop and that he wanted him in his kitchen. He offered seventy-five thousand dollars a year, twice what any cook got at Fontanot's, and so Bishop had to go.

Michael Cotter was hired to take Bishop's place.

Michael was different from the other smokers. Miranda, Ben, Parker, Penelope, and Thomas Grant were all in their late fifties up to sixty. Bishop was that age too. And even though Thomas was only twenty, he had what Fontanot called an old soul, and because of his scars and limp he seemed more like one of the older workers.

Cotter was young, not quite thirty, and handsome, black as glowing tar and lithe like a panther. He was always laughing and quick to lend a hand. The waitresses from the restaurant would come out to the yard just to look at him when he'd take his shirt off to move the heavy metal smokers or large bundles of meat.

Cotter got along with everybody. He and Thomas became fast friends.

One day, after his first few weeks on the job, Michael offered to drive Thomas home. Thomas took the ride because he liked to hear Michael's tales about the streets. They were different streets from those Thomas had inhabited. Michael told stories about tough men and fine women that loved and fought in the clubs and bars. Thomas knew what happened outside, and Michael knew what went on indoors.

"So you stayed in that alley and didn't evah go to school?" Cotter asked on that first day he gave Thomas a ride.

"Uh-huh."

"That's wild, man. And nobody nevah knew?"

"Not until Pedro killed himself and I tried to stop him and fell off the roof. Then they knew . . . about me not goin' to school anyway."

MICHAEL COTTER LOVED a good story. He had been in the army for a spell, as a sniper. He told Thomas that they had him "all ovah the niggerlands from Afghanistan to Sudan, from Argentina to North Korea."

"And you shot people?" Thomas asked.

"Oh, yeah, man. Sometimes, though, they'd put a twist on it."

"Like what?"

"Sometimes," Michael said, "when they didn't wanna kill somebody but just shake him up, they'd have me shoot his wife or young child. Sometimes I'd just wound a dude so he'd miss a meetin'."

Most of the other smokers liked Cotter, but they didn't believe his stories.

"He just a blowhard," Parker had said to the other smokers one day before Cotter had arrived. "I mean, he tell a good story all right. And I believe he had some time in the armed services. But the United States government ain't nevah gonna have no sniper shoot no child."

"I'ont know," Miranda said. "Maybe not a white child, but if it was some little black boy or Arab girl they might not care."

"What do you think, Lucky?" Ben asked Thomas. "You the one he talk to the most."

"He prob'ly did all that," Thomas said.

"Why don't you think he lyin'?" Penelope asked the youngest smoker.

"People lie to impress people," Thomas said, paying very little heed to the words as they came out of his mouth. "When they lie they sneak a look to see if you're impressed. But Cotter don't care. He just talkin'. I think he did alla what he said. All of it and more."

ERIC WAS HAPPY to have his brother back in his life. He still lamented Christie's death, still felt guilty about it. But he didn't feel alone with Raela as he had with Mona's mother. If he was sick she nursed him and never got a sniffle. When they went skiing together he broke his leg, and she didn't even sprain an ankle. And she was forever surprising him with her views of the world and her conviction that they were meant to be together.

"But do you love me?" Eric asked her one day.

"Sure," she said.

"But I mean really, deeply."

"That's not the way you and I think," she replied. "I'd kill for you if I had to. I'd die for you too. Isn't that enough?"

"When I was in New York I slept with a woman, a stock-broker named Connie."

"So?"

"Does that make you jealous?"

Raela gazed up at a spot somewhere above Eric's head.

"If I smelled her on you I might get violent," she speculated. "Yeah. If I smelled her on you, you might have to hide for a while."

"But you didn't smell her?"

Raela pressed her face against his chest and inhaled deeply. Then she exhaled and said, "All I smell is me."

Eric was reminded of Ahn's story about the tiger. Looking upon this girl and remembering that, the young man felt real fear for the first time that he could remember. It exhilarated him, made him shiver. Raela put her arms around him and pressed his head to her breast. From there he could feel the strong beat of her heart and somewhere, far away, the muted thudding of his own blood.

"What we have is what we need," she said with conviction.

Eric thought that he was directionless in this jungle of a girl, directionless but not lost.

★　★　★

A YEAR PASSED for the brothers. Thomas went twice to New York and found Clea there waiting for him. In that year he had not cut himself or fallen down, nor was he stopped by the police even once. Every day he woke up early and sat with his stepfather. They read the newspaper and talked about the events in the world. Minas seemed infinitely interested in Thomas's ideas and point of view.

"You're so much like your mother that it's uncanny," Minas said to Thomas.

"She was the kindest person in the world," Thomas would say.

"Yes, she was," Minas agreed, "and as long as you are here she will never be gone."

Eric relaxed. He experienced a profound love for his daughter now that he wasn't afraid he'd do her harm. They'd spend hours playing games and going to amusement parks and the zoo.

His feelings for Raela never changed, but this didn't bother him. She was his sail, he thought, and he was her ship. They were ancient archetypes instead of real people.

Sometimes when thinking this, Eric became terribly sad. He'd see himself like a reflection in a mirror, unable to reach out into the world of flesh and bone. But at those times Raela would come to him, and he realized that even in isolation he wasn't completely alone.

And he also had Thomas. The brothers saw each other at least three times a week.

"You know, the more I think about what you said," Eric was telling Thomas at the stone animal park, "the more I think that it's true."

"What?"

"That you're the one who's lucky. You loving life makes

you like that. There's nowhere you can go where you don't feel at home."

"Like a snake," Thomas said, happy to continue the conversation he'd had so many years ago with Bruno. "A snake can go anywhere he wants to."

"See that? If somebody called you a snake, even that would make you happy. You can't get much luckier than that."

MICHAEL COTTER WAS driving Thomas every day by the end of the year. Thomas had talked to Michael almost as much as to his brother or Clea. He'd told him about the alley parrot chanting "no man" and Alicia in her cinder-block tomb. He talked about his years as a drug dealer and in the youth facility and as the child husband of Monique and de facto father of Lily.

"I called Clea at lunch, and she told me that she applied to UCLA and that they accepted her," Thomas said to Michael on their ride home after work one day. "She asked me if I wanted her to come out here and live with me."

"And what did you say?" Michael asked.

"I said absolutely."

"Congratulations, my man."

"Thanks. You know, she says that after she graduates, we'll figure out whether or not to go back to New York."

"Hey, man, that's great. We should celebrate that. I got to see somebody today, but why don't we have a drink tomorrow to toast you and your girlfriend."

"Okay. Great."

THAT NIGHT THE whole family got together to celebrate. Eric, Mona, Raela, Ahn, and Minas were all there. Michael came with

Doris. Michael had gone to live on a date farm in the desert. He'd grown a beard and dropped out of college. He no longer communicated with Raela's parents (that's how he began to think of Kronin and Maya). Doris drank too much sometimes, and when she did she got rowdy. But Michael said that he loved her, and Raela spent weekends with them once a month.

"It's been a long journey, Tommy," Minas said, holding up a glass of cognac. "But I think you've made it through."

They all drank and cheered.

Raela played the piano for them, and Ahn sang a Vietnamese song that she remembered from her youth before coming to America.

Sometime late in the evening, Eric took his brother into the garden.

Eric seemed older. There could often be seen a slight smile on his lips. His shoulders sagged slightly, and he paid a lot of attention to people around him.

"You think you'll marry Clea?" Eric asked.

"She's too young," Thomas said. "She just wants to go to school and have some fun."

"Will you live together?"

"Yeah. Maybe we'll get a place near Fontanot's or some kinda student housing thing."

Eric put his arms around Thomas, kissed his cheek, and whispered, "You're my brother, Tommy."

Thomas went to bed happy and fell into a dream.

He was in his alley valley again, and all the trash was gone. No Man and his wife were in the oak tree with a dozen parrot chicks crying for food. Skully was there and so was Pedro. Bruno was sitting on the other side of the fence reading a Fantastic Four comic. Thomas was sitting in the shade of the big oak watching the sun creep across the floor of the alley toward his feet. He was feeling completely relaxed when the surface he was sitting on started to shift.

He jumped up and realized that he was sitting on Alicia's tomb. The head cinder block fell away, and Alicia sat up. At first Thomas was happy to see his old friend come to life, but then he noticed that the tattoo on her left breast no longer read *Ralphie* but now said *Clea*.

"Don't touch me," Alicia said in a voice much like his mother's.

He wanted to obey, but his hands moved forward with a will of their own, and even though she screamed, his fingertips grazed her neck. Instantly she fell back dead. An earthquake shook the alley. Tall buildings that had never been there before began to fall. No Man flew away, and the oak toppled upon Bruno — Thomas came awake unable to breathe, unable to yell, but the shout was in his throat.

"HELLO?" ERIC SAID, answering the call. It was 3:27.

"Eric."

"What, Tommy?"

"If something bad happens I want you to tell Clea that I really love her."

"Nothing's gonna happen, Tommy."

"And I want you to know how grateful I am for you going back East with me and helping me."

"What's wrong?" Eric asked.

"I just had a dream. But it was really real. Everything went wrong all at once. The whole world fell apart in a earthquake."

"You remember what you told me about the moon, don't you?"

Thomas took a deep breath, another.

"Yeah, but . . . things have been goin' so good, Eric. A whole year now and nothin's wrong."

"That's okay, Tommy. You just had it bad, that's all. Bad things might happen again but not so bad that you won't be happy."

"No?"

"It was just a dream. Just a dream."

"Just a dream," Thomas echoed. He could feel the sleep returning behind his eyes.

"Go back to bed, man," Eric said. "It'll all be fine in the morning."

BUT THOMAS WAS upset all day at work. He knocked over a steel smoker filled with chickens. He cut himself in the afternoon, and if it wasn't for the fast work of Michael Cotter he might have lost a lot of blood.

At the end of the day, when Michael was driving him back, Thomas said, "You should have turned left."

"Aren't we gonna have that toast? There's this great bar I know on Little Santa Monica."

"I don't know, Mike," Thomas said. "I don't feel much like celebrating."

"Aw come on, Lucky. It was just a can'a chickens and a slip. You're gonna be fine."

Cotter pulled into an almost invisible driveway and up next to a beautiful fountain. A doorman wearing a uniform came out and opened Thomas's door. Another uniformed man opened Michael's door and said, "Welcome back, sir."

"What is this place?" Thomas asked his friend.

In the foyer there were several well-dressed men and women walking, talking, waiting for an elevator.

"It's a hotel bar," Cotter was saying. "You know, hotels have the finest bars and restaurants."

The handsome young smoker led Thomas into a large room filled with small tables. At a table in a far corner sat Kronin Stark.

"What's goin' on?" Thomas asked. He stopped walking.

"Mr. Stark has something to tell you . . . about your brother."

For a moment Thomas was half back in his dream. He felt as if the hotel floor were buckling under his feet. He pitched forward, but Cotter caught him and helped him to a chair in front of the giant.

"I hear congratulations are in order," Stark rumbled. "Clea Frank is coming to California to be with you."

"What do you want with me?" Thomas said. "And what about my brother?"

"Your brother is about to go to jail for quite some time," Stark said.

"You're crazy. Eric hasn't done anything."

"As you will," Kronin replied with a slight bow. "Take a ride with me and I will explain the details."

"I'm not goin' anywhere with you."

"Fine. Leave then."

Thomas looked at Michael, who smiled and shrugged his shoulders.

"What's going to happen to Eric?"

"Come with me and you shall be enlightened," Stark said.

A CAPE HOTEL doorman opened the back door of the silver Rolls-Royce, and Stark crawled in like a badger waddling into his hole.

"Get in on the other side," he said to Thomas. "Terry will drive us."

"I'm not gettin' in the back with you," Thomas said.

"Suit yourself. Sit next to Terry then."

Thomas got in the front seat next to the man he knew as Michael Cotter.

"Your name is Terry?" Thomas asked.

"Sure," the sudden stranger replied. "Where to, Mr. S?"

"Let's go up into the canyons. I like it up there."

The one-time smoker drove off, turning right on Little Santa Monica.

Stark leaned forward and handed Thomas a large red envelope.

"Take it," Stark said. "Look through the photographs."

There was a thick sheaf of eight-by-ten glossy photos. They were pictures of Monique and Madeline, Harold and Clea, Minas Nolan, Ahn, and another half dozen people that Thomas did not recognize. He paused at the photograph of a black woman in a straitjacket who was screaming hideously.

"That's Nelda Frank," Stark said. "Your girlfriend's sister. A nice group, isn't it? Good-looking people. You would never think that that sweet-looking Vietnamese woman is in the country on forged papers or that stolid Harold Portman has been embezzling funds from his boss for years. Your grandmother's insurance company doesn't know that she lied about a preexisting condition when she bought her policy. The doctor that kept her records back then has recently agreed to make amends for his wrongdoing."

They were crossing Sunset, beginning an ascent into the hills.

"What I do to you, man?" Thomas asked, sitting with his back against the door, looking into the backseat.

"Three nights ago I sat with your brother and my little girl.

She smiles at me. She kisses me hello, but her joy in me is over. She's moved out of my house and chosen her man. My life is empty because of Eric Tanner Nolan."

Stark brought both hands to his face as if he were about to melt into tears, but he did not cry. Instead his fat hands folded into fists.

"She's gone from me and is never coming back. If your Eric died tomorrow, she wouldn't even cry on my shoulder. He has taken her heart from me."

"You crazy," Thomas said.

"Yes, I am," Kronin conceded. "That's an important fact for you to understand. I am crazy, and I will destroy the lives of everyone you know if you don't do exactly what I tell you to do. That's just how crazy I am. Your former nanny will be thrown out of the country or into a federal penitentiary, and Harold will be in prison too. Your grandmother will die from the cancer in her stomach. Your stepfather will be sued by half a dozen angry patients, and Clea's sister will fare far worse."

Silence settled in on Thomas. All the words he knew dried up and flaked off in his throat.

"You yourself will be tried for the murder of a Jane Doe buried under cinder blocks in an alley inhabited only by you. There's no statute of limitations on murder, is there, Terry?"

"No, sir," the man once known as Michael Cotter said.

"The district attorney will soon begin to seek charges against your brother for helping a wanted felon escape from the authorities," Stark said. "He will be sentenced for that felony and spend quite some time behind bars."

They'd made it up into the hills. The road looked down on the desertlike slope of the mountain.

"And you, Thomas Beerman, will testify at your brother's

trial that it was he who suggested and financed the escape. It was he who masterminded everything."

"You crazy." Thomas found the words even in his silence.

"If you don't do it," the billionaire warned, "he will still be convicted, and everyone you know will be destroyed along with him."

"But why? Why would you do this?"

"Because it will break your brother's heart to see you turn on him. And I want to do to him what he has done to me."

When Stark leaned forward, and Thomas was nearly blinded by the light off his skin. He averted his eyes — Kronin thought he was crying — and wondered about the moon.

The tide'll come in, the sun'll rise . . . He remembered the words he'd spoken to his brother. Now he realized that he was wrong. They were entering a sharp curve over a steep incline. Thomas pushed both his normal and shorter leg against the door, propelling himself against the steering wheel. Terry grunted and tried to keep the steering wheel straight, but Thomas's hands were too strong for the self-proclaimed assassin. There was no way to stop the car from careering off into free flight. Thomas was weightless. He floated into the backseat. Stark was yelling and so was the man he called Terry. When the Rolls hit the first boulder, Thomas slammed into Kronin's belly and smelled the acrid stench of the fat man's belching breath. He also felt a severe pain in his good leg. It felt wet and he thought of blood, but then they hit the second hard rock and then the third. No one was crying out now, and darkness was all around them. Then suddenly there was a wrenching sound of metal tearing, and Thomas was dimly aware of flight and then light. There was a flash of heat across his face, and he remembered the fear in Stark's face when the big man realized that he was about to die.

20

H E WAS in a hospital bed once more, looking at the light through the window again. He turned his head to the left and there was someone there. Clea — her hands clasped together and her eyes too sad for tears.

"Hey," Thomas said.

"Hi. How are you?"

"That depends. Am I gonna die?"

"No. They said that you're really banged up but that there's nothing life-threatening."

"Did I lose my leg?"

"You lost a lot of blood, but the doctor says that the leg'll be fine," she told him. "He also said that he might be able to fix the other leg with a hip replacement."

"And are you still moving out here to live with me?"

"Of course," she said.

"You will?"

"Of course. Why would this accident make any difference?"

"Does your sister have a gap between her front teeth?"

"Yeah. How did you know?"

"Stark."

"What about him?"

"He told me. He said . . . he said . . ."

"He said what?"

"He knew about her. He had a picture of her. He knew about everybody I knew, and he was going to hurt all of them unless . . . He wanted me to testify that Eric helped me to escape from the police."

"Stark's dead. So's his driver."

"They're dead and I'm not?"

Clea stared at Thomas, not comprehending the meaning of his question.

"You were thrown clear," she explained.

"But we crashed. The car crushed in around us."

"You were thrown clear. After that the car fell on its back and then the gas tank blew."

"So the pictures were burned?" Thomas asked.

"Yeah, I guess. Everything burned."

"I killed them."

"Don't be crazy, Tommy. It was an accident. The police think that it was because of dirt on the road. The driver hit the brakes and slid off the side."

"I grabbed the steering wheel," Thomas said.

"I would have too, but you couldn't stop it. You're lucky that you weren't killed with them."

Clea went over to Thomas and kissed him, but in his mind he was still in that careening car, crashing into boulders, counting out the last beats of his life . . .

"REALLY?" ERIC SAID that evening when he and Thomas were alone in the hospital room. "He wanted you to testify against me?"

"I think that he planned to marry Raela one day. He said that you stole her from him."

"And then you grabbed the wheel and ran the car off the mountain?"

"It was the only thing I could think of. I murdered him, Eric. And I didn't even lose a leg or nuthin'. And everything burned up; even the steering wheel melted. The pictures all burned. What should I do?"

"What do you wanna do, Tommy?"

This set off a series of thoughts that went all the way back to Thomas's earliest memories: Eric running fast; Eric laughing out loud; Eric falling and rushing into Branwyn's arms yelling for her to make the pain go away. He remembered a recurring childhood dream about a wasp as big as a horse chasing him, intent upon stinging him in the chest, in his heart. He ran into a cave that was too small for the hornet to get into, but the enraged insect jabbed its stinger in after him again and again. It stung Thomas in the hand and the leg, in his eye and mouth, but it never got him in the chest and finally it died from all that stinging. That was always when Thomas would wake up, after the wasp had defeated itself. In the dream he never left the cave.

"Tommy?"

"Yeah?"

"It's not your fault, man. You had to do it."

In his mind Thomas emerged from the cave. The huge insect lay dying, vibrating its wings in sporadic fits. The stinger had come loose from the abdomen, with the slick entrails following after.

"It's like nuthin' makes any sense anymore," Thomas said to Eric. "Like I fell out of a airplane but then I was okay."

"What's wrong with that?"

"It doesn't make any sense. You're supposed to die if you fall like that."

For some reason Thomas thought about Alicia then. He remembered struggling with the heavy cinder blocks that he and Pedro used to make her tomb. She was dead. She fell over the fence and never got up again.

THAT AFTERNOON AND night Thomas had four visitors.

The first was Clea Frank. She came into his room and sat next to his bed.

"I love you," she said. "I just came by to tell you that I'm going back to New York to pack, but when I come back we'll get a place together and you'll go back to school or whatever you want and I'll finish my degree."

Clea kissed Thomas and said something, but he'd been on painkillers and fell asleep, missing her words. He remembered her reassuring tones, though, and he felt that maybe things might be okay.

WHEN HE WOKE up again, Raela was standing there.

She gave him a serious look and then sat down next to him.

"Eric told me what happened with my father," she said.

Thomas didn't question why his brother would do such a thing. He didn't utter a sound. He wondered, dispassionately, if the girl had come to get revenge, not because she was angry but because it was the right thing to do.

"He told me about the pictures and his wanting to send him to jail," she said. "I believe it because that would have been just another day of business for my father. He destroyed people and businesses all the time. He sent men to jail, and then he'd come to my room and tell me how they'd begged and cried. He said that he was building a great treasure and that it would one day be mine."

Thomas wondered at the little girl in her bed hovered over by the giant who was trying to woo her with treasures. He thought he understood her steel will then.

"He would have gone on doing that, but you stopped him," Raela said. "I thought about it for a long time after Eric told me. You grabbed the wheel and ran off the road. You expected to die along with him. He was trying to destroy you like he did everybody else, and you grabbed him so that he'd go with you."

Raela was gazing directly into Thomas's eyes. He felt a greater intimacy with her than he'd ever experienced before. It was a terrible intimacy, a frightening knowledge.

"I loved him in a way," she said. "He made me the most important person in his whole world, and his world was everything. There was nothing I couldn't have, and no one would hurt me as long as he was alive. He was a monster, but he loved me. But I want you to know that I don't hold his death against you. It was his own fault, and he's the only one to blame."

WHEN THOMAS WOKE up again, Ahn was sitting in a chair where Raela had stood. The Vietnamese nanny was knitting. Thomas gazed at her for a long while before she looked up at him.

"You were asleep," she said.

Thomas wanted to speak but he didn't.

"I came to tell you a story," Ahn said.

Thomas felt his smile rising. Ahn's stories were the most important tales in his life. He knew that he would get something wonderful from her words.

"Five years after my parents were killed, I lived on a beach in the south. I lived by myself in a refugee camp. American soldiers would come to us to visit the young women and girls there. One night I was hiding in the trees watching a beautiful young woman named Min. She was . . . was making love with a soldier in the sand. I was watching because many of the young girls did this thing to make money to pay for food and clothes and maybe a way out of Vietnam. I was thinking that maybe I could do like Min and make money to buy my passage.

"I listened to the words she said and I watched the things she did, trying to see if I could do that when a gang of boys ran up to them. The boys were shouting, and the man tried to stand. But before he could get up one boy hit him in the head with a rock. Another boy stabbed him, then another and another.

"Min ran away naked except for the soldier's pants that she held against her breasts." Ahn's breathing was coming fast, and her eyes were looking back more than thirty years. "The boys were from the camp. I knew their names then, but by now I've forgotten them. They were all stabbing the soldier, and when they were finished, they ran off in the night screaming like ghosts.

"When they were all gone I came out and looked down on him. He was still alive, but the blood was bubbling out. His eyes were wide open, and he looked at me, begging me. He grabbed my arm and squeezed hard. I just sat there telling him that he would be all right. And then his hand got weaker until it finally fell away."

Ahn turned her gaze to Thomas then. "He died, and I stayed with him for a long time. I could not save him. The boys that hated him could not stop themselves. The girl who ran away could not save him or stop the boys. Everything that happened was going to happen, and there was no other chance. He had just been making love with a beautiful Vietnamese girl and then he was attacked and then he died holding on to my arm."

Ahn held up her arm, showing it to Thomas.

"It was our fate."

LATE THAT NIGHT Thomas came awake suddenly. In the corner of his hospital room stood his mother. She was wearing her white slip and the house shoes that Minas Nolan had given her. She was silent, staring at Thomas, and he was just as quiet returning her gaze. As he watched her the color slowly drained away from her image. She turned gray and then slowly became transparent, like glass. When she was almost completely clear, her form began to sparkle from the inside. The cloud of iridescent light then drifted toward the window, out through the glass, and away into the dark sky. The lights kept moving until they covered the nighttime horizon, becoming stars.

WHEN THOMAS AWOKE in the morning, he was exhausted and felt more alone than he'd ever been. It was as if his body had been cut away from his soul and he was floating somewhere above himself on the bed. He knew that he'd been crying, that he'd lost everything that he'd held on to since he was a boy, running like Ahn had taught him to do. He knew that his mother was dead and gone, and that he was a criminal, a murderer.

He looked out the window into the light-filled sky and thought about dying. Then he was filled with wonder at all of the pathways that came together in him on that day in grace.

ABOUT THE AUTHOR

Walter Mosley is the author of numerous best-selling works of fiction and nonfiction, including the acclaimed Easy Rawlins series of mysteries. The first Easy Rawlins novel, *Devil in a Blue Dress,* was made into a feature film starring Denzel Washington and Don Cheadle. Another novel, *Always Outnumbered, Always Outgunned,* for which Mosley received the Anisfield-Wolf Book Award, was made into an HBO feature film starring Laurence Fishburne. His first novel for young adult readers, *47,* was published in 2005. Walter Mosley was born in Los Angeles and lives in New York.

BACK BAY · READERS' PICK

Reading Group Guide

FORTUNATE SON

A novel by

Walter Mosley

A conversation with
the author of
Fortunate Son

Walter Mosley talks with John Orr
of the *San Jose Mercury News*

We aren't yet halfway through 2006 and the talented Walter Mosley has already published four books: *The Wave* (science fiction), *Life Out of Context* (political meditations), *Cinnamon Kiss* (an Easy Rawlins mystery), and his latest, *Fortunate Son*, which is literary fiction, a beautiful, involving, and touching parable about blacks and whites in America.

Don't blink: he has a Fearless Jones novel coming out in September. There are eighty-three books by Walter Mosley — mysteries, literary fiction, science fiction, fiction for young adults, collections of short stories and political essays — listed at Amazon.com.

And he is not publishing hackwork. He has been called "brilliant" by the *Washington Post* and other newspapers; the Associated Press has said about him: "Only Mosley has employed detective fiction as a vehicle for a thoughtful, textured examination of race relations in the United States. Only Mosley puts white readers, if just for a few hundred pages at a time, in a black man's shoes."

We spoke with Walter Mosley recently by phone about *Fortunate Son* and other matters.

Do you ever sleep?

You know, I only write about three or four hours a day, but I do it every day — and that seems to be enough.

When I read Fortunate Son, *I thought: parable.*

Well, listen, what else can you think? I told my publisher, "Well, you know, it's a parable." He said, "Don't say that!" [Laughs.] He said, "Don't say that, people won't want to read it!" I go, "What am I gonna say? It seems like a parable to me."

Though not a parable in such a way where at the end of it you're going to say, "Well, this is right and that's wrong." It's the kind of parable where you'd say there's possibility and there's choice. And there's probability. There's possibility, probability, and choice. And that's the world you live in.

According to Milton, that's what God gave us, choice. Correct me if I'm wrong about Fortunate Son: *Black man and white man in the United States are bonded and even though sometimes that bond in this culture leads to danger for both of them, they have to stick together to survive. Is that too simple? Am I misreading?*

When you say "have to," you know, I wish that were true, that people had to. They don't have to. They can choose to, but they don't have to. There's a bond of love between the two brothers, Eric and Tommy, and that's what they want, they want that love, they want each other in their lives.

I wouldn't want to say that their relationship is inescapable; that would be a little too optimistic, actually.

Tommy is this great example of somebody who really sees deeply into the world. He's an unbelievably unlucky person.

3

But he's also incredibly fortunate because he's able to take actions into his life and to see things, and to see beauty in life. No matter how bad things go, he's able to see and understand beauty, and he's able to maintain a certain innocence. Whereas his brother, Eric, is so lucky that it really strains the imagination to believe in his luck. But then you see, well, this is not helping him. This does not give him a better life. The fact that he's bigger, stronger, smarter, more beautiful, more talented, and luckier than everybody else doesn't give him a good life. That's why I called him Eric, which is the name that is embedded in our nation's name, the name we call ourselves, America. Without the beauty that Tommy brings, Eric's life is nothing.

And that's certainly a direct criticism of the country. But, you know, hey, you can have everything, it doesn't mean anything.

Again, parable. I've come to think there's no difference between the races, but in America — and in other countries — because of color of skin people have been forced to be raised in different cultures. It's the cultural differences that make the difference.

Yeah, it's what people believe. If you believe it, in your mind and in your heart, there's a certain truth to it. Whether or not there's any kind of objective truth to it in the world in general.

Except — if you're a poor kid raised in South Central — some of that area is nasty, it's really tough. It's a hard life to be starting out in. You don't get the breaks you get if you're raised up in Sherman Oaks and go to a nicer public school, or you're raised up in Beverly Hills and have a lot of money, like Eric.

But, you know, there's another thing. Using that kind of equation doesn't cover all the bases, there's a few others to be covered. For instance, you're a poor white kid in Bellflower. You know, living in a tiny little house, or living in a trailer, let's say. Your father's gone, your mother's not treating you right, the school you're going to is filled with poor kids that are also not being treated well.

So you could say, well, the poor white kid and the poor black kid are the same. And the truth is there are a lot of similarities and there are a lot of problems that either one of them might carry through their lives. But there are also racial overtones in this country.

I agree.

It's important to remember, because, you know — a lot of times black people will say, "Those white people, they're all rich." Well, no, they're not. A lot of them are poor. Go to Appalachia. There's some *poor* white people in Appalachia.

If you're black or Asian or Latino, you get the fact of your racial profile thrown in your face a lot of the time.

But, you know, Tommy in this situation, in this story, represents something other than that. Tommy doesn't pay too much attention to race. Eric is his brother. Eric's father is his father. Tommy has friends who are black, he has friends who are white, he lives in a world where there's all kinds of people and he deals with people individually, which you have to do.

There's an understanding that Tommy has of being in the world, the greatness and the beauty and the excellence of being alive. And how small we are in relation to the rest of the world.

Do you think Eric lacks that?

He doesn't understand it because his mind has been made small. I think he has an inkling of it, which is why he always wants to get back to Branwyn, and he always wants to get back to Tommy, because they showed him a larger world. But in his own world, he's the best — everything happens for him, nothing happens for anybody else — you know, until he meets his girlfriend. There's nobody who can stand in his way. And so his world, kind of contradictorily, becomes smaller.

Like the top of a pyramid.

But a really tiny pyramid. Eric doesn't see the whole world around him.

Race is not an issue to either of the brothers in the book.

But there's tons of racism in the book.

Certainly. Tommy's father. There's an angry guy for you.

Yeah.

What was your life like as a kid?

My life was actually very simple as a kid. You know, listen, I lived in the '50s and '60s in South Central, among an immigrant black class from the western South — from Louisiana, from Texas, some from western Mississippi. And these people came to work! And there was lots of work! This was when

America had hegemony over global politics. So there was a lot of work. Everybody I knew worked two, three jobs. Everybody owned their house, everybody had, you know, notions for the future.

There was still racism. Racism? That's why the Watts riots happened. There was more of a glass ceiling than there is today.

But, you know, it's interesting. In the end I don't think you can make simple statements, like it's better now, it's worse then. Certainly, if you look at the slave quarters in South Carolina in 1810, yeah, we're better than that. But there are a lot of bad times and there are people who are suffering who have become invisible and who are vilified for their situation, not for their potential, character, or personality.

There are lots of good mystery writers out there, but as far as I know, you're the only one who's writing brilliantly about what it was like to be black in L.A. in the time of Easy Rawlins.

I'm just writing about my character.

But it's a great thing, and you're educating people. Somebody from Iowa, maybe, is going to read your book and learn something worth learning.

That's the wonderful thing about mysteries, you can bring people into different worlds.

Regarding Fortunate Son, *who's going to read this book? Are you preaching to the choir?*

Anybody who likes literature, right?

One of my editors wanted me to write about you because she says, and I agree, that you are one of the most important writers working today. In that sense, I put you right up there with Toni Morrison and E. L. Doctorow.

Well, thank you very much, I appreciate that.

Adapted from John Orr's interview with Walter Mosley, which originally appeared in the *San Jose Mercury News* on May 14, 2006. Reprinted with permission. A transcript of the entire interview is available at http://triviana.com/books/mosleyqa.htm.